ALSO BY JESSICA PARK

NOVELS
Clear

Relatively Famous

FLAT-OUT LOVE SERIES
Flat-Out Love

Flat-Out Matt

Flat-Out Celeste

LEFT DROWNING SERIES
Left Drowning

Restless Waters

180
seconds

a novel

JESSICA
PARK

SKYSCAPE

SKYSCAPE

Published by Skyscape, New York
www.apub.com

Amazon, the Amazon logo, and Skyscape are trademarks of Amazon.com, Inc., or its affiliates.

ISBN-13: 9781503943360
ISBN-10: 1503943364

Cover design by Adil Dara

Printed in the United States of America

This book is dedicated to Danielle Allman. Because she is brave, she is brave, she is so ferociously brave.

CHAPTER 1

LITTLE BIRD

Junior year of college starts now, which means I have two years left until I am free. Every day is a reminder of how completely different I am from my peers, a constant sense of my inability to be social and happy and emotionally unchained. It can be a challenge to isolate myself here, but I do what I can.

It takes Simon twenty minutes of circling Andrews College's campus to find a place to park. Arrival day is always utter chaos, with students spilling from cars, arms laden with boxes and bags; cars double-parked up and down the streets; and tearful parents milling around and clogging the sidewalks. The drive from Boston to northern Maine has taken almost five hours, and this early September day feels more like August than it does the start of fall. Welcome to New England. I am sweaty from the lack of good air-conditioning, but I try to subtly fan my shirt when I step out of the car, relishing the faint breeze.

"Sorry about the AC," Simon says apologetically. "This car's an oldie but a goody." From his spot outside the driver's side, he looks over the car at me and half smiles as he taps the hood and looks unreasonably fresh, given the heat. "Bad timing for it to go out, I know. We could consider it some kind of fashionable spa detox. I'm sure Volvo would approve."

I smile and nod. "Sure. Junior year should start with a cleanse of some sort."

"Right? Before you do all sorts of college things to pollute your system. Parties, cafeteria food . . ." He waves a hand around, and I know he's hoping I will continue with the joke.

Simon tries very hard, and I routinely fail him. I know this, but it's all I can manage. It's not his fault; it's mine. He's a very nice man. Too nice, probably. Too giving and too understanding.

Simon, I silently remind myself, *is also my father.* It's embarrassing how often I have to remind myself of this, because I've seen the adoption papers. I was there, for God's sake, when they were signed and when I officially—and finally—left the foster care system at the ripe old age of sixteen and a half.

I catch my reflection in the window of the car. My long dark hair is pulled into a ponytail, the weight leaden on my back, my thick bangs stuck to my forehead with sweat, my cheeks flushed.

My reaction is not from the heat, though. This is anxiety building. I need water.

Not only do I have to meet a new roommate, but I'll have to part ways with Simon. I'll hate putting him through an awkward good-bye, so I resolve to perk up and do a better job. I'm just not very good at being a daughter, but I want to try. I care about him so much, but I still struggle with how to show him that.

I plaster on a smile and round the car to the trunk. "Think we can make it in one trip?" I ask. "If we do, I'll buy you lunch."

"At your nasty student union? That's no incentive." Simon retrieves a box from the trunk. He's trying to hide it, but I can see him grin. "I'll carry one shoe in at a time if that'll save me."

"Actually, I was thinking about the Greek place down the street." The suitcase I pull out doesn't weigh much. I'm a minimalist, and so I travel light.

Simon stands up and tips his head to the side, raising an eyebrow, no longer concealing his happiness. "Greek place? With gyros? And hummus?"

I nod. "And baba ghanoush."

He shifts the box to rest on his hip, freeing up a hand. His voice elevates. "Grab everything you can and run! Only take what you need! Run like the wind!" He yanks a small duffel from the car and dashes to the sidewalk, calling out over his shoulder, "Come on, Allison! There's no time to waste!"

I laugh and take the only other bag I have from the back of the car and then slam the trunk. Simon is teasing me, because the truth is that his car is now empty of what I've brought to school. My adoptive father is trying to make light of my inability to plant real roots anywhere, how I allow myself a fraction of the things other students stuff in their small dorm rooms, and I'm reminded of how sweet and understanding he is when it comes to my personality flaws. While most students take hours to unload cars and retrieve boxes from campus storage, we've unloaded the car in five seconds.

It takes scrambling to catch up with Simon—who has raced so far ahead that I'm chagrined by my inability to keep up with him—and my suitcase bumps up steps and over a good deal of grassy lawn as I shortcut between dorm buildings to reach mine. I'm breathless when I reach Kirk Hall, where he is sitting on the box, looking all sorts of casual and relaxed.

"Really, Simon?" I gasp. "How . . . how did you even know where you were going?" I pant.

"I studied the campus map last week. And perhaps yesterday. And again this morning before we left." Simon manages to look as cool and handsome as ever, with no hint of a sweat stain on his button-down red linen shirt. The hair that is always stylishly whooshed back from his forehead is still in place. His effortless ability to always look so poised, even when not warranted, is admirable. Aviator sunglasses turn toward me. "I've only been up here a few times before, and I can't look like the average bumbling family member, following blindly while their child leads the way. I want to look like I know what I'm doing."

I feel bad for not inviting him up to visit more often over the past two years. Maybe this year will be different. Maybe this year I will be able to let him in. I'd like that.

My heart rate is returning to normal, but I'm sweating again. "So, you thought you'd scamper wildly across campus like a lunatic?"

He grins. "Yes. Now, let's go see your room."

It was my hope that I'd land a good room-lottery number last spring and snatch up a coveted single room, but, unsurprisingly, I'd been at the bottom of the barrel. I'd waited hours in line to choose my room from a poorly drawn map, only to find that all the singles were gone. The fact the dorm-room selection couldn't be done online was beyond belief, and I cursed the archaic system as I ran through the remaining room choices. The student in charge asked repeatedly if I had a friend I could room with, and I tried brushing him off five times before I practically had to holler, "No, okay? No, I don't have anyone to room with! That's why I want a single room!"

Some might say I created a bit of a scene, but I was too busy panicking to care. I finally chose half of a two-person suite that at least afforded me a private bedroom, along with a common room. I'd have to come in and out through that small shared common area, but I could probably keep to myself easily enough. In more positive moments, part of me dared to hope that this mystery roommate and I might hit it off. Wonders could happen. Still, today I am anxious about meeting her.

It only takes a few minutes to sign in at the dorm and get my key. Then, with significant trepidation, I enter my basement suite.

Simon laughs when I audibly exhale. "Relieved she's not here yet?"

I roll my suitcase into one of the barren bedrooms and then plunk down on the rock-hard, hideous orange sofa in the lounge. Simon takes a swivel chair from my room and slides it in front of me, where he then plants himself. "Why are you so worried?"

I cross my arms and look around the concrete room. "I'm not *worried* at all. She's probably very nice. I'm sure we'll become soul mates, and she'll braid my hair, and we'll have pillow fights while scantily clad and fall into a deep lesbian love affair." I squint my eyes at a cobweb and assume there are spider eggs preparing to hatch and invade the room.

"Allison?" Simon waits until I look at him. "You can't do that. You can't become a lesbian."

"Why not?"

"Because then everyone will say that your adoptive gay father magically made you gay, and it'll be a big thing, and we'll have to hear about nature versus nurture, and it'll be soooooo boring."

"You have a point." I wait for spider eggs to fall from the sky. "Then I'll go with assuming she's just a really sweet, normal person with whom I do not want to engage in sexual relations."

"Better," he concedes. "I'm sure she'll be nice. This kind of strong liberal arts college attracts quality students. There're good people here." He's trying to reassure me, but it's not working.

"Totally," I say. My fingers run across the nubby burned-orange fabric covering the couch, which is clearly composed of rock slabs. "Simon?"

"Yes, Allison?"

I sigh and take a few breaths while I play with the hideous couch threads. "She probably has horns."

He shrugged. "I think that's unlikely." Simon pauses. "Although . . ."

"Although what?" I ask with horror.

There's a long silence that makes me nervous. Finally, he says very slowly, "She *might* have *one* horn."

I jerk my head and stare at him.

Simon claps his hands together and tries to coax a smile out of me. "Like a unicorn! Ohmigod! Your roommate might be a unicorn!"

5

"Or a rhinoceros," I point out. "A beastly, murderous rhino."

"There is that," he concedes.

I sigh. "In good news, if I ever need a back scratcher, I have this entire couch." I slump back against the rough fabric and hold out my hands before he can protest. "I know. I'm a beacon of positivity."

"That's not news to me." Simon's blue eyes meet mine. His skin is tan and weathered from a summer spent sailing off the coast of Massachusetts, his brown hair lightened in places where the gray has not taken over. I should have joined him on these excursions more than the few times I did. Next summer, maybe next summer . . .

"I think a back scratcher is a great luxury provided to you by Andrews College," he says. "Enjoy."

As I look around the concrete room, I make a resolution: I am going to give this unknown roommate a chance. I will push myself to be open and friendly. We might be very compatible. There's no need for this collegiate relationship to become a be-all, end-all friendship, because I already have that with my one true friend, Steffi, and my heart has no room for more than one. But a good, working relationship with a roommate? That could actually be enjoyable.

Well, *enjoyable* might be pushing it. I'd shoot for *tolerable*.

There is a loud knock on the door, and it swings open as a tall boy with a scraggly beard and rows of beads dangling around his neck pokes his head into the room. "Yo, are you Allison?"

I nod.

He beams. "Hey! Great to meet you! I'm Brian, your RA. Listen, my friend, welcome. We're so happy you're in Kirk Hall. Gonna be a rockin' year." He makes a little fist pump in the air, and I try not to recoil. "So, dude, one thing? Your roommate? Small hitch with her."

"What do you mean by *hitch*?" I ask.

"Yeesh, she sorta isn't going to be coming to school this year. Something about an Antarctic trip and a sea leopard." His face contorts. "Sounds unappealing to me, but she's gonna be holed up in a lab studying this creature for a few months before she takes off to see 'em in person."

Simon wrinkles his face. "Sea leopards?"

"Dude, yeah." The boy with the necklaces pinches the bridge of his nose. "I bet they smell. Guess you'll be flying solo this year, little bird." Suddenly he brightens. "But hey! We've got a killer welcome-back party here in this very dorm tonight! Third-floor lounge! See you there!" He points a finger at me and then vanishes, letting the door slam behind him.

While Simon looks stricken that I will not have a roommate, my spirits are undeniably lifted. *I'm a little bird who is going to be flying solo this year!* "Let's go get some baklava," I say with too much enthusiasm.

"Allison . . ."

"What? Oh." I force myself to look forlorn and try to hide that I actually find a degree of comfort in this turn of events. "I mean, it would have been nice to live with someone, I guess, but it's all right. I'm sure this girl will have a unique year. So, good for her, right? Did you know that sea leopards are also called leopard seals? I like that name better."

Simon tosses his hands in the air. "I didn't." He searches for something appropriate to say. "Look, I know you don't like people, but that doesn't mean you should be happy if—"

"If someone chose a year of living in a lab and then in the frozen tundra, studying a vicious and creepy animal, over living with me?"

He looks sad. "Yes. But it's not as though she knew you and . . . rejected you. She's just following some dream of hers or whatnot."

We sit without speaking, and eventually my butt hurts enough from the scratchy couch that I stand and walk the few steps to what would have been my roommate's bedroom. I lean my head against the doorjamb and look at the floor. "I'm sorry that I don't like people. I'm sorry that I look clearly relieved that I'll be living alone."

"It's okay," he replies gently. "I get it."

"And I'm sorry I'm pessimistic."

"I get that, too."

"And I'm sorry . . ." I can't find the words. "I'm just sorry. I think you made a mistake. A mistake with *me*." This is the first time I say what I have been thinking for years. I'm not sure why it comes out now, but, generally speaking, I'm not sure of much.

From the corner of my eye, I see Simon rise from the chair and turn my way. Softly, but very assuredly, he says, "No. I definitely did not make a mistake with you."

Because he knows me well enough, he doesn't step toward me expecting an embrace or some other emotional or physical display. Simon gets a lot of credit for respecting my boundaries. He knows that connection is not my thing.

People are not my thing.

Trust is not my thing.

"What I also know for sure," he continues, "is that you owe me lunch."

So, we walk to the little Greek place a block from campus, and we order a crazy amount of food. I spend a lot of time stuffing my face and little time talking, but Simon manages to make our silence feel less uncomfortable than it should.

"I wonder what she's like," I murmur between bites. For a few seconds, I imagine having a typical college experience, complete with a bang-up, awesome roommate, with me actually welcoming that experience. My past two roommates and I made zero connection, unsurprisingly. I know that was my fault. "Maybe she was really cool. Maybe we would have been friends."

Simon clears his throat. He knows I'm full of shit.

"But," I continue factually, "leopard seals are obviously the love of her life, and since I find them terrifying, I suspect a friendship wouldn't have worked out anyway. This is for the best."

My head starts to hurt. I down my drink and then focus on filling and refilling my glass with the bottle of sparkling water.

"How much do you actually know about these animals?" Simon interrupts my obsessive water consumption. "I've barely heard of them."

It takes only a minute for me to pull up a picture on my phone, and I stick the screen out in front of me. "Teeth. That animal has mini spears for teeth."

Simon casts a look of defeat. "Okay. You're right. That's an unpleasant animal. She might not have made the best roommate."

I sit back with immense satisfaction, my headache now subsiding.

CHAPTER 2

WE GET ONE

At nine o'clock at night, I'm in bed, smoothing down the crisp sheets, ensuring that the perfect fold resting on my chest holds its form. A small desk fan circulates enough air to keep me from suffocating on this hot night. Something about the sounds of students whooping it up and celebrating their return to campus makes my stomach knot up, so I don't open the small window. The whir from the fan doesn't quash the revelers' drunken partying much, but it at least helps.

A sudden pounding on my door startles me, and it takes me a second to squelch my panic before I tentatively open the door.

"Allison! How was your summer? You coming to the dorm party upstairs?" A petite girl with a plastic cup stands before me. Her bleached hair spikes in dramatic chunks from her head and then lands just on her shoulders. I recognize her from a few of my classes last year. Becky? Bella? Brooke? Some kind of *B* name. She catches herself when she notices my tank top and pajama bottoms. "Oh. I guess not," she says.

I form a big smile. "Hey! It's so good to see you. Oh my God! You look gorgeous! Check out that tan!" I manage to sound so overzealous that even I'm surprised at the squeal in my voice. "I'm seriously beat from all the end-of-summer parties." I give a knowing look, trying to convey the idea that I've been engaged in such wild and scandalous activities over the past few weeks that I cannot possibly haul myself to one more social event. I pretend to yawn.

B-name girl raises her cup in understanding and nods her head so vigorously that a strand of her hair bounces into the liquid. "I hear you. Well, rest up. Next time, 'kay?"

The idea that I am going to have to spend another two years here, deflecting social interaction, is daunting. If I could throw an invisibility cloak over myself and attend college that way, I would.

"For sure . . ." I make the horrible mistake of pausing, letting her know that I cannot for the life of me remember her name.

"Carmen," she says with a splash of annoyance. "*Carmen.* I lived next to you last year, and we had lit and British history together."

"I know your name, silly!" I scramble to think of something else to say. While I don't want to go to any parties, I also really don't want to hurt her feelings. It's moments like this that I so wish I could be less awkward and weird. In a scramble to be friendly, I blurt out, "I just . . . I was just noticing your cool earrings. They're so unique."

She touches a hand to her ear. "They're plain silver hoops."

"Er, I didn't mean *unique*, really. I meant . . . that . . . they're the perfect size. Not too big, not too small, you know?"

Carmen looks at me skeptically. "I guess so."

"They're really nice. I've been wanting a pair like that."

"My mom got them for me. I can ask her where she bought them if you want."

I smile. "That's so cool of you. Thanks!" I'm too chipper, I realize, so I bring it down a notch and fake another yawn. "Anyway, I'm sorry I'm so lame tonight. But drink a beer for me, will you?"

"You got it! I'll start now!" She takes a big drink from her cup and goes down the hall, turning back after a few paces. "Nice to see you, Allison."

"You too, Carmen!"

I lock the door and turn off the light. The door to the empty second bedroom is open, and I stare at it. Leave it open, or shut the door? I can't decide what to do. Closed will make it seem as though someone is in there. sleeping, studying, hooking up, wanting privacy . . . As though maybe I have a friend in there with whom I have an actual connection. Something. Open will remind me that there is no one in there.

Truly, I have no idea what to do. Minutes tick by.

Suddenly, I lurch forward, grab the handle, and slam it shut. That room does not exist.

I rush away and quickly close my own door. I cannot get back into bed fast enough.

I scramble to pull the bedding up to my chin in some kind of crazy fit. *Why would Carmen come by my room?* It's inexplicable. My toes are wiggling wildly, and I clap my feet together to calm them down.

I fan my body with the sheets before again smoothing the fabric, making sure the top fold is exact. Simon insisted on getting me new sheets, even though I already had one set, and he washed and even ironed these for me before we left home. He looked terribly disappointed when I tried to turn down these new sheets. "You can't have just one set of sheets! Please? For me? Just this one year, have a second set," he'd pleaded. "The thread count is off the charts." So, I'd thanked him and accepted the gift of high thread count.

The feel of the heavyweight cotton is less familiar than the inexpensive, scratchy sheets that I'd often slept on when growing up, and so I am moderately uncomfortable and tempted to pull the old ones from my closet and remake the bed, but in an effort to make Simon happy, I stick with these. He's been trying for years to give me a new normal.

I wish I could let him, but my history is too tainted for him to fix.

I stopped hoping for stability when I was ten. It was a good, long run of optimism, if you ask me, but when I turned ten, it became obvious that I was unadoptable. No one would want a shy, uninteresting, skittish child who was well past the cute baby stage.

I close my eyes and stroke the sheets over and over, trying to manage the anxiety that always comes with revisiting the past.

I remember a very kind social worker who picked me up from a home placement when I was around eight. It was New Year's Day, with sleeting rain stabbing at the mounds of snow, and she must have adjusted her pink wool scarf a dozen times a minute in her nervousness. What a depressing job she had. I can still see the smiling faces of the parents and their two biological children as they all hugged me good-bye and waved, wishing me well and thanking me for staying with them. *Thanking me*, as though I'd been an exchange student who'd just stopped in temporarily to experience the culture of an upper-class Massachusetts family. As though they'd been hosting me for fun. But at least I ate well, went to a good school, and got to take ballet for those six months. Ballet classes, however, were not worth the heartbreak that came with being told it was time to go.

My childhood was a constant exchange of new schools, new rooms, new houses, new neighborhoods, new families. I think about how many teachers and classmates I had to meet, how many times I had to start over.

Then there were birthdays. Either overly celebrated or entirely forgotten.

My breathing picks up, and I squeeze my fingers over the fabric, trying to remind myself that I have more now than I ever expected. I should be reassured. There is Simon. He promised he wasn't going anywhere. He adopted me. He signed papers, for God's sake. Legally, he *can't* go anywhere.

So, he is stuck with me.

My phone jars me from my impending escalation.

Steffi. She's the only person in the world I'd talk to now.

I wipe my face and cough to clear my throat. "Hey, you!"

"Hey, back!" Steffi shouts happily. Immediately, I am comforted.

Steffi has been the one exception to the endless proof that the world is unstable and unreliable. From the moment we met when we were fourteen, we have been partners in survival. For only three months, we lived in the same foster family with four other kids, but three months were all we needed to cement our friendship.

"How is California?" I ask.

"Stupidly sunny and gorgeous. Just like me." Steffi lets out her gravelly laugh, and I can practically see her flip her long blond hair. "I was made for Los Angeles, you know that. And you are, too. You'll see that once you graduate and get your ass out here."

I smile. "That's the plan." I hear music fade in and out and the sound of hangers being pushed along a closet rod. "You going out?"

"You betcha. I'm putting you on speaker while I get dressed, 'kay? So, what's going on with you? How'd drop-off with Daddy go?"

"Fine. You know . . . We had lunch."

"Simon still as hot as ever?"

"Oh my God, Steffi! Don't be gross!" But I can't help laughing.

"He's not *my* daddy," she says, making her voice all sexy and borderline creepy. "If I had my way, I could be Mrs. Simon Dennis. And be your mommy!"

"Shut up! That's weird. And he's gay," I remind her. "You're not exactly his type. Thank God."

"There is that," she says, sighing dramatically. "Dammit! Is he still wearing those adorable aviator glasses? Don't answer that. Why is romance so unfair?"

I roll my eyes. "I think you'll survive not capturing Simon's heart."

"It's fine. I plan to drown my sorrows in a slew of vodka sodas and pick up the hottest piece of ass I can find. And you? Will you be getting some college-boy action yourself this fine evening?"

I refrain from snorting. "Classes start tomorrow. Just taking . . . it . . . easy tonight." For some reason, I stumble over my words, and it's the only thing Steffi needs to know something is off.

"What's going on, Allison?" She's gentle now.

"I'm okay."

"You having a hard night?"

It's useless to lie to her. "Yes. A little. I don't know why."

The music in the background stops. Like it or not, I have her full attention. "You want to run through it again?" she asks.

I can't speak, but she knows me well enough to know that I'm nodding.

She begins to tell me what I already know—or what I should know, but what she must remind me of all too often. "We are not statistics. We beat the system. Nobody wanted us for all those years? Fine. So, we blew apart the system. We grew up alone, rejected, unwanted. But screw everybody. We graduated high school, and we're both in college. We haven't gone to jail. We don't use drugs. We've never run away or been on the streets doing Lord knows what. We are not statistics," she emphasizes again. "We lived with some rotten families. We lived with some cool ones. The details do not matter. Do you hear me? The details *do not* matter. I don't want to live in the past. Neither do you. We're not going back there. It's over. We are not goddamn statistics. We will never be. We are the exception, and we are exceptional. Got it?"

I nod to myself again. "Right." I had become a shell of a kid until Steffi showed up and rocked me into life. At least to a degree.

"So, what else?" she prompts. "What do we do? Each and every day?"

I roll onto my side and reach to turn off the small desk light that shines over me. "We focus on the future, and we don't look back."

"Big futures," she corrects. "And why do we have big futures waiting for us?" she asks me.

"Because you made us study. Because you knew that our education was the most important thing. That it would save us."

She's not bragging when she makes me say this; she's only pushing me to validate what we both did. She should take more credit, though, because Steffi threatened, cajoled, and bribed to get my contact information with each move. She was relentless in keeping us together even after we were apart. And Steffi is the only reason that I threw myself into school because she instilled in me how crucial this was to survival.

"And you got into college. A damn good one."

"And you got a full scholarship to UCLA. Nobody does that. *Nobody*," I stress, almost as if to remind myself of what she's accomplished. Steffi's hard work and ferocious determination have indeed paid off well. She, much more than me, is the exception to the foster-kid rule.

"We got where we are," she continues, "because we stayed focused."

I stare at the ceiling above me. "And because you took care of me."

"We took care of each other." Steffi pauses. "Do you remember what you did for me?"

"I don't want to talk about that."

She's silent for a bit. "Okay. But you took care of me, too."

"Why don't you let me take care of you more now?"

"Because I'm a tough shit."

I can't help laughing. "You are. I just want you to know that I'm here for you. That I'd do anything for you."

"Of course you would! I know that. Allison?"

"Yeah?"

"You got a good ending, okay? You got Simon. Don't forget that. Even when we thought it was too late, even when it felt like it didn't matter anymore, you got a father. You have somewhere to call home, somewhere to go during breaks and summers. Just because he showed up late doesn't mean that he doesn't matter. You defied some crazy odds by getting adopted in high school."

"It's not fair." I cannot stand when Steffi says this, because my guilt is uncontrollable. I cup a hand over my mouth to stifle the sobs that threaten to come through, and it takes me a moment until I can speak without emotion. I wait until my voice is flat. Factual. "But you didn't get adopted."

"I didn't need to. I was a sick little kid, Allison. Nobody wanted a kid who'd had cancer. And then, years later, even when I was better, I didn't need *them*." The *them* she refers to are Joan and Cal Kantor. Steffi moved into their house around the same time I moved in with Simon. Simon adopted me, but Joan and Cal did not adopt Steffi, instead letting her turn eighteen and go off on her own. No support, no family, no sense of safe haven.

As hardened and independent as Steffi was, even she was shaken when they politely let her know that their time as foster parents was done. It was not a happy graduation from high school.

I will never forgive them.

I'll never know what to say about Joan and Cal. What to say about how they discarded the most tremendous girl. A could-be daughter.

As always, Steffi steps in to fill the void I create. "Look, Allison, I was a dud, okay? A risk. And why would I want to settle down with a nice family and their three dogs when I have you, right?"

"Right." But I'm not sure.

"Hey! Snap out of it!" she says sharply. "I got you! What do I always say?"

My head is spinning. "I don't know . . ."

"Hold on to your one. Remember? I have you, and you have me. And when you're lucky enough to find one—*just one*—person in this unforgiving life who makes everything worth it, who you love and trust and would kill for, then you hold on damn tight, because that's probably all you get. We got this," Steffi says with conviction.

"Okay."

"It's going to hurt until it doesn't anymore."

"Okay."

"Say it."

"It's going to hurt until it doesn't anymore." I repeat her words, but I'm not sure I believe them. I'm not as strong as Steffi, and my past does still hurt. Even though the worst should be over, it all still hurts with a relentless, enduring power that I cannot match.

It's possible that I'm too broken.

"Steffi? You're not a dud. You never were. You are more perfect than any parents could handle. That's all."

CHAPTER 3

MOTIVATION

I learn a troubling thing during the first week of school: it's harder to find upperclassmen courses that are jam-packed with students. I'm a big fan of lecture halls and classes that facilitate anonymity. As much as I avoid people, certain types of crowds are ironically my friend.

On Friday morning, I spend thirty-five minutes in the campus registration office, going over the course options with an eye for the best chance at being able to blend in. I refuse to drop my Hundred Words for Snow: Language and Nature class, because it's all about how language influences the way we see the world, and I find that irresistibly intriguing. Plus, the course seems to involve a lot of listening, with minimal class participation, and I'm totally on board with that. I do, however, give up Cultures of Neoliberalism, because it meets in a conference room in the library, and there is no way I am going to discuss "the relative autonomy of the economic sphere" with only six other students and a professor. Instead, I swap that out for the very popular Social Psychology. Between those classes and the Eating for Change? Food, Media, and Environment in US Consumer Culture, as well as Probability and Mathematical Statistics, I should have a perfect balance between being safe from too much interaction and having really interesting classes that I'll enjoy.

With my schedule in place, the next few weeks go smoothly. I settle into a pleasing routine of studying, visiting the library, and reading during meals in the cafeteria. I suppose I come off as a quiet, nerdy girl, but that's nothing terrifically unusual at Andrews College.

I'm in a surprisingly good mood one late-September Friday as I move fluidly through the crowded student union and outside to the quad. I only have psych class left today, and the upcoming weekend means less pressure to interact. The union's café makes a good iced coffee, and I suck the straw hard as I walk to the sunny lawn area and find a spot to myself under a large oak tree. I have a half hour before class, so I lean against the knotty trunk and retrieve a library book from my backpack.

I'm probably the only person alive who still prefers print books over e-books, and overall, I'm not much into technology. Obviously, I use e-mail and the Internet for research and news, and I have a cell phone, but that's about it. Steffi has been hounding me to get on Facebook and Twitter and such for years, but the mere thought makes me want to hurl. As someone who stays on top of celebrity gossip, Steffi can't understand my desire to avoid social platforms. While she doesn't have any particularly close friends in Los Angeles, she's well entrenched in UCLA's superficial social scene, and she's always busy going out with groups of party acquaintances.

My iced coffee is the right amount of both strong and sweet, and I draw another big taste as I kill time before class. The air has begun to cool a bit, and it finally feels more like autumn. I look up and watch the oak leaves flutter in the slight breeze, letting sun and shadow flicker across my face. There's a feeling of peace. It's so quiet here.

I scan my surroundings and, as always, admire the beautiful old stone that makes up the original buildings on campus. Andrews College could not look more classically collegiate, and even the newer buildings were designed to fit in with the old. Trees and shrubs, brick pathways, and ornate lampposts all add to the atmosphere. Inspired by this glorious day, I decide that I should spend more time out here before the brutal Maine winter arrives. Holing up in my room so much is probably not smart, and from my spot under this tree, I can at least watch the world go by, even if I don't participate. I realize that when I pay attention, I actually hear a lot: Frisbee players calling back and forth to each other, the chatter of students traversing the nearby walkway, guitar notes floating my way from a musician under another nearby tree . . . I'm taken aback at how much sound I usually shut out. Great. Another thing that's probably not indicative of sound mental health.

I watch the guitarist. He's clean-cut, with short, perfectly trimmed hair, and wearing a plaid button-down shirt tucked into jeans. The guitar rests in his lap as he strums and sings to a girl lying on her side in the grass and gazing up at him. The boy doesn't strike me as a typical guitar player. He looks like an economics major who picked up the guitar to get girls. But apparently it's working, because the one he's playing for appears utterly smitten.

This should be a sweet scene to witness, but instead all I feel is my good mood starting to sag. For a moment, I'm jealous. I can't imagine that I'll ever have a boy sing to me, much less look at me the way he's looking at her. But I shouldn't be jealous, because odds are this thing between them will end badly. That's how life works.

They have no idea how naive it is to believe, to trust.

I try not to flinch when he sets aside his guitar and crawls her way, laughing as he rolls her onto her back before lowering his mouth to hers. God, I really am jealous. And sad. I'm sad that I can never have that.

I throw my unread book into my backpack and forcefully zip the bag closed. I pound across toward a trash can to dispose of my iced coffee, which I have now lost the taste for. I toss it toward the bin, but it ricochets off and explodes in a mess of liquid and ice that smatters against the sidewalk.

"Nice shot," someone says rudely as he passes by.

"Thanks! So much!" I call to his back.

I sigh at the coffee disaster. I can't just leave ice cubes all over the walkway, so I crouch down and start to collect them, cursing under my breath as more than one slips from my hold.

"Slippery little guys, aren't they?" A pair of legs appears next to me, and I glance only for a second at ripped jeans and red Converse sneakers.

I don't say anything as I continue my desperate attempt to clean this mess. Without looking up, I manage to locate a few napkins in my backpack and do what I can to blot up the liquid.

The person bends down next to me, and I watch as he deftly picks up every stupid ice cube that has fallen through my fingers and plunks each one smoothly into the cup in my hand. His forearms are tan, toned, with leather cords and thin rope bracelets around each wrist. Like superhero cuffs or something. He probably thinks he can deflect bullets. My head involuntarily turns a smidge, and I catch sight of a bicep peeking out from the hem of his white T-shirt. Quickly, I look away. I wish this guy hadn't stopped.

I wish I wasn't instantaneously having lurid thoughts.

I wish he didn't smell like cookies and love.

When he gets the last of the ice cubes, I manage to toss the cup successfully into the trash bin without catastrophe. "Thanks for the help. I assume nine million ants will soon be here to celebrate Sugar Fest," I mumble.

Cookies-and-love boy smoothly begins pouring water from a stainless canister and washes the pavement clear. "Not to worry."

It becomes obvious that I must acknowledge this person who is being unnecessarily kind. It feels like a burden to do so, for which I'm ashamed, but I put on a smile and face him. Well, actually look up to him, given that he's got a good half foot on my five-feet, four-inch stature.

This boy looks at me. He really *looks* at me. I shift a bit to avoid eye contact, and while I would love to turn away completely, his soft, deep-brown hair frames his face in a way that prevents me from doing so. His curls are too long, the shorter ones framing his face, others tumbling recklessly over his ears, almost touching his shoulders. I suspect it's been a few days since he's shaved, but the scruff suits him, and it takes all of my will not to get drawn in by his unusual amber eyes that pierce through me. I am entirely discomfited and displaced by this person. And yet . . . I stare. Only for a short spell. For a matter of seconds, I let myself follow the shape of his face, the way his cheeks are full and how they lead into a jaw that makes me want to insist he shave so that I can see it more clearly.

This is bananas. *I'm* bananas. Some sort of psychotic hormonal surge has temporarily engulfed me, and I will knock this nonsense away now. Like, right now. Really.

Finally, I avert my eyes and throw away a soggy napkin. "Thanks again. Gotta get to class."

I sense he is about to say something, so I pivot and slip into the flow of students heading toward the other side of campus. As if I'm not already out of sorts, Carmen walks by, heading in the other direction, and waves. I wave back politely and say nothing, yet I'm actually dying to scream about what a hot mess I am after spilling coffee and having some unknown, sexy boy help me.

My Social Psych class is held in one of the biggest lecture halls on campus. Even though the class is huge, there are still plenty of empty seats, and I take what's become my usual spot at the end of a middle row. Immediately, I flip open my binder and make as if I'm intently studying notes from the last class. Most students take notes on their laptops, but Steffi told me she'd read that writing things down makes you learn them better. I put in earphones and play my white-noise app for added security from interruption while the room slowly fills.

Someone taps me on the shoulder, and I jump. It's just a girl wanting to get past me to take a seat. I nod and stand, and it's then that I hear voices that pass the sound in my earbuds and make me glance up.

The boy who helped me with the ice cubes is walking into the room. My stomach drops. Poised on the steps that run up alongside the rows, he is surrounded by students, all animated and talking effusively, and—it's clear—fussing over him.

Without thinking, I mute my app and slowly sit back down.

The boy smiles as someone pats him on the back in greeting, then lifts up his chin to acknowledge the clapping coming from a row of students. *Who is this guy?*

Students begin chanting, "Esben! Esben! Esben! Hashtag rock yourself! Hashtag rock yourself!"

So, his name is Esben. Ice-cube plucker is named Esben. *Huh. Well, whatever.*

I frown and shrink lower into my seat. I don't know what is happening, but it's making me horribly agitated. This Esben boy laughs and waves away the attention. A girl in the third row calls his name loudly enough to be heard over the ever-growing chanting and beckons him to a free seat next to her. He's clearly some kind of überpopular campus icon.

I'll just ignore him. It'll be easy. We have nothing in common.

Yet, I find myself staring at the back of his head for the hour-and-a-half class, and I have to work hard to stay on top of my note taking. Against my will, I'm intrigued when the professor raises the concept of charismatic leadership and then gestures toward Esben, eliciting laughter and applause from the entire room. By the end of the class, my heart is pounding, and I practically leap out of my seat the second the professor finishes assigning our reading. I reach the door in mere seconds, pushing through the flood of exiting students to get outside.

God, I need air. I need air.

My pace quickens as I separate myself from the mass of students, and I make it back to my room in record time. I deposit my backpack onto the sofa in the middle room and look in the mirror while I calm down. My bangs are still neat, my long ponytail has held its place, and my mascara has not smeared or left disgusting, goopy clumps in the corners of my eyes. I breathe in and out, in and out, until I begin to feel settled.

It's then that I notice a not-insignificant coffee stain on my yellow top.

Goddamn it.

I tremble as I rip the shirt over my head and dash to my closet to find a clean one. My emotional reaction to a simple stain is extreme; I know that, but I also know that I have my reasons.

When I was eleven, I lived with a foster mother who was obsessive about me never getting dirty. A mere smudge on my shoes was catastrophic, so in an effort to avoid dirtying white sneakers, I developed this odd style of walking that looked more like stomping. A visible spot on a shirt was cause for alarm, so I learned to be continuously on the lookout for anything that might strike me off her adopt list. That woman was constantly pointing to minor marks on my clothing while wincing and gently encouraging me to change outfits. It's impossible to shake the belief that she returned me to the foster system because of my inability to keep my clothes spotless.

So I rifle furiously through my closet for the most pristine top I can find. Even though I know *why* I'm freaking out, it doesn't help. My crazy reaction is one of a million dysfunctional ones that I have perfected over the years.

I really am goddamn irreparable.

I take my coffee-stained shirt into the bathroom down the hall. Holding the stain under the faucet, something dark on the underside of my shirt catches my eye, and I groan. *Great, what bizarre stain is this now?*

My fingers glide under the fabric, and I feel something plastic. I am mystified, so I flip over the shirt.

Stuck to my shirt is a button pinned to the side hem. It's pale blue with white lettering.

YOU CAN'T REACH WHAT'S IN FRONT OF YOU UNTIL YOU LET GO OF WHAT'S BEHIND YOU.

I stare at this in disbelief. Why is there a motivational button stuck to my shirt?

YOU CAN'T REACH WHAT'S IN FRONT OF YOU UNTIL YOU LET GO OF WHAT'S BEHIND YOU.

The statement is crap, because some of us will never be able to let go of what chases us.

YOU CAN'T REACH WHAT'S IN FRONT OF YOU UNTIL YOU LET GO OF WHAT'S BEHIND YOU.

The words nearly scream at me. Against my will, I smile.

This is so weird, a button showing up on my shirt. So random. And yet, I admit, sort of wonderful. It's a nice sentiment, and I should probably take it to heart.

This button is probably smarter than I am.

CHAPTER 4

WHITE NOISE

I decide to go into full shut-in mode over the weekend, planning to leave my room only to pay for pizza deliveries and to hit the shower. However, it's nearly impossible to sleep on Friday night, and I'm tortured by the sounds of joyful drunks roaming the halls. As I toss and turn, I make a mental note to either turn into a joyful drunk or invest in some earplugs.

Earplugs it is.

There are no knocks on my door, though, so there's that.

My sleep is restless and tainted by bad dreams, dreams in which I am driving a car I cannot control; dreams in which I am racing through an airport with no luggage and no ticket, unable to find any departure gates; dreams in which I am faced with an endless series of locked doors for which I have no keys.

I'm exhausted when I get out of bed at eight on Saturday morning, and there's no way I can get through the day without coffee, so my hopes for being a shut-in are dashed. The nice thing about waking up early on a weekend is the silence that overtakes the entire campus. Only a handful of people are outside when I make my way to the student union. The air is crisp, the leaves starting to turn, and I welcome the impending arrival of true fall. The Andrews College campus is always attractive, but the light this morning is exceptional, the quiet desertion appreciated, and my fatigue feels less painful.

But there still must be coffee.

Given how much I like the quiet, I should probably consider moving by myself to the middle of nowhere when I graduate next year. I could live off of Amazon deliveries and never have to leave the house. It's a highly appealing idea, but I've promised Steffi that I will move out to Los Angeles. That's always been our plan, but I'm not sure how I'm going to deal with such a heavily populated city. Of course, we'll be together, and she'll help me figure things out. Steffi's my rock, and she will not let me crumble.

The union is empty, and there's no wait to place my order with the grouchy student who is working at the café today. He looks pissed and more tired than I am, and he knocks down the brim of his baseball hat before taking my money and slamming buttons on the register. *There,* I think with satisfaction, *this is someone after my own heart.* Unlike that Esben. Carefree, happy, people loving, he's an enigma. I don't know why I'm thinking about him, anyway. He's obviously insignificant in my life. I want to fist-bump the sullen café boy for his outward display of crankiness.

I take my quadruple cappuccino and check my PO box to find that I have one notification slip.

Simon has sent me another care package. This is the fifth so far this year. It's not that I don't appreciate the thought, but I don't know how to respond to his generosity. I collect the box and tuck it under one arm, noticing that I'm oddly comforted by the sight of Simon's usual white packaging and handwritten address.

My walk back to the dorm is slightly awkward, and I have to set the box down while I fish out my key to get into the building. While I'm bent down, the heavy metal door flies open and smacks my right shoulder. As I'm pushed off balance to land on concrete, I'm not sure what hurts more: the pain from that or the burning cappuccino as it splatters across my left hand.

A couple who were holding hands and giggling when they first emerged are now gasping and apologizing profusely. The smell of alcohol and sex is heavy on them, and I move quickly to pick up my box and scramble inside, telling them not to worry.

I get back to my room and glare at my now-topless and half-empty coffee. I shouldn't be surprised because at this point I understand that I am not allowed to have caffeine without some kind of major incident. Very carefully, I set down the cup on the small table, treating it like liquid gold.

"Stay," I command it.

I open the door to the second bedroom and set the latest care package on top of the other four boxes from Simon. It's very wrong of me, I know, but I cannot get myself to open the boxes. Seeing what's inside them, understanding how much thought he gave into putting these together would make me feel guiltier than not opening them. Something catches my eye, though. The return label is slightly different than usual. I lean down and squint. Instead of the usual peony by his name on the return address label, there is now a leopard seal. He has a messed-up sense of humor, but I like it. Still, I leave the box where it is.

The door shuts behind me, and I have to laugh: I am rooming with care packages.

My shoulder is aching pretty good, my hand is stinging, and the cuff of my sleeve is soaked with coffee. I yank my sweatshirt over my head, grumbling over what is becoming an annoying routine, and replace it with a loose-fitting printed top. As I'm washing out the sweatshirt, I can't help but feel around in the rest of the jersey. Clearly, there is no silly motivational button, but I look anyway. Just in case. I could use one today. The disappointment I feel at not finding one is embarrassing, but I keep grabbing at the fabric just to be sure I didn't miss one. Why? Because there may be a motivational-button angel watching over me, right?

No.

I'm being nuts.

I finish up with my sweatshirt, then take what's left of my coffee and sit on my bed. After I text a polite thank-you to Simon, I don't know what to do with myself. My room is ridiculously clean, as always—overly organized, truth be told. My closet is only half-full and already arranged, with my clothes hanging by color and other items stacked neatly on the high shelf, so there's no excuse for a Saturday cleaning spree. The supposed common room in this suite is empty, save for the furniture supplied with the room, so there's nothing to be done in there. I could ice my shoulder, but that's hardly an activity. Although, given my options, it's not a bad one, so I pull a cold pack from the minifridge next to my bed and stare at the wall for fifteen minutes until the cold becomes more painful than the injury.

My clock might as well be shouting at me that it's early, and I have a full day to get through.

Well, there's always studying.

For hours, I read and reread textbooks and class notes and then jump ahead to next week's work. Statistics are delightfully dry and unemotional, and I spend extra time drowning in numbers and graphs until my growling stomach makes it impossible to keep my eyes glued to the page. I could call for a delivery, but . . . the walls are closing in on me. It's unlike me to feel unsettled when alone in my room, but I am. *I'm unsettled.* And it's disturbing.

The short walk I had this morning was nice enough to make me decide that I could tolerate leaving the dorm again. Something about that air this morning got to me. I can't stay on campus, though. I'll walk into downtown Landon, which is not exactly a metropolis, but it's as much of a city as we've got around here.

A block from school, I pick up a veggie pocket at an organic café and eat as I walk. I'm not exactly sure where I'm going, but I know that I'm at least walking in the direction of downtown. When I'm done eating, I try to video call Steffi, but she doesn't pick up. Probably still asleep after a late night, if I know her. I guarantee that she was out dancing until three in the morning, surrounded by adoring guys who paid for her drinks all night. There's a good chance one of them is with her now, and I'll dig for details later.

My earbuds are in, and I switch on my usual white-noise app. I let the whirling sound infiltrate my being, and I walk. And I refuse to think. About anything. I've felt restless and antsy, unable to fall into my usual routine, since I returned to school, and I've about had it. I need to get back to being satisfied by schoolwork and schoolwork alone. School and Steffi, those are my saving forces. Those are what keep me steady.

After a much longer walk than anticipated, I find myself at the outskirts of Landon, on a wide street lined with small shops, restaurants, and bars. This is an old town, and the sidewalks are cobbled brick, with lampposts evenly spaced down the street and lots of vintage-style signs calling out store names. It's cute. Yet immediately I wonder what in the world possessed me to come downtown, because I don't want to shop or sit in a café and converse with the locals. But I'm tired from my hour-plus walk, and my shoes are rubbing against my heels, so I've got to rest for a few minutes before I turn around. I think I remember a park at the end of this street, so I keep my head down and dodge pedestrians until I pass all the shops.

Sure enough, there is a park. Not only that, there is an enormous lake. I frown. How did I not know there was a lake here? *God, I'm so oblivious.* I take a seat on one of many benches and stare out at the water. The sun is high, casting sharp rays onto subtle ripples in the water. I turn up the volume on the background noise in my ear and watch the bits of white light fluttering before me. It is such an expansive circle of water I can barely make out the houses on the opposite side. Dark-blue water beckons only feet from where I sit, and I think how much more enticing the water is than the stringy blades of grass that meet it. The lake has a tranquility that I envy. *How deep is it?* I wonder. *Deep enough to swim? Deep enough to disappear? Deep enough to drown?*

But I do nothing but watch. I do not think.

I do not remember.

I do not plan.

I empty my mind until I am barren, until I don't feel like me, until I don't feel like anyone.

I just exist. Barely.

At some point, I close my eyes and drift further into myself. This may not be peace, this mind-set I'm in, but it's stable, and so I stay, refusing to leave even when my hands begin to chill. Eventually, though, the light filtering through my eyelids fades, and that pulls me back.

When I open my eyes, I realize that it's close to sunset. I have evidently been on this bench for hours. Not that it matters, really. Shadows are falling over the water, making the blue closer to black. I turn away as my vision begins to refocus on the real world.

I wish I liked the real world more. I wish I could embrace life. I wish for so many things, and I have no idea if it's possible for me to have them. I could try, maybe, but I have no clue where to start.

I shake my head and snap out of my dreaming. It was dumb to go so far from campus, and now I have an hour walk home in temperatures that are dropping into the low fifties. I cross my arms for warmth, and I make my way back to the main street. I forgot that traffic is barred from this street after five o'clock, and so now people wander freely down the middle of the road. College students are already invading the area, ready to hit the bars for the night, and I keep my head down, focused on getting past this scene as quickly as possible. A few people bump against me, but I don't react, even when a burly guy knocks against my sore shoulder. In fact, I feel nothing. I suppose that should be concerning.

I'm midway through the chaos, still keeping my attention on the cobbled bricks under my feet, when someone grabs my arm and drags me off the sidewalk. "Can you help? We just need one more person. It'll only take a few minutes, promise! He's my brother, and I swear he's cool." The girl's voice is friendly and animated, but I look up reluctantly.

"Um, what?" I say rather blearily and give her a cursory glance.

Her honey-colored hair is tucked behind her ears in a short bob, and a strand comes loose as she practically dances backward while tugging at my hand. "Come on. It'll be fun. Just sign this. It's a release form, nothing crazy."

I barely hear what she's saying, because I'm too busy trying not to trip over my own feet and also considering how to escape. She stops after a few yards and grabs a clipboard from her bag. "Name?" she asks.

"Huh? Me? Oh." I have no idea what's going on. Probably a petition of some sort. "Allison Dennis," I mutter.

She has me sign my name. I hope I didn't endorse a group supporting whale hunting or tempeh-only meals being served in the cafeteria. "So, all you do is sit in a chair and hold eye contact for a hundred and eighty seconds," she says. "No talking, no vocalizing of any kind, no looking away, no touching. Just don't break eye contact."

I snap out of it. "What are you talking about?" There are too many people gathered here, and I want more than anything to run, but I suspect she is the sort who would chase after me. Better to placate her and then make my exit.

"It's just a social experiment of sorts. It's cool. I'm Kerry, by the way. I take the video." She smiles broadly. "Now, go. Sit before it gets too dark." Kerry pivots my body toward a chair at a small card table.

"Video? Wait, no! I don't want to do any social experi—" I start to protest, but before I know it, she's plunked me down.

There is a matching empty chair across from me, and I clutch my hands together as mounting anxiety takes over. Clearly, I am doing something besides signing a petition. What did she say? A hundred and eighty seconds? And I have to look at somebody? Great. But that's only three minutes. In three minutes, I will be done with whatever stupid thing this is, and I can go back to my room, crawl into bed, and disappear again. I want to return to where I was only a short time ago. That place of nowhere. I fidget with my fingers and concentrate on spinning the rings I wear on my right hand while my foot taps repeatedly and uncontrollably.

Even without looking up, I see someone take the seat across from me, and hesitantly I lift my head.

Esben sits in front of me.

My insides clench; a surge of adrenaline and a sense of danger take over. Everything in me tenses and braces. For what, I don't know.

A hint of recognition crosses Esben's face. He remembers me from yesterday, a fact that only serves to stress me out more. This is the first time I've looked at him head-on, and his presence both alienates and beckons me. Instantly, I am horribly ashamed because I want to run to him and I also want to shove him so forcefully that he careens back in his chair and cannot do whatever we're about to do. Instead, I try to tolerate the ice that now seems to be running through my veins. Esben shifts in his seat to get comfortable and casually runs a hand through his mop of curls, pushing the hair from his face so that I have a full view of how irritatingly striking he is. I frown. He appears utterly relaxed, now leaning back in his chair as though this bizarre arrangement is the most normal thing in the world.

My desire to bolt is now threefold.

I could run. I don't have to sit here.

I retain the power of free will despite the circumstances.

Yet, I don't leave. Inexplicably, I am tied to this chair.

I turn and look for Kerry, but she's already poised with a video camera, standing in a now-silent and very large and observant crowd that has formed a circle around us. As if I'm not already feeling out of my element, the expectant silence that spreads among them is unnerving.

Esben speaks softly, his voice incredibly silky and reassuring. "You ready? One hundred and eighty seconds."

CHAPTER 5

ONE HUNDRED AND EIGHTY SECONDS

One hundred and eighty seconds. That's not long. That's nothing.

Slowly I shift my gaze. I start at his hands, both resting casually on the table, and then move to the bracelets. A few inches to the right, and I see the bright blue of his soft shirt over his chest. I lift my chin, see the stubble on his cheeks, the barest smile on his lips.

Fine, I tell myself. *He's just a boy. He can't do anything to me in three minutes.*

I meet his eyes, and in the beginning of the sunset light, their amber color is even more brilliant. He raises his eyebrows, silently questioning.

I glare at him and nod, as though he's challenged me to a fight for my life. As though getting through the next three minutes will somehow make me less weak than I am. "One hundred and eighty seconds," I affirm.

Bring it.

There is a blip in his confidence. But he gives me an inviting smile that I cannot take personally. He's probably done this countless times. I'm just another participant.

Esben signals Kerry, and she says, "Time starts now."

Ten seconds. His eyes practically bore through me. Esben is not screwing around here. He means it when he makes direct eye contact.

My hands tighten together. Despite how much I hate what is happening and how awful it is to force myself to not look away, I keep my expression blank, and I do not break from him. I don't know how I will get through this. He's making it worse by looking so at ease, so comfortable taking me in. But I will not back down.

It's simple really, I remind myself. *Just keep staring, stay solid and unbreakable. Feel nothing, because there's no reason to.*

Twenty-five seconds. I know little about him, but I do know for sure that he is nothing like me. That he is everything I am not. And mostly that this is an idiotic exercise in staring at a near stranger. After another few seconds, I resent him. I resent everything about him. Because, as his eyes are locked on to mine, I feel as though he sees more than the blue of my irises. And that makes me nervous. Vulnerable. Angry. He has somehow violated my protective shield, and in retaliation, I lock down even more.

Thirty-three seconds. I can't block out my growing rage. How dare he put me in this position? Me, of all people? He reeks of freedom and generosity and openness. And I hate him right now. And he must sense that, because his head moves back ever so slightly.

Fifty seconds. I have hardened my look, but it is draining me. It's more of a struggle than I would have thought to dislike him. Esben's look is gentle, soulful even, and I am wearing down, because even more than his expression, it's the feel of *him* that's starting to wreck me. It's undeniable that, as much as I want to dislike him, he exudes an energy, a spirit that overtakes me with calm. The area around his eyes moves just a bit, as though he wants to smile but he's stopping himself. Somehow, he is feeling good; he is lifted by the show of whatever he has created in this face-to-face experiment. Trying to move as little as possible, to convey that I haven't been affected, I inhale deeply through my nose and release the breath slowly through barely parted lips. *I can't hate him.* As much as I want to, I just can't. How can I hate someone else's happiness? Or, I realize, joy? That's it. Esben has joy about him.

Maybe what I feel is envy for what he has that I don't. I try to lock down my emotions.

Seventy-three seconds. Despite my resistance, I cannot help but be pulled into this. Into *him*. I'm sure the onlookers are making noise, but I can't hear anything except the even ebb and flow of my breathing. An unfamiliar sense of peace and relaxation has taken over me, and I let it stay. It's so rare to feel like this, especially with someone else along for the experience. Yes, I can get to some version of quiet on my own, but it's more about dead space. Nothingness. The absence of pain. What I am engulfed in right now is different. Not only am I swimming in a new version of serenity, but I have a partner in this. Esben is with me, no question.

Ninety-four seconds. Esben tips his head ever so slightly, as though he's seen something in me. How could he?

But quickly, I understand. Whether I like it or not, he is taking in pieces of me, just as I am taking in pieces of him, too. Without talking, I am still internalizing this boy in front of me. I study his look more intensely.

Oh. It's not that he sees something *in* me; he's *searching* for something in me.

Esben must feel how high my walls are, and I am equally ashamed and grateful that my secret is out. A kind of disturbing relief washes through me. For the first time, I believe that someone wants to experience me. To value me.

One hundred and eight seconds. The openness in his demeanor, his willingness to be so present, to want an exchange of some sort, is stronger than I am. But he has no idea what he's asking of me, what he'll find. My attitude shifts. *You want to play?* I dare him. *You want to use me for some kind of class project or whatever this is? You want inside my head? Fine. You have no idea how messed up I am. Go ahead. Drown like I do.* I step out from behind my walls.

For the first time, I look at him as I am. I give him me. I'll feel everything that I do on a daily basis and send it his way. We'll see if he can take it. Wordlessly, I can slay him with my anger and pain. And that's what I want. To take him down, to lash out at him in anger.

It takes only a few heartbeats for the twinkle in his eyes to dissipate. For a moment, it's as though the wind has been knocked out of him. I know that look because it's how I feel most of the time. His energy is more serious now, more intense. As if to punish him, to drive him away, I concentrate on how much I loathe myself, my inability to be anything resembling what he is. I flash through every house I've lived in, every school, and every family that was never really mine. Across the board, my life has been an accumulation of dysfunctional puzzle pieces that will never fit together. I will him to feel my repeated traumas.

One hundred and twenty-nine seconds. Yet what Esben is doing cannot be ignored. Even by me. Not for one second has he left me. Despite the horrific energy I am hurling at him, Esben is holding us together emotionally, giving me an unspoken promise that he will not drop me. The traumas that bind me every day, every hour, every minute soften until I barely feel their presence.

For reasons I cannot comprehend, I am lost in him. Safe. Right now, I am without a past that I hate. Right now, I am only here with him.

One hundred and forty-seven seconds. Even without taking my eyes from his, I see his shoulders move with his breathing. In addition to his kindness and sincerity, there is now an added element. Desperation? Need? He is not, I suddenly understand, freakishly perfect.

Esben has his own vulnerabilities. Apparently, we do have something in common.

One hundred and sixty seconds. We are engaged in a form of intimacy that scares the absolute hell out of me. It's as if there is a weight on my chest that I want to shove off, and I've never been this terrified before.

Or this whole and hopeful and connected.

My body starts to tremble. I want more of what I'm feeling, and I also want none of it.

I don't want to be so scared all the time; I don't want to be terrified that the earth could splinter apart under my feet at any given second. I want to be happy, really happy. *Dammit.* If only I could hide from the shards of hope that are piercing through my defenses. I feel tears build, and I clench my jaw to fight them back. Esben lifts his head a bit and rubs his lips together. There is a mix of concern and empathy and promise and . . . oh God, there's yearning . . . in his expression, and I know I am not mistaken about the shimmer that appears in his eyes. He takes a hard breath, as if trying to contain himself, and the sound of his jagged exhale courses through my body.

He, like me, is fighting something.

Together, we battle.

One hundred and seventy-three seconds. Emotion is going to swallow us whole, and I cannot survive this intensity any longer. I may break down under the ache that has settled over my heart. It will happen; I know it. I will succumb to the force, the pull, and I won't emerge victorious.

It becomes hard to breathe normally as terror rips through me. I'm going to collapse because I am goddamn alive, and I have barely felt life until this. Until *him*.

Kerry's voice is timid. "Time," she says softly.

We both stand. Esben simultaneously kicks his chair over and flips the table on its side, and I choke back a sob as we rush to each other. Esben moves like lightning, and his body crashes against mine as he wraps his arms about my waist and lifts my feet off the ground as though we have waited an eternity for this, as though this is a reunion that couldn't be delayed any longer. I throw my arms around his neck, embracing him more tightly than I've hugged anyone. In fact, it's been ages since I've had human contact this close, and the feel of him is almost too much. I cling to Esben with a blind, irrational trust, operating solely on instinct. Keeping me against him, he eases my feet onto the ground, and I knot my fingers together to make sure our hold doesn't break. He is shaking, maybe even more than I am, his breathing accelerated and uneven, and I bury my face against his chest. I could hide here forever. Or maybe it wouldn't be hiding. Maybe it would be living. Maybe . . . maybe . . .

I can't. I can't go there.

But my hands involuntarily move over his shoulders until I am tucking my arms between us, pressing my palms against his chest. I see what my touch looks like against him, how my hands sculpt to the shape of him, how I gather the fabric of his shirt and pull him in closer. His head dips down, and I respond by raising mine until his cheek is pressed against the side of my face, his embrace never faltering. I like the roughness of his stubble, the sound of his trembling breath, and the security of his grip on me. And even more, I like the heat of his mouth and the soft way he moves his lips when they brush against my cheek.

Because I am not myself, I don't have the sense to stop when I turn my mouth to his. His lips are poised as though waiting for me, as though he'd known what I would do. We move seamlessly into a kiss. It's not slow; it's not gentle. It is a kiss filled with unexplainable need, a kiss seeking salvation and healing and surrender and . . .

God, I can't think. I can't do anything but submerge myself in the taste of him. His hands go to the side of my face while his lips move against mine, and his tongue continues to send a flood of heat through me. I cannot get enough of this kiss, my starvation making me crazy and compelling me to slide my hands to the back of his head to ensure he does not stop.

Because if he stops kissing me, this will be over. Everything will be over. I will return to a life I am not equipped for.

That's all that I can process, all that I can understand right now.

So Esben needs to keep kissing me.

His thumbs move over my cheeks, then under my eyes, and I feel him wipe away tears. One of his hands brushes back my hair, and he softens the kiss. His lips begin to move more slowly, more passionately, more precisely. He can't let this end either; I can taste that in him. I don't know how long we are entrenched in each other like this, but it isn't long enough.

It's only when someone breaks the silence with a loud whistle and the large circle of people around us erupts in cheering and clapping, with a few lascivious noises thrown in, that I am harshly jerked back into reality.

Sharply, I push away from Esben and gasp for air. *What have I done? Oh God, what have I done?*

This is insanity. He doesn't want to let go, but I take three steps back and watch as his face registers as much confusion as mine likely does.

Just enough for him to notice, I shake my head. *No, this never should have happened.* I take another step back, and then another. Esben shakes his head now, asking me not to leave. Begging me.

But I do. Because that's what people do: they leave. When things are good, when things are bad, people leave.

But this time, I leave first.

CHAPTER 6

CURIOSITY DIDN'T KILL THE CAT

It takes every ounce of willpower I have to go to Social Psych class on Monday. I didn't leave my room for the rest of the weekend after the . . . *incident*. The ridiculous, stupid, inexcusable incident. Clearly some sort of temporary insanity took over my brain, and I'm terrified that other students may have witnessed my coming undone, so I walk to class with the hood of my sweater pulled up, big sunglasses covering nearly half my face, a patterned scarf wrapped around my neck and bustling up over my chin. It occurs to me that I may be drawing attention to myself with this silly outfit, but I feel more protected this way. Nothing out of the ordinary happens on my walk, though.

My cell rings just as I near the spot where Esben picked up my ice cubes, and I answer distractedly. "Hi . . ."

"Hiya!" Steffi says. "Where've you been, girl? You didn't take my calls or reply to my texts at all yesterday! Whatcha been doin'? Cozied up with some campus hottie?" she asks all too hopefully.

I trip over my own feet and nearly lose hold of the phone. "Wh . . . what? No! God, no. I just . . . uh . . . well, so much studying to do. I was at the, um, the place with the books . . ."

"The library?" she prompts.

"Oh. Yes, that." I stare at the concrete where my coffee had splattered. "All the books . . ."

"Allison, I told you not to get drunk in the morning. It's uncouth."

"What?" I snap my head up. "I'm not drunk!"

"Then why are you being all spazzy? And I can hardly hear you."

I push the scarf from my mouth. "I'm not spazzy! I'm very focused on school. That's all. This is an important year, and I have to make sure my grades are perfect, and the library has so many resources, and it's quiet, and I met a study group, and after that I found a comfy arm-chair by a window with a great view, and then I checked out a really old Shakespeare edition." This is a series of ridiculous lies that I can't seem to stop myself from telling. "Have you read Shakespeare? I haven't much—"

Steffi breaks through my babbling. "Holy hell, you are *so* spazzy."

She's right. "It's just a Monday thing, I guess."

"This is not a Monday thing. Something is going on. Spill."

"Nothing!" I say too loudly. "Gotta go! I'll call you later!"

Good God. I tell Steffi everything, not that I usually have tons of crazy stories to share. But this? No. I simply cannot tell her. The best approach is to pretend it never happened. There is the looming issue of having to face Esben in the next few minutes, but I will simply pretend that there is no Esben. Easy.

It turns out that I didn't need to worry. I get to the lecture hall and hunker down in my seat, but Esben is not here yet, and he does not come in late. A wave of relief should sweep over me, but I've been anticipating this moment for a day and a half, and now I'll have to go through this again on Wednesday. In no way am I disappointed that he's not here today, of course. Not in the least.

On Tuesday night, Steffi video calls me while I'm up late, typing up notes from the day.

As always, she looks impeccable; even the loose bun with stray blond tendrils falling out is perfect. Her tight pink tank top shows off her long neck and full cleavage. If I didn't adore her so completely, I would be riddled with envy. As it is, seeing her face on my screen always makes me happy, and I smile at her. "What's up? How are you?"

It's then that I notice she's leaning back in her chair, arms folded, with an undeniable smirk on her face.

"Steff?"

She bunches her lips together and cocks her head. "'What's up?' Seriously? What's up with *you*? Is there, oh, any chance you'd like to share something massively huge and crazy with me?"

I freeze, my smile vanishing. I cannot get myself to say anything. Something very bad is about to happen; I can tell.

Suddenly, Steffi flails her hands about wildly, and she begins talking with such a shocking level of delight that I can hardly follow what she's saying. "Did it occur to you to tell me that you'd become a viral-video sensation? That you're plastered all over the Internet, getting all schmexy time with the one and only Esben Baylor? Ohmigod, could he be any freakin' hotter? How was the kiss? What the hell was that? Oh wait! Is he there right now? Am I interrupting anything?" She claps her hands together and leans in to the camera, pretending to peer around my room.

I can't process this. "I'm a what?" I ask flatly.

"You're a viral-video sensation! All over Facebook and Twitter and BuzzFeed! Upworthy!" She's screaming and laughing, and I feel as though I might pass out.

"No. No, no, no." I start shaking my head. "What are you talking about?"

"Hold on." She starts clacking furiously on her keyboard and messages me a link.

Hesitantly, I move my mouse and click.

Oh hell, no.

I don't know what this BuzzFeed thing is, but even I can tell that the site is huge, with links to stories about celebrities I know nothing about and lots of headlines and exclamation points. And smack at the top of the page is a video with the headline, "180 Seconds: Interactions between Strangers That Will Make You Melt."

I clap a hand over my face in horror and scream in protest. "Nooooo!"

"Watch it! Watch it!" Steffi demands with delight.

I glance at the chat window and roll my eyes at the way Steffi is bouncing around idiotically.

"Have you seriously not seen this?" She is obviously in disbelief. "If I were you, I'd be throwing this around all over the place!"

Of course she would. She's gorgeous and confident and loves nothing more than to be the center of attention. I shake my head and hit the "Play" button, peeking out between my fingers. Music begins, and I barely make out the words that scroll by in what's presumably some kind of introduction. Then a video of Esben seated in an all-too-familiar chair begins to play, and the camera pans to an older man in the chair opposite him.

"This cannot be happening," I whisper.

"Jump to the end! It gets better!" Steffi squeals.

"I bet it does *not* get better," I say angrily, but I drop my hand from my face and click to a later spot in the video.

Esben is smiling and nodding at a middle-aged woman dressed in business attire as she gets up from the chair and leaves. The screen goes black, and more text appears: Sometimes, the unexpected happens. Sometimes, someone makes you break your own rules. And suddenly, there I am on-screen. I watch the moment that I first see Esben.

"Nooooo!" I yell out again. "Oh God!" I hit the "Stop" button. "I am not watching this! Steffi, what am I going to do? Why is this online?"

"Do you really not know who Esben Baylor is?" she hollers, while looking way too happy.

"He's . . . he's just some guy in my psych class." I pause as I process what she's said. "Wait, how do you know his name?"

"Seriously? Honey, I know you aren't an online social butterfly, but really? Esben Baylor!" She flops back in her chair, clearly exasperated with me but still smiling. "This is what you get for being so out of it."

"No, I really do not know who he is," I say impatiently. Now is not the time to scold me for my failure to be on top of Internet trends. "So, who is he? And why do you know about him?"

"I assumed that even you would know who Esben is. I mean, hello? He posts tons of stuff online. Twitter, Facebook, he's got a live blog . . ." She waves a hand around. "He's all over the place. And plenty of other sites pick up his posts. Esben 'Hottie' Baylor does videos, pictures, starts hashtag trends. Stuff like that. Bios of interesting people he meets, things that help people, posts that raise awareness of issues. All really touching, feel-good stuff. And now you're in one of his videos! God, I'm so jealous I could lose my mind, but I'm also totally excited for you! This is the best thing ever!"

"Okay. Okay, it's fine. This will be fine." I try to calm myself down. Maybe this isn't so bad. Maybe it won't be a problem. It's just a dumb video.

"He's got a huge following." Her beaming smile is beginning to really irritate me. "Like, *massive*."

I prop my elbow on the table and drop my head into my hand. "Awesome."

"What are you so upset about? You made out with Esben Baylor! The only thing to worry about is all the girls who are going to hate you for this."

"Again, awesome." I close the browser window.

"It *is* awesome," she insists, but her voice is gentler now. "Allison, this is all very cool. You needed a little spice, don't you think? Something to mix things up?"

"No, I did not." I pout. "Listen, I gotta go. I'll call you tomorrow."

"You didn't even watch the whole video. Your scene is amaz—"

I stop her. "I don't want to watch it. I don't want to talk about this again, okay?"

"But everyone else is talking about it! People love it, and—"

"Steff, please!" I beg. "Everyone will forget about it soon enough. This is not going to be a big deal, okay? I won't let it. I don't need this right now."

"Well . . . all right." Her disappointment is palpable. "You just looked so . . . different in the video. So . . . so . . . ."

I sigh. "So what?"

"Open. Real. Emotional." She casts an undeniably sweet energy. "Vulnerable and so connected."

"I wasn't any of those things." This is a lie, but I'm going to hold to it.

"And in case you didn't notice, Esben is gorgeous. Like, supergorgeous. Hot. Breathtakingly handsome. And he goddamn flung himself at you! I have never seen anything more romantic in my life, and neither has the rest of the Internet. He's a heartbreaker, for sure."

"He is not!" I shout defiantly.

"He is." She is calm now. "And more than that, Allison? Esben is as perfect as anyone gets. That boy has heart like I've never seen."

"How nice for him. I don't care."

She glares at me, and I look away when she says, "You were glowing."

"I was absolutely not glowing!"

"Honey, who cares if you were? You looked beautiful. And passionate."

"Seriously, stop it. It was nothing." I'm so over talking about this mess, and I can't stay in this conversation any longer—even with Steffi. "I love you, but I've got to go. I'll talk to you soon." Without giving her a chance to say anything else, I end the video call.

I turn off my computer, throw on pajamas, hit the lights, and get into bed. I don't care that I haven't brushed my teeth or that I totally need to pee. There is no way that I'm leaving this room to go down the hall to the bathroom. Who knows who I might run into? What if Steffi is right and some girl accosts me for . . . for the . . .

I scream into my pillow.

For the kiss.

I scream again.

How could I have let this happen? I have worked so hard to set up a life that I can manage, and all it took was three minutes to undo that. Three stupid, dumb minutes that I would kill to undo.

I have to regroup. People are fickle, and this is bound to blow over soon. I will simply pay no attention to Esben or this mess. I will not search the Internet or—God forbid—read comments. I will not watch this video. It will not exist. Problem solved.

Except that I toss around in bed for more than an hour, unable to relax, unable to shed my throbbing anxiety. When it's obvious that I am not going to sleep, I notice that my cell phone is within arm's reach, with moonlight practically shining a spotlight on it. I look away and wiggle my toes nervously. *No, I will not.*

But I do. I can't help myself. I click my phone on. Curiosity may have killed the cat, but I've got a lion's roar going on in my head.

It takes two seconds to search for Esben's video, and I find it on a different site from the one Steffi sent me. I groan. How many places is this posted? Now that I've given in and gone to this page, though, I still can't get myself to watch. I don't know what I'm afraid of. I was there. I just don't want to relive it.

But I also kind of do.

I scroll toward the end and let it play for only a few seconds. I hit the "Pause" button and look at the image before me. And I can't stop looking at it.

Esben's hands are on my face, our kiss well in progress, and both of our expressions clearly show that this kiss is more than just any old kiss.

Was more, I correct myself. *It's not anything now.*

Still, I allow myself to look at the picture, to hold the phone in my hand as I fall asleep, and to dream without nightmares.

I give myself that much. Just for tonight.

CHAPTER 7

JUST TRYING TO BREATHE

Never during my two years at Andrews have I skipped a class. Not once. But I skip Wednesday's Social Psych class. I'm tempted to skip my next class, but that seems phobic and weird, even for me, and missing two classes would probably make me more anxious than braving leaving my room. Besides, having missed breakfast and lunch, I'm ravenous. There have been near-relentless knocks at my door all morning, and I put in my earphones and jack up my white-noise app to block out the demand for me to say something profound or meaningful or whatever these people want from me.

When there is a lull in the hammering on my door, I realize that I have a little time before my class, so I decide to stop by the Greek place where I ate with Simon. Nothing bad can happen when surrounded by falafel. At least, that's what I'm going with.

I am only halfway along the path that leads from my dorm to the street, when a guy with a biker jacket and a messenger bag strapped snug across his chest holds up his hand for a high five. "Nice going!"

This is the sort of thing I was afraid of. My hand only raises limply, my unhappiness making me almost nonfunctional, but the guy claps our hands together and cheers.

"Very cool video," he says.

"Oh. Well, thank you."

He releases his hold, pats me heartily on the back, and gives me a weird salute as he continues on his way.

One down, who knows how many to go. I cannot hate this day any more.

Just outside the Greek place, three girls ambush me.

"You're the girl from the video with Esben!" one says.

"Is he the best kisser ever? You have to tell us! He's got to be, right?" A girl with flowing red hair makes a ridiculously dreamy face.

The third looks borderline pissed. "Why did you leave? Oh my God, I would have ripped his pants off right there if I'd been you!"

"So"—the first leans in conspiratorially—"are you a couple? Did you go back and get him?"

This is horrendous. "What? No! God! We are not a couple!" I say too defensively. *Be polite. Be polite!* I remind myself. I clear my throat. "I'm so pleased you enjoyed the video. I'm going to eat falafel now."

I turn and yank open the door to the restaurant. The elderly Greek man who takes my order lights up when he sees me. "Hey, hey! It's you!" He signals to the kitchen staff behind him. "Look! It's her!" The Greeks all cheer, and my cheeks flush hotly.

I pay as quickly as possible and grab a seat. I have only taken one bite of my food, when two girls I recognize from my psych class plop down at my table, squealing, "So amazing. I cried!" and "What was it like? The whole thing?" I stand up, toss my uneaten food, and bolt.

The rest of the day continues this way, but thankfully my professor gives a detailed lecture that I lose myself in for an hour. I don't look up from my note taking, but I can feel the stares from my peers. After, I grab a premade sandwich from the student union for dinner and retreat to my dorm.

Thursday is equally bad, and it occurs to me that I may be forever trapped in this hellish vortex of attention and have to drop out of college and go live in some remote part of the world without Internet access. I will live in a hut and forage for berries. Again, I think about the possibilities Amazon gives me. I can order everything I might ever need. Total isolation is doable. I could live like that.

By Friday, I am just plain mad. Seething and stoic, I go to my Social Psych class. I radiate stay-away vibes, but this does not stop people from looking at me way too much. All eyes turn to Esben when he walks in, and I see him scan the room. He stops when he sees me, his face brightening and hopeful as he starts to walk my way. Esben likes eye contact and silent communication? Fine. Two can play at that. I shoot him a glare full of rage, and he stops in his tracks. The chatter in the large room lulls, but right now I don't care if everyone sees the rejection I hurl at Esben. His face grows worried, confused. Then apologetic. But my expression does not change, and when the professor walks in, I sharply pull my eyes from his and refuse to look back. Without words, I have told him and everyone watching what I need to.

So there. That is that. This is over.

My steely aura does a good job protecting me from further comments, and I get through my next class, pick up yet another care package from Simon at my PO box, and walk back to my dorm without harassment.

I should feel better now that I've asserted myself and shut down some of the drama surrounding the video. Instead, I feel like crap. Utter crap. *I got what I wanted, right?* No Esben, no connection, no one talking to me. World order has been restored.

This should feel better than it does.

I hear a familiar voice call out my name. "Allison! About time! I've been sitting here for twenty-five minutes, and I gotta pee like nobody's business."

I jerk my head up and stop in place. My heart soars; my emptiness washes away. "Steffi!"

Perched on the front step of my dorm is my best friend, looking for all the world like a rock star in her red leather pants and sleeveless black shirt. She's got a small suitcase next to her. I can't tell if I want to burst into tears or start laughing.

She stands and opens her arms wide. "Come to Mama!"

I run the short distance between us and hug her fiercely. "What are you doing here? Oh my God!"

"What am I . . . doing . . . here? Right now, I'm trying . . . to breathe . . ."

I release my grip on her and step back, laughing. "Sorry." I shake my head in disbelief.

Steffi tosses her hair and puts her hands on my shoulders. "I. Have. To. Pee."

"Okay, okay!" I unlock the front door, take her to the ladies' room and then to my suite, all the while hurling questions at her.

"For real, what are you doing here? I cannot believe this!" There is genuine happiness flooding from me right now. I automatically set the latest care package on top of the others in the spare room. When I turn back to Steffi, she's making quite the face. "What is it?" I ask.

She gestures behind me. "Um, are you building an oversize game of Jenga in there? What the hell is up with the boxes?"

"Oh." She's got a point. The box tower is a little weird looking. "They're from Simon."

"I see." She flashes a curious smile. "We'll get back to that later. I did not take a red-eye to Boston and then rent a car to drive a million hours because you have a hoarding problem."

We both sit down on the couch. "So, why come? And why didn't you tell me?"

She shrugs. "I wanted to surprise you."

I'm still flabbergasted that she's in front of me. "But, but . . . how did you afford a ticket and a car?"

"Do you have any idea how much money my scholarship gives me to buy books and stuff? Way too much. I'm not buying every single thing on the syllabi. You know how it is. Half the time, we don't use a book for more than a day. So, I traded in unnecessary books for a trip."

"I'm very glad you did." I hug her again. As I do, I can't help but search for the scar that is imprinted on her shoulder blade. A reminder of the challenging childhood she has survived. "And we need to feed you. You're skin and bones."

"And boobs! Don't forget the boobs!" She smushes her chest against mine, and I laugh.

"I could not forget the boobs," I assure her as I sit back. "I can't wait to hear everything that's going on with you! You hungry? What do you want to do for dinner?"

"Tequila," she states.

"Could we have a food component, too?"

"Maybe. I'll think about it."

CHAPTER 8

TEQUILA AND THINGS

The food component turns out to be Italian food from a restaurant down the street that I'd never tried. Steffi inhales her plate of fettuccine Alfredo, and, in between bites, chastises me for never having been here. "I mean, really? Do you now understand what you've been missing out on?" Then she stabs one of my meatballs and shoves the entire thing in her mouth.

A quick pit stop at the liquor store (where Steffi is handed flyers from three different guys for various parties), and we are back in my room, with Steff now pouring us our first tequila shot. I haven't had a drink since this summer, and the alcohol burns down my throat. I smile. "God, I missed tequila."

"And tequila missed you." She bites a lime wedge and winces. "Know what else missed you?"

"What?"

She reaches into the paper bag next to her and raises a bottle. "Gin!"

"Yay!"

Her other hand goes to the bag and emerges with another bottle. "And tonic!"

"Yay!"

"And yay for my bangin' fake ID."

I pour us strong drinks and get some ice cubes from the minifridge while Steff makes a playlist on my computer and blasts music from my bedroom.

"Oh, hell. Is today Friday?" she calls out.

"Yeah, why?" I step into my bedroom and set down her drink on the desk. "Why are you on Amazon?" I squint at the screen. "And why are you buying a roll of cartoon sheep stickers, duct tape, and a nose-hair trimmer?"

Steff takes a large swig and then spins in the chair to face me. "Remember the apartment that I lived in last summer? Well, after I moved, I accidentally sent some things there because I forgot to update my address on some websites. Including, I will have you know, a site where I bought a megahot and not-inexpensive dress. The two stupid girls who moved in after me never sent back anything." She takes another drink. "Or they would just claim things never arrived. Liars. So, every month I send off something addressed to me at my old address. I like the idea that they get all excited, thinking they can steal more of my purchases, and they probably get hyped up, thinking it's something cool—because I always order cool things, right?—and then they open the package, and it's striped tube socks and a poop emoji pillow or whatever. So I am punishing them forever."

Oh, how I have missed this girl.

I sit on the bed. "That's kind of goddamn brilliant. I want to help!"

"Go ahead. Pick out something. Aside from buying plane tickets, this is also what I do with the extra financial aid money." She puts her hands behind her head and stretches. "I really am a genius."

After some browsing, I add a no-solicitors sticker and a box of poorly reviewed quinoa crackers, and when the confirmation e-mail dings on her phone, telling us that her order was received, we celebrate by slamming down our drinks and both burping at the same time. Soul sisters, we are for sure.

I'm a definite lightweight, so by nine thirty, I am beyond tipsy, and it feels fantastic. Steffi is doing some crazy dance that is predominately defined by Hula-Hoop hip moves and Superman arms. It's superodd but rather entertaining. From my spot on the couch, I suck an ice cube and watch my friend move through the common room as she dances off the beat. I am still gobsmacked that she is here, and the smile plastered on my face is a welcome respite from the events of this past week.

It's that thought that makes me sit bolt upright. "Hey! Wait a minute!" I yell, my voice garbled from the ice cube in my mouth. "Stop!"

"Huh?" Steffi pauses her dance. "You cannot handle my sexiness?" She shakes her hips.

"You!" I thrust a pointed finger her way. "You are not here because you had extra money!"

Her face drops. "What do you mean? I wanted a long weekend with my best girl. That's all." But she reaches for the gin bottle and starts to pour a drink.

"You are here," I say forcefully, while repeatedly jabbing my finger at her, "for nefarious reasons!"

Steff laughs. "Nefarious reasons? Oh really?"

"Stephanie Elinor Troy! You are sneaky! 'Fess up, right now!"

But she can barely talk because she is doubled over, laughing and trying to breathe.

I frown. "What is so funny?"

Finally, she answers. "My middle name is not Elinor!" Then her fit of hysterical laughter continues, and she sits beside me.

"It's not?" There is the beginning of a slur in my voice. "Why do I think it is? Who is Elinor?"

The poor girl might hyperventilate, and it takes her forever to answer. "Remember that weird family I lived with in Watertown? Elinor was the name of their Jack Russell terrier."

"Oh." I grab her cup and take a drink. "Who names a dog Elinor?"

"A proctologist and a psychic who live in Watertown and wanted a fake daughter for five months."

"Do you even have a middle name?"

She takes back her cup and shrugs. "Not that I know of. I don't even know how I have a last name. *That's* weirder than a dog named Elinor. Remember, I got dropped at one of those safe-harbor haven thingies where you dump off babies without any questions, so I doubt there was a sticky note on my head with a full name. Hey! So, who named me? Who named us? You were left at a hospital, too!"

She's right. This has never occurred to me before. "Yeah! Who named us? We should have been able to pick our names!"

"But you took Simon's last name, so now you are Allison Dennis, and it suits you." Her eyes light up. "Hey, I have an idea. Let's play care-package Jenga!"

"Stop it." I giggle.

"Come on. It'll be fun. I take out a package near the bottom and hope the tower doesn't tip."

"We are not playing care-package Jenga!"

"Then you take one, then me . . . honestly, why haven't you opened any of 'em? Simon probably got you good stuff. Ramen and cookies and lice treatment."

"I don't have lice!" I shriek.

She nods very seriously. "Not yet. But college campuses are notorious breeding grounds for lice."

Maybe she's right. Maybe Simon has sent me true necessities that I didn't even realize I need. God, Steffi doesn't have anyone sending her care packages, and she really deserves it. And maybe there are cookies in there . . . I should consider opening them. Or maybe just one.

I'm a little wobbly when I stand and start pouring a gin and tonic. Halfway through making it, I spin around and slosh gin on the carpet. "Heeeeeeey! Wait a minute. You are trying to distract me from the crucial subject at hand."

"Which is crucially what?"

"The reason you are here." After I manage to make my drink, I sit back down next to her. "Let's have it."

She gives me a blank look and says nothing.

I lightly shove her shoulder. "Do you have fabulous news or something? Oh, did you apply for that magazine internship you mentioned last summer? Did you get it? Oh, oh! Or there's a boy. It's a boy, isn't it? Tell me, tell me!"

Steffi grins and claps her hands together. "Well, yes. There is a boy."

I'm about to burst. Despite numerous and entertaining flings, Steff hasn't had a true boyfriend in ages. "Tell me everything!"

She is still grinning and stares at me for way too long, and it's only when I throw my arms up in frustration that she answers me. "The boy's name is Esben Baylor, and you sucked face with him, became an Internet sensation, and you won't talk about it. Something major happened! Something wonderful! This was totally unlike you and totally awesome. Cheers!"

I cross my arms with irritation and sneer. "No, no cheersing! We are not cheersing!"

"That's not a word."

"Whatever. I thought you had good news about yourself or something. I thought we were celebrating. This is totally disappointing. You're actually here to make me talk about that Esben boy and the stupid thing I did?"

"Yes." Steffi takes out her phone, taps the screen a few times, and faces it my way. "Look. Just look." It's a freeze-frame of Esben and me.

"It's nothing." But my denial sounds weak, and I take the phone in my hand and study the image.

"It is *not* nothing."

I snap out of it. "He made my life hell this week! Do you know how many people were bothering me about this on campus? Wanting gory details and being all probing and whatnot? Ugh. It was awful. I finally got it to stop."

She practically snorts. "Well, the Internet hasn't stopped."

"What are you talking about?"

"The tweets, the comments on every site that picked it up . . . people are still loving it."

"There are comments?"

"Yeah, dummy! Like, thousands." She squints at me. "We need to do something about your makeup. And hair."

"Huh? Who cares about my makeup and hair? Thousands of comments? How are there thousands of comments?" The gin is not helping me feel less freaked out, and I barely notice Steffi pulling my hair loose or reaching into her purse to retrieve a makeup bag.

She has me close my eyes, and I feel her brushing eye shadow on my lids. "Sweetheart, Esben has over four hundred seventy-five thousand followers. And that's just on Twitter. Then there's Facebook, where he's got over three hundred thousand. Plus, his live blog."

I open my eyes and ignore her irritated expression at my interrupting her crash makeover. "Hundreds. Of. Thousands. Oh, Steff . . ."

"If you'd pay attention to the online world, you would've known. Esben Baylor is a social icon! And he's right here on your campus! I'm so jealous I could scream."

Yeah, I could scream, too.

She goes to her phone again and taps around. "Here. Read. These are the comments under his original Twitter post."

Silently stewing, I begin what could be an endless process of scrolling while Steffi lines my eyes with dark-brown eyeliner, dusts blush over my cheekbones, and then turns on a big curling iron and starts fussing with my hair while I read.

Stunning. Heartfelt. Touching. Keep doing what you do, Esben.
You go! The entire montage is extraordinary. Thanx for sharing.
Showed this to my mom, and we both cried, lol!

Who's the girl? She's a babe! Right on, brother! Not a bad start to a romance, huh?

Plz come to Chicago! We want u! I'll volunteer to do whatever u want! Kiss me!

Is the girl on Twitter? Want to follow her.

Now THAT was a kiss. But . . . then what? Did she come back? Have you talked to her?

I scoff and keep scrolling and reading. The tweets are, by and large, raving and supportive of the video. There are, of course, mean tweets, too: That girl doesn't deserve you. Glad she bolted, and I hate all your lame stuff and UR a moron, and This is so corny and schmaltzy. Get a life.

They all make me sick.

Steffi gets the iron too close to my scalp, and I let out an "Ouch!" then take the last now-watery drink from my cup. "You know what?" I say too loudly. "What he did is not okay! I didn't ask for this attention. Fine, if he likes being at the center of the universe, that's his prerogative, but how dare he suck me and other unsuspecting people into his crap, right? He's a horrible, horrible person!"

"Oh, well, yes. Horrible." She pauses. "You should tell him that, don't you think?"

I slap the phone down on the couch. "I should! I should, dammit!"

"Yes, right now!" Steffi is on board with this. She must be coming around to sharing my anger. "Let's find out what dorm he's in. The student directory is online?" she asks.

"I dunno. I guess. I haven't looked anyone up before."

We log on to the Andrews student portal, and it takes Steffi only seconds to learn that Esben lives in Wallace Hall, which is a dorm not far from mine. "Bingo!" she says before zooming in on his profile picture. "Good Lord, that boy is easy on the eyes . . ."

"Hey! Knock it off!"

"I mean, he's still a very bad person, of course, but he is one hot piece of ass."

"Now you're making me hate him more."

"Well, then you need to go tell him how awful he is right now."

"Right now?" I hiccup.

"Yes. Seize the moment!" Steffi leaps up, pulling me with her, and runs a hand through my now-curly hair. "You go watch that video with him and point out all the jerky things about it!"

"Aren't you coming with me? As backup? You know, you can yell, 'Yeah, good point!' and 'Buuuuurn!' when I say smart things."

She pulls a red lipstick from her tight pants pocket and freshens her color. "I'm gonna pop over to one of those parties we got invited to. There are some damn cute boys on this campus. Text me when you're on your way back."

"I'm gonna go kick some Esben ass!" I sing out proudly. "Like a vigilante!"

"Esben's ass, drunk vigilante, yes, yes. Now, let me just throw a bit more lip gloss on that pouty mouth of yours . . ."

CHAPTER 9

MACARONI AND VIDEOS

Steffi and I part ways in front of Esben's dorm, and I march confidently (if a bit clumsily) up the stairs. At his room, I do not hesitate before slapping the door with the flat of my hand. I mean business tonight.

The door opens, and I am momentarily taken aback, unable to ignore that we are again only a few feet from each other. And also unable to ignore that his shoulders are broad, but not too broad, and that I know what it's like to be crushed against him, feeling him hold me. I literally shake my head and look up at the obviously startled boy in front of me. "You and I need to have a conversation, buster!" I push past him and find myself in a single room, with barely enough space for the bed, desk, and dresser. His bed is unmade, a navy comforter scrunched over plaid sheets; his laundry is strewn around; and his desktop is so beyond cluttered that I verge on having a panic attack. "You're a slob," I say without thinking.

He takes a second to reply. "I . . . am. Sorry. I didn't know you were coming by. Obviously." There's a beat of silence before he says, "Allison."

It's the first time I've heard him say my name, and I'm moderately shaken. "Ohmigod, I'm sorry. You're not a slob. I'm awful." I look around the room. "But you're not a neat freak. Not that there's anything wrong with that. It's a style choice. Very relaxed."

"Here, let me just . . ." Esben sidles past me and begins furiously straightening the sheets and comforter to give some semblance of order to the room. "Would you like to sit down?" Without looking at me, he gestures to the bed.

"Fine." So, I do, and he sits in the desk chair. Automatically, I begin smoothing the comforter with my hand and watching the way the fabric ripples as I skim my hand over it. Eventually, I look around his room. I can barely make out the small microwave propped up on milk crates because it is so covered with clothing, notebooks, and discs. I also spy a video camera on a shelf, and I look away.

The quiet goes on for longer than socially appropriate, yet it doesn't feel as strange as it should. He's just waiting. The way Simon waits for me, I realize.

"I have some questions," I blurt out. Gin is making me annoyingly direct. I can't face him, so I stare down at my hands.

"Okay."

"Do you ever wear your hair in a man bun?"

He laughs. "I do not. It's not long enough, but I highly doubt I would even if I could."

"That's good."

"Next question."

"Why don't you have a poster of a kitty hanging from a tree limb, with some hideous font that says, 'Just hang in there'? Or a poster of Gandhi and some sort of freakishly smart quote? Instead you have a black-and-white print of Lenny Kravitz."

"I'm allergic to cats, and Gandhi was less photogenic than Lenny Kravitz."

"Funny," I say in a monotone. At last I raise my head. "Why did you do it? Why did you do that to me?"

"I don't understand," he says softly.

"Why did you put me on the Internet? Why did you make me a part of that whole thing? What did I ever do to you?" My voice is rising.

"I was, you know, doing just fine, and then yoooooou made it so everyone was bugging me and asking about me and"—I drunkenly wave my hand in the air—"tweeting things and commenting about stuff and all that. I didn't ask for any of that."

"Allison, I'm so sorry," he says gently, but with an air of surprise. "I . . . I . . . you signed the waiver. You . . . I assumed you knew who I was."

"Ohhhh, well, don't we think highly of ourselves!"

He laughs lightly. "I didn't mean it like that. It's just . . . I do a lot of these social experiments and such, and it's a relatively small campus . . ."

"So, then you should have known that I like to be left the hell alone! That I don't want people seeing me act like, like . . ." I don't even know how to say what I mean. "No one should have seen that. Because it shouldn't have happened. You did something," I say too accusatorially. "I don't know what, but you did something. Why? Did you need someone to be your big finale, so you had your sister grab the most introverted person you could find to see if you could . . . I don't know. Break me?"

Esben actually looks hurt, and I feel a hard pang of guilt. He shakes his head over and over. "No, no. God, no . . ." He glances to the side as if searching for what to say.

"What happened that day? You have to tell me," I plead. "Because I don't get it, so you must. Why did we . . ." I can't bring myself to say it. "Go on. Tell me everything, Mr. Esben Baylor. Maybe you think everyone knows you, but I do not know anything about you except that you're a big jerk." I hiccup, and he politely does not comment. "So, you start talking right now!" I am so crazy and not nice right now, but it's impossible to stop the words that spill out.

"Okay." He takes a deep breath and exhales slowly. "I never know who will be involved in any of my projects. Really. Even though there were a lot of people there last week, we were having trouble getting volunteers. I think people get nervous when they've been watching me for a while. Besides, it's usually more interesting with people who haven't had a lot of time to think about what they're doing beforehand. Kerry said she just grabbed you from the crowd. It wasn't planned. Honest." Esben looks at the floor and rubs the legs of his jeans anxiously.

"It still happened, though." My voice is gentler than I'd planned. More scared, too, maybe. "It still happened, and I didn't want it to."

"If I'd had any idea that you didn't want to be there . . . I didn't know anything about you except that you spilled coffee one day." A half smile peeks out. "I wanted to do that social experiment because I thought it would be a great way to see how two strangers can communicate and feel and maybe even find common ground, all without talking. How prejudgments about others sort of get washed away in the process, how a relationship of sorts happens in that short time. I didn't know how anything would play out. How could I?" His sincerity is undeniable. "I included the video section of us because something very unique happened. Something that affected me that I was totally unprepared for. You want me to explain it? I don't know that I can. I just . . ." He's getting uncomfortable now. "Something about you reeled me in fast. I'm not sure I've ever been that hyperfocused on anyone. It's like you were totally in my head, hearing me, questioning me, comforting me, reaching for me." Esben laughs with a disbelief that I understand, and he runs a hand through his hair and shifts in his chair.

I scoot back on the bed and help myself to one of his pillows for support. "I may or may not get that," I admit. "Keep saying things." I want him to continue talking because the liquor has loosened me up enough that I'm quite enjoying watching how he moves his hands while he speaks, how his voice is a bit husky without being too deep.

"Just because there isn't a rational explanation for what went down between us doesn't mean that I can't appreciate and be grateful for those three minutes. How often are we *that* moved?" He looks shyly at me. "I did, you know, have other great connections that day. Like the man who must've been six and a half feet tall, wearing a bandanna on his head,

65

sporting this studded motorcycle jacket and looking mean as all hell. To be truthful, I was a little scared when he sat down. I've got unfair reactions to people, just like anyone. Anyway, I cleared my head as best I could and tried not to assume I was about to be murdered. Then the coolest thing happened. I don't know why, but at some point, he started giggling. Then so did I. And soon we were both laughing our heads off and having the best time."

"And apparently he didn't kill you."

"He did not."

I focus on his wrist and the leather and rope bracelets for a while before I move back to that endearing face of his. "And then there was me."

He nods and leans forward, resting his arms on his legs.

"You kicked a chair," I point out.

When he smiles, those damn amber eyes of his offer very little to make me angry. "I did. That was out of my control."

"And flipped a table."

"Also out of my control."

"You kissed me."

"How could I not?" Esben locks eyes with me. Again. "Was I alone in that? Because I'm pretty sure you kissed me, too."

I am counting the seconds in my head. *Six, seven, eight, nine, ten . . .* I nod. He's right, but I can't say that out loud.

"Wasn't that kind of beautiful?" he suggests. "It was for me. Maybe not for you, though. I thought it just felt like too much right then, and that's why you took off. And it's why I didn't try to find you after."

I glance over at the video camera. "You weren't in psych class on Monday. Were you hiding out?"

"I just wasn't feeling well."

"Great. Am I gonna get mono now? Or the bird flu?"

He laughs. "No. Just some late fall allergies that had me feeling rough."

"Oh." I fidget with my hands, then face him again. "Sorry you weren't well." I study his face until I realize that too many seconds have ticked by, and it's getting weird. "I hope you're better now?"

"I'm good." Esben is calm and steady. "And you weren't in class on Wednesday. And then you were obviously not happy to see me this morning." The way he sighs with apology now is totally beyond sweet. "Allison? I am truly sorry that you are upset by all of this. I can take the video down in two seconds."

I straighten up and look around the room. Something catches my eye, and I scoot off the bed and snatch a small container of microwaveable macaroni and cheese. It takes some squinting for me to read the instructions. "'Cook for three minutes.' How ironic." I rip back the top and take out the foil package of gooey cheese sauce. "Do you have some water?"

Esben raises an eyebrow, and I freeze. "Oh God, I'm sorry." I glance down at the open container. "Apparently I just got supercrazy hungry when I saw this and grabbed it. How rude of me . . . um, let me just put this back." I attempt the impossible and try to reseal the mac and cheese.

He laughs. "It's all right." Esben takes a bottle from his small fridge and adds water to the cup.

I crawl back to my spot on the bed, now decently mortified. Again. My phone dings. Steffi has messaged me from the party. She's sent a picture of herself and a good-looking guy in a plaid shirt with the message, "I met me a cutie boy!"

Esben holds out the water bottle. "You might want to have some of this."

Oh God. "Sorry. I know I'm a little drunk. Or a lot. Either way." But I take the bottle from his hand and drink. I rub my lips together and watch him watch me.

"Your hair . . . it looks very pretty like that. The curls."

"Steffi did it."

"Is Steffi your roommate?"

"No, she's my friend from California who apparently flew in to badger me because I wouldn't talk to her about you."

"I see." Esben shuts his eyes for a second. "Again, I'm really sorry if all this has upset you. Some of my projects ask a lot of the participant. You have to be open and . . . willing to give of yourself. Sometimes people aren't quite ready, or they're surprised by what happens, but it's usually in a good way." He pauses. "Even if they're resistant at the start, sometimes it's their transition that is worth it."

"Like with me?"

"Like with us," he corrects me. Esben gets up and paces as much as he can in the small space his room allows. "Why did you sign the waiver?"

The condensation on the water bottle is wetting my hand, but the cool feels nice. "I wasn't paying attention. I'd been in a . . . mood. I didn't know what I was doing." I hiccup again. "Walls . . . you said something about people with walls. That's me."

"You don't like that you let those walls down."

"No."

He sits again. "Why not?"

"There's no way you would understand. You like people. That's obvious. You're curious. You want to investigate them, delve into layers of humanity and crap, right?"

"I suppose that's a good way to look at it." Esben suppresses a smile as he spins his chair and retrieves the mac and cheese and a plastic spoon, then trades them out for my water.

"I'm not like that. I don't much care for people because they kinda suck." This microwave meal is the best thing I've ever eaten. I point my spoon at him in between bites. "They are unreliable, selfish, and they lie all the time."

"That's a rather negative perspective."

"*Now* you're feeling me!" I say happily. "So I don't get what you do. At all. Like, I can't even watch this eye-contact thing you did. *We* did."

"Wait a second. You haven't even seen the video?"

"Just bits and pieces." I wipe my mouth with the back of my hand.

"Okay. How about this? You watch it and see what you think. Then I'll take it down if you want. Say the word. But, Allison? At least watch it."

"Fine. Fire 'er up!" I get up and drunkenly wave him out of his seat. He kindly accommodates my gin-laden attitude, but I do notice a well-deserved eye roll.

"Oh awesome. A giant desktop screen so everything will be huge and even more traumatizing!" I shout.

"It won't be traumatizing." Esben is laughing as he leans over my shoulder and moves the mouse. I am profoundly aware of his proximity, and I don't know what to make of the fact that there's an unpreventable flutter in my chest. "So, is Steffi a friend from home?" he asks.

"I told you. She lives in California. Los Angeles."

"Is that where you're from?"

"Massachusetts," I mutter as the video pops up. "Foster care."

Esben pauses the video before it even starts. "Yeah? Wow. For how long?" His question is not dripping with fake compassion or asked because he wants grisly details. He is just curious.

The screen in front of me is frozen on the intro image, and I let it get blurry as I stare too long at it. "Foster care? I was there forever. Well, until I was a junior in high school. Steffi, too. She was sick when she was little, and that probably scared off potential parents. I wasn't sick, but nobody wanted me either. I guess we were duds. Anyway, we lived together for a bit. She saved me. As much as I can be saved." I state the truth as easily as I breathe. "My birth mother dropped me off at a hospital in Boston, and that's all I know about her. Maybe she was young or broke. Or a criminal. Maybe the mistress of a senator who had a secret love child? That'd be kinda cool, huh?"

"It would certainly add some scandal to your story, I guess," he answers with amusement.

I sigh. "That one's unlikely, I suppose, but it's the most intriguing of options. In the end, it doesn't really matter. The point is that I was not wanted by anyone. I lived with seventeen families. That's a lot, huh?" I burp and clap a hand over my mouth. "Excuse me. Anyway, some of the families were okay. I know what other foster kids have gone through, and I never had it as bad as many. Still, sometimes I never even unpacked my suitcase. Too scared to. There was no point." The gin is becoming a nuisance, but I can't fight it.

"That's why you have walls," he says.

"Yes," I agree. "It's why I have walls."

I feel him come closer, his mouth now not so far from my ear. "But you lowered them, even for a little bit. So maybe you want them to crack."

Without my usual filter in place, I reply, "Yes. Maybe. It's very tiring, keeping them standing. I just don't know what would happen if I let them fall. I haven't been without them in a very long time," I murmur. "Maybe ever."

"I understand. And I'm honored that you gave me a glimpse behind them, because I've never felt anything like that. So, watch." He hits "Play." "This is the original. Other sites that picked it up gave it gross clickbait names and whatever. I can't control that—"

"Shhhh!"

Music plays, and I tense but do not turn away. Esben is right. I need to watch this because I need all the information. I must know what is out there about me.

The title slams out of darkness: *It Only Takes 180 Seconds.*

Videos and words wash by. Clips of the first seconds of people who sat with Esben, interspersed with later moments from his other sittings.

There's the elderly man that I saw when Steffi first sent me this link. His cane stands next to him, and he smiles peacefully throughout his time with Esben. He exudes a kindness and approachability that touches me. Like a grandfather I will never have.

The text reads: Some people share their contentment and absolute joy with the world so easily. It's infectious.

Then there's a woman in her business suit, who looks exhausted beyond reason. I watch her focus, the way her face softens, and the way she relaxes into eye contact.

A mother with four children under the age of five. She works during the day as a manager at a department store, and she never has weekends off. She also works three nights a week as a hostess so that her family can pay their bills. Because her husband works nights, they only see each other for a handful of hours per week. But she says that's enough because love always wins. Or, rather, she clarifies, she wants it to.

A firefighter who is still in a sooty uniform appears; his hardened and defeated face is gutting.

This man just got off a fifteen-hour shift. He rescued three people from a building engulfed in flames. He's proud, but he's also upset because he missed his six-year-old's birthday. He's worried that she will remember that forever.

Then there's a middle-aged woman with beautiful braids and skin the color of coffee. Her face blank, she shows almost no expression in the clips we see, just flashes of watery eyes on occasion.

This woman lost her husband exactly one year ago today.

She says this is the first time she's been able to escape the worst of her grief, even for a few minutes.

I watch the rest of the clips—including the one with Esben and the guy wearing the motorcycle jacket—both anticipating and dreading my appearance.

He's saved me for the end.

My fingers brush against his when I take the mouse and pause the video. I turn to him. "You mean a lot to these people," I say, a new understanding coming over me.

"They mean a lot to me." Esben looks at me with such warmth and sincerity that I can hardly take him in. "I just gave them a chance to let the world stop spinning. What they did with that was out of my hands."

I get what he's saying. I've lived it.

"Keep watching." There's a nervous yet hopeful edge to his whisper.

Hesitating, delaying this, I cannot get myself to start the video because I fear the world—or *my* world—might blow up if I do. The computer's mouse feels hard and threatening against my palm.

Esben's hand goes over mine. "It's okay."

Together, we hit "Play."

CHAPTER 10

ROBIN HOOD

Sometimes, the unexpected happens. Sometimes, someone makes you break your own rules, I read.

My body is tense when I begin watching, but my intrigue leads me forward. Although I lived these moments, seeing them from this new perspective is fascinating. This is how others experienced my three minutes with Esben. And, I learn quickly, he's included the *entire* three minutes, not just clips as with the rest of the participants. I am glued to the video this time, desperately wanting to not miss a second of the replay. There are near head-on shots of my face, Esben's, our profiles as we face each other, and I see now that there must have been more people shooting footage than just Kerry. It's more than unpleasant to watch how cold I am during the first few moments I face him, but the way I shed my armor and defenses—the way I eventually allow myself to be with him—is intoxicating. It's a side of myself that I am terribly unfamiliar with.

The video shows him flipping the table, kicking the chair, and how we run to each other as if we need each other in order to breathe. I am less frightened by seeing this than I would have thought. In fact, my emotions swell, and a warmth courses through my body that has nothing to do with all the alcohol I've had.

On-screen, Esben's mouth touches my cheek. I remember that well. It's just before I lost my mind, and I cringe, knowing what's coming. But I don't look away as I see myself lift my mouth to meet his. The kiss goes on and on. Right now, I shudder a bit. Never have I kissed anyone like this. With the few people I have kissed, the kisses never looked like this. They never felt like this either.

I finally understand how the Internet was spellbound.

The most painful part to watch is when I push from him and leave, when my fear and confusion become too strong for me to fight.

I'm disappointed in myself. Ashamed. Anyone else in my shoes wouldn't have broken that tie.

"I shouldn't have done that," I say.

"Kissed me?"

"No. Backed away."

"It's all right," he tells me.

Incredible sadness and frustration engulf me. "No, it's really not. It's not okay that I have never kissed anyone with a fraction of that urgency before. It's not okay that I'm afraid of people and relationships and interaction. None of it is okay."

Esben kneels next to me and tries to soothe my growing upset. "Look, I'm not a shrink, but . . . hell, you've kind of been through a lot, and if you ask me, it *is* okay that you've been in a shitty place. Just because that's where you've been doesn't mean you have to stay there if you don't want to."

I think for a few minutes.

"Play it again," I say quietly. "Play it again."

Three more times, I watch the video, and Esben stays right beside me. After, when I have memorized every second of our airtime, I turn in the chair. Esben is very calm, I notice. Very together.

Steffi was right, I admit. Maybe it's my gin haze letting me acknowledge this, but he is gorgeous. Slowly, I lift a hand and place my fingertips on his cheek. Esben does not move while my touch grazes down his face, and I trace the line of his firm jaw and trail down to under his chin. The back of my hand moves inch by inch back up, the feel of his skin enough to keep me there forever. "You shaved," I say.

He cracks a smile. "I did."

"Esben?"

"Yeah, Allison?"

"Could I have some more macaroni and cheese? I'm still a little drunk and hungry."

"Of course," he answers with a laugh.

Just for a heartbeat, his hand goes over mine, and he gives me a little squeeze.

While the microwave hums in the background, I look through comments under the video. The sheer number of them is incomprehensible. There are over ten thousand. I keep scanning lines, scrolling down, reading a few more.

"What is instalove?" I dive into the second mac and cheese, and Esben lies on his side on the bed, his head propped in his hand.

"Oh . . ." An actual blush floods his cheeks, and I suspect this does not often happen. "Um . . . this is sort of awkward—"

"A lot of people are hashtagging us with instalove." Now I'm the one blushing. "I mean, not hashtagging *us*. Hashtagging you. Your video." I take a large bite and unceremoniously talk with my mouth full. "Why are people doing that?"

"Oh. Yeah. Well, it means, you know, instantaneous love. It's often used as a derogatory phrase to say that two people fell for each other too quickly. That it is fictional and would never happen in real life. But there's also a lot of cheering about us. About us and instalove. Because some people believe in that. They say they've lived it."

A rush of humiliation tears through me. Again. I should be getting used to the feeling. But I also feel a teeny bit . . . I don't know. A good kind of embarrassment.

"The kiss," he tries to explain, "got to viewers. The video captured the . . . the pull between us. There are a lot of people who latched on to the idea that we should be together."

"Together?"

"Allison," he says rather bashfully. "They think we fell in love that day."

I let this sink in. "How could that happen? That's nonsensical. And why do they care?"

"That's a good question. They saw something that reminded them of someone. Something they wanted. They projected their own emotion onto us. Or," he says cautiously, "they saw something real take place."

"But . . . I walked away."

"You did. But people want to believe in love. They want to believe that you walked away for a reason. That maybe you'd come back." Seeing Esben rattled is sort of cute. "Oh, and before you see it yourself, I should probably tell you that there's another hashtag floating around." He literally clears his throat, presumably to buy time. "It's *thiskissthiskiss*, along with people wishing for *thiskissthiskissparttwo*."

I have to control my voice. "Do you believe in this . . . this instalove?"

"Insta*love*. No, maybe not love. It's called that, but it's sort of obnoxious and thoughtless, if you ask me. It discounts that powerful things can happen in a matter of seconds. I've seen it over and over. Not quite what . . . um . . . what happened here, but I've been pretty stunned by how people's raw feelings come out in only a few minutes." He pauses. "It's what you do *after* those moments that matters."

My world seems to spin harder and faster, and I could slam it to a stop, but I don't. I take a risk. "So, what are you going to do?" I ask.

Esben looks at me thoughtfully. "Wait. I'm going to wait."

"Wait for what?"

"You."

"Oh."

He smiles lightly. "You've obviously not been having the best reaction to everything that's gone down, so I'm just going to wait and see where you land. Or maybe you already know what you're going to do?"

"I'm not sure. I thought I knew, but then you fed me macaroni and cheese and haven't been at all the jerk I thought you were."

His eyes sparkle. "I'm happy to hear that."

"I'm sorry for being so rude earlier. Tonight and in class. That day . . ." I sigh at myself. "I'm kind of a mess."

"You don't need to apologize."

"I'm not like you, Esben. I'm not social or happy or at ease with myself. With the world."

He gives me a cocky smile. "Not yet."

"Don't get ahead of yourself." But I smile anyway.

I go back to the website and scroll all the way to the top. This page, I realize, is Esben's home page, where everything he's done is centralized. I click a past post that's titled *Saving Private Parrot* and read for a minute. "You found someone's parrot?" I ask.

"Yeah. It was pretty cool. Someone who lives a few towns away messaged me and asked if I would help get the word out about his escaped parrot. Cute little thing named Peep. Somehow, he got out of his cage, and his owner was really upset. So, I posted about it, and then someone shared it on Facebook and got a comment about seeing a parrot on a parking meter outside of a tattoo shop. So, I tagged the tattoo shop, and the owner went out to look for him, but before he could catch him, he flew away. However"—Esben is getting more and more animated as he talks—"he did see the bird fly to the top of the building across the street. There's a dance studio on the third floor, and some ten-year-old ballerina commented that she was at the studio, and she has a pet parrot and knows all about catching them. So, the kid goes up to the roof." He stops and gives me a reassuring look. "Don't worry. Flat roof. And, sure as hell, she holds out her arm in some way the parrot must've liked, and he flew right to her. The tattoo guy got a picture of it. See?"

I glance back at the computer and scroll down. There she is, tutu and all, holding a parrot.

"And in class the other day?" I ask. "People were yelling something about a hashtag. Rock yourself? Is that right? It's something you started, yes? What does that hashtag mean?"

"Yeah, that was fun, and it got a lot of comments. It was about asking people to post pictures of themselves and to say what they were proud of, or what they loved about themselves. Sort of a time to throw out stupid social standards and appreciate who we are. So, I asked followers to celebrate what they loved about themselves with pictures that weren't overly filtered. Or brag about something cool they'd done for themselves, for a friend, for a stranger . . . whatever made them feel good. Anything, really." He laughs.

"So, what happened?" I ask. "Give me an example."

"Oh, um . . . well, one guy posted a picture of himself with his daughter. She's probably only five or so, and this dad let her put bows in his hair and beard, and he had some feathery boa thing around his neck and a tiara on. He posted the picture from a crowded pancake house and said that he was proud to be a single father who would do anything to make his daughter happy." He grows serious. "This dad sent me an e-mail. The girl's mother left when she was six months old. He was inspired by the rock-yourself hashtag, and when his daughter wanted to play dress up, he went with it. When she then wanted to go out for pancakes, he did. And they had a blast. I shared his picture as a separate post, and people loved it. He wrote me again afterward, telling me that because of all the online support and how validated he felt, he and his daughter are going to make every Sunday Glamorous Girls Pancake Day."

"I love that. You must be proud." I'm barely comprehending the enormity of what Esben does.

"I don't know about proud. I just enjoy putting stuff out there. Giving people the opportunity to shine. To feel good about themselves."

"You give people hope and . . . joy," I say incredulously, "and comfort in what is usually a crappy world."

He thinks for a moment. "I wasn't able to do that for you."

"You did. I just don't like that you did," I say reflexively.

"Why?"

"Because those things are temporary for me." I rub my eyes, aware now of how utterly exhausted I am, and more so, of how frightened I am to leave this room. To leave Esben. Suddenly, I want Steffi. She will make everything better. "I need to go home."

He nods. "Okay. I'll walk you back to your dorm."

"What? God, no. What if someone sees us together? Everyone'll go all hashtag crazy. I'm fine."

Esben rises to a stand and shakes his head. "It's late, and there is no way I'm letting you walk across campus alone."

"Okay," I agree as I step tipsily into the hallway and send Steffi a quick text. "But walk twenty feet behind me."

"So it looks like I'm stalking you?"

"Yes." I giggle. "I mean, no. Just be casual, and don't look crazy. Don't pull out a knife. Or a bow and arrow or whatever." I start toward the stairwell.

"A bow and arrow?" he asks with a laugh.

"I dunno. Like Robin Hood." My footsteps echo as I go down the stairs, and then I hear Esben begin the descent.

"Because I steal from the rich and give to the poor?" Esben asks from behind me.

"Because, knowing you, you'd still look good in tights." I shove open the dorm door. The evening air is chilly, and I cross my arms for warmth.

The sound of his chuckle dances in the night. "Thank you, I guess?"

I walk a bit more and then glance back at him. "You do give to the poor, too, in a way."

The short walk is silent, and I can feel his eyes on me as I fuss for my key. My movements are clumsy, and it takes a stupidly long time for me to retrieve the key.

"Found it!" I yell in celebration. I undo the lock, pull open the door, and halt. I'm not sure how to say good night. My fatigue and emotional confusion and the leftover effects of alcohol are weighing me down and making it hard to be socially smart. So, I just stand there, with my back to him, and debate what to say.

"Allison?"

Slowly, I turn and lean my weight against the open door. "Yeah?"

Esben is standing with a good distance between us. He really did stay twenty feet away from me as he walked me home. "I'm glad you came by."

"Okay."

"I am." He tucks his hands into the front pockets of his jeans. Light from one of the lampposts casts a glow over him. "I'll see you Monday?"

"Okay." I start to turn inside, but then I stop myself. "Esben? I'm glad I came by, too."

I go downstairs to my room. Steffi is wearing my robe and emerging from the second bedroom, her hair messed up.

"Well, there you are! Did you let him have it?" she asks.

I squint at her. "What are you doing?" Then I look past her and see a blanket tossed on the bed. "Oh my God. Did you have sex next to care-package Jenga?"

She makes a mock shocked face. "How dare you suggest anything of the sort."

I raise my eyebrows.

"Okay, fine, yes!" she squeals and begins jumping up and down. "And it was superfun!"

"And how was it?" I ask with a laugh. "Details, please, my dear."

"More important than my sexual prowess, though, is what happened with you?"

I stumble in my place a bit, fatigue taking over. I'm not sure how much longer I can stand. I'm crashing hard in more ways than one. "I just want to go to bed. So sorry. Can we just go to bed?"

She comes over and holds my face in her hands while she examines me. "You look wiped. Yes. And you'll tell me everything tomorrow. But it was okay?" she asks gently.

I nod. "Yeah. It was okay." A yawn overtakes me, and I feel crazy needy and helpless all of a sudden. "Will you sleep with me like we used to?"

"Of course."

When Steffi and I lived together, we shared a room, and I used to crawl into her bed. It made me feel safer, less alone. I need that now.

She is part sister, part best friend, part mother, and tonight, when we crawl into bed together, she lets me snuggle into the crook of her arm, as she has done so many nights before.

Steffi smooths out my hair as I begin to drift off. "I'm glad it was okay," she says quietly. "That's a good start."

CHAPTER 11

―――――――

BRAVERY

We both sleep until after noon, and I'm disoriented when I wake. This is the latest I've slept in ages, and I'm surprisingly not very hungover. Even more surprisingly, I seem to have gotten the best sleep I've had in ages, and I feel deeply rested. My brain is a scrambled mess from last night, but I'm rested.

Steffi and I spend the day in our pajamas, and while she paints my toenails deep burgundy, I hear details of her evening with plaid-shirt boy that both make me blush and make me happy for her. I ask to hear about her classes and her cramped studio apartment that she loves and about the taco truck that parks on her street every Tuesday, and she answers all of my questions. I give her a lot of credit for giving me space today, because not once does she ask about Esben.

When the sky begins to darken, I am finally ready. Casually, I say, "So, it turns out that Esben is not a terrible person."

"Oh?" Steff is rooting through my closet and trying hard not to frown at my unfashionable clothing.

"I watched the video."

"Did you?" She takes a red top off the hanger and holds it against her torso and assesses herself in the mirror. "This is actually cute."

I laugh. "You can stop pretending that you don't want to know what happened with Esben."

She flings the top at me playfully. "Well, thank God!" Steff jumps on the bed and crashes down to a sitting position. "Tell me. Tell me!"

So, I do. Every detail that I can remember, although I do leave out the part when I set my hand on his face. And the part when he put his hand on mine . . . I don't want her to get the wrong idea.

Steffi leans back against the headboard and hugs a pillow while she listens. "So, he's really not a monster. Who knew?"

I roll my eyes. "*You* knew!"

"Fine, yes. But you had to see with your own eyes." She looks at me directly. "Allison? He's as perfect as they come. He is."

I don't know what to say to this.

"Look, I doubt people as much as you do, but Esben is not like most people. Even I can see that."

I nod.

"You don't need to keep pushing him away. He's not a threat."

"Maybe."

"Might be nice for you to have a friend."

"I have you."

"Allison, of course you have me." She reaches for her shoes. "But Esben is special. You know how you and I are exceptions? Esben is, too. Just a thought." She stands and throws on a coat.

"Are you going somewhere?" I ask.

"Chinese food. Last night's fling recommended a place a block away. I'm starving, so I'll go pick up dinner. We need at least five orders of fried dumplings."

"I'll come with you." I start to get up, but she stops me.

"My dear, I love you, but you need a shower. You reek."

"Well, thanks. You don't smell so hot either."

"I smell like sexy sex. But I'll shower after dinner. I've got an early flight, so I'm going to have to get up at the crack of dawn to drive to

Boston. No drinking tonight. Or not much drinking. We're cutting ourselves off by eleven. Midnight, let's say midnight."

"You're out of your mind if you think I'm drinking after last night. I don't need to do anything else idiotic."

"You need to redefine idiotic." Steff swings open the door to the hall. "Back soon, smelly girl."

She is right. I do stink, so I strip down and put on my robe. The women's bathroom is crowded this evening, with girls primping for Saturday night parties. Carmen is leaning into a mirror and applying lipstick. Here hair is shorter now and colored a light purple that's very pretty. I walk past her, then think twice and decide to make eye contact in the mirror.

"Hi, Carmen."

She stands up straight. "Oh, hi, Allison." I don't blame her for looking tentative.

"Are you going out tonight?" I ask. "You look nice."

"Thanks. Yeah, I have a date. Or sort of a date." She smiles a little. "Meeting him at a party."

"Cool. Have fun."

She assesses her appearance in the mirror and rubs her lips together. "You want to come with me?"

I don't have my usual urge to run away screaming, which I find interesting. "I actually have a friend in town this weekend, and we're still recovering from last night. But thanks." I start toward a free shower stall and then look back. I'm nervous and shaking a bit, but I say, "Maybe next weekend?"

"Yeah. That'd be great."

I set my bath products on the floor of the shower, hang my robe, and turn the faucet to just below scalding. A shower has never felt so good, and I take my time, praying that this shower will clear my head of the jumbled mess that's swirling around inside. I wish Steffi could stay longer, especially with what's been going on. My usual quiet college life has been turned upside down, and I don't know what's going to hit next. Although, I must admit I don't actually feel unhappy right now, and not just because Steffi is still here. Now that I've at least had a conversation with Esben, the entire video incident feels less unpleasant, and I don't have constant waves of anger or shame crashing over me the way I did before. Perhaps, as Steffi suggested, Esben is an exception. I don't know.

When I get back to the room, Steffi is still gone, so I text her. My stomach is growling like crazy, and I hope she actually did get five orders of dumplings, because I could down them all in a flash. After a few minutes, she replies that she got lost going to the restaurant, and now they're backed up. I set to tidying up the common area, and the box tower grabs my attention. I debate for a bit, then take a box from the top of the pile and bring it to my bedroom.

I set it on the bed and stare at it. Then I move it to the desk, and I sit on the bed and stare at it. Then I stand up and pace back and forth like a tiger in a cage. For the first time, I am yearning to open one of these boxes, and it also feels like I'm up against a challenge, as though I'd promised myself that I wouldn't open any of these care packages because I don't deserve them. Now I'm tempted to cave.

Screw it.

I grab some scissors and slice the tape. After a few deep breaths, I open the box.

Immediately, I start laughing. The top layer of the care package is made up of microwavable macaroni and cheese cups. It's so perfect. When I've got my giggling under control, I see what else Simon has sent. Plastic spoons, lemon cookies, and tea bags (for a tea party, Simon insists!), instant soups, hair ties, body lotions in various fruit scents, socks with monkeys on them, a ten-cup coffeepot, a bag of ground Sumatra, two red mugs, individual raw sugar packets, and a twenty-dollar bill earmarked for pizza. He's included a card, and on the front is a picture of a leopard seal. Inside, he has written:

Allison—

Do you have any idea how hard it is to find a card with a leopard seal on it? Very. In fact, they do not seem to exist, so yours truly made one using an online photo service. THAT'S DEDICATION!

Let me know if there are other things you would like me to send for you, even though that is unlikely, because I know that you are not opening these boxes, and that's okay. I'm still going to send them, because that's what fathers do for their daughters. Or maybe it's just what I do for you, my sweet girl.

I hope one day you'll be ready to open these, but if that day never comes, that will also be okay.

Much love,

Simon

Five times I read the note, and then I cannot get to my phone fast enough.

"Hi, kiddo. How are you?" Simon answers with his usual cheer.

"How did you know I wasn't opening the care packages?" I demand.

He laughs. "Well, honey, every time you call to thank me, you are very polite but very vague. I figured that if you'd been opening them, I would have heard something about the inflatable unicorn, which I knew you wouldn't find funny, but I do."

"I've only opened one box." I pause. "You sent me an inflatable unicorn?"

"Maybe . . ."

"Simon?"

"Yes?"

"I really like the coffeemaker."

"I'm so glad."

"And I'm going to open the rest of the stuff you sent."

"Whenever you want."

I realize that I am smiling broadly. "Hey, know what? Guess who is here?"

"Santa Claus? The Easter Bunny?"

I laugh. "No. Steffi. She flew in for the weekend to surprise me."

"Wow, that is a surprise. That's a long trip for such a short time. Anything urgent going on?"

"No," I say too quickly. "No, it's just . . . well, she got all worked up over something that happened. There's this boy, and . . . I don't know."

"Ahhh," he says. "A boy. A boy you like?"

"I don't *like* him like him. It's just something weird happened between us, and Steffi got crazy over it."

Simon's voice grows concerned. "Something weird meaning that I should be mailing a box of condoms instead of coffeepots?"

"What? Simon! Oh my God!"

"Just checking."

I hear rattling at the door. "Can I explain another time? Steffi is back with dinner. But don't worry. Everything is fine."

"If you say so. Call again soon, will you? I miss you."

"I miss you, too."

I am frozen with the phone in my hand after I hang up. I don't believe I've ever told Simon I miss him. But I do. I realize that now. I'm allowing myself to miss him.

Clearly, I am having some kind of bizarre midcollege crisis in which my mind is being taken over and replaced by someone else's.

Steffi is now kicking the door from the outside and hollering at me. "Hello? A little damn help here would be nice!"

I jolt from my poor attempt at self-analysis and rush to the door. Steffi is holding an enormous paper bag in one hand and a plastic bag from the liquor store in the other. "The handle on the Chinese-food bag ripped, and we're about to have a lo-mein disaster of epic proportions."

"Where have you been?" I ask as I take the bag of food. "You've been gone for ages."

"I told you. Got lost, long wait, blah, blah. Let's eat. And drink!"

She sits on the floor and pulls out a bottle of tequila. "Picnic time. Let's just set everything out here."

"I guess. I'll get a towel or something—"

"Stop being so uptight. Sit. Eat. Don't worry about messes. There are bigger problems in the world than a bit of soy sauce on the rug."

I frown but sit down anyway and start to set out the cartons of food. "You're as slobby as Esben."

She unscrews the cap from the tequila and takes a long drink. "Esben's a slob? I knew I liked him. And you got past my lack of obsessive-compulsive tidiness, so you can get past his."

I can feel her staring at me with hopeful eyes while I locate chopsticks and dig in to the carton of dumplings. "He helped find a lost parrot once. Using social media. I looked through his old pages. Stuff that he's done."

"I saw that parrot one!" she squeals. "Did you see how he started a dance party in a mall once?"

I laugh. "No, I missed that."

"Insane! I'll show you. And that boy's got some moves, by the way. Just so you know."

For the rest of the night, we eat way too much food, Steffi drinks way too much tequila, though I only have a few shots, and we cruise the Internet and read about Esben Baylor and his various social projects. At two in the morning, when both of us are overtired and simply cannot stay awake, we get into bed.

I stir at six in the morning. Steffi is sitting next to me, her hand on my arm.

"You ready to go?" I murmur.

She nods and squeezes my arm. "Yeah."

My eyes adjust to the dark. "Text me when you land in LA, okay?"

"Of course." Then she leans over and puts her arms around me, hugging me tightly.

"I love you, Steff."

"I love you, too, Allison." She holds me more tightly. "Be brave. With yourself, with Esben, with everything. Okay? Tell me you will."

"Okay . . ."

"No, tell me that from now on, you will be brave. Take more risks. And mean it. It's time. You can't live in this room and never go out. You're going to miss too much. So tell me."

My thoughts are still foggy in the early morning, but I know this is important to her, so I agree. I promise. "I'll be brave, Steffi. From now on, I'll be brave."

CHAPTER 12

BEAR

Monday morning arrives both too quickly and not fast enough. I jolt awake at five in the morning, unable to fall back asleep. This is a pivotal day for me. It's a day when I will either crawl back into my hole or make massive changes in my life. Both options ripple terror through me, but I am truly more scared to retreat than I am to advance. I promised Steffi that I would be brave, and I need to do that, but not just for her. The ache for more, the ache that I have been pushing away for so long now, has become too strong to ignore. It was already growing, but I'm finally admitting to myself that those one hundred and eighty seconds with Esben somehow threw me into a whirlwind.

Either I get slammed to the ground by that force or I soar. What I'm going through is not Esben's fault, and I'm not angry with him anymore. Esben caught me on a vulnerable afternoon. He couldn't have known that I'd be so fragile and fearful.

Of him, of everything.

Hurt, rejection, and emptiness made up my childhood, and they have controlled me for so long now that I don't know if I can stop them.

But, God, I want to. I don't want to live like this.

I throw my arm over my eyes to dam the tears that threaten to come.

I am so ashamed of how cold I am. That I have only one friend. That I live in a bubble of my own creation.

I am brave. I am brave. I am brave.

But I cannot stop the tears. "I don't want to live like this," I say out loud over and over through my sobbing. I cry for who I have been, who I am, and who I could be. However, I also cry with an iota of relief, because a change is about to happen. I know this. A change that has the possibility of lifting me from the wreckage. What it will look like is very unclear, but I have to take a chance.

I am going to hope again.

I am brave. I am brave. I am brave.

Much later, when my tears subside, a degree of calm takes over. I crawl from my bed and take the coffeepot that Simon sent and start a very strong brew. I leave the box and packing material on the floor in an intentional effort to ease up on my strict sense of order. I head to the shower, and the hard waterfall against my skin refreshes me some, but my eyes are horribly puffy, so when I return to my room, I run an ice cube over them while I sip coffee from one of the red cups. I dry my hair and then attempt to replicate the curls that Steffi gave me the other night. I put on a sleeveless white mock turtleneck and a camel-beige open cardigan and pair those with jeans and brown boots. Then I put on some makeup. It's less than Steffi would suggest but more than I usually do. I want to feel pretty today, because I need any boost I can get.

I open another one of Simon's care packages. In this one, I find a fabric-covered journal, three kinds of new tea and a squeeze bottle of honey, microwave popcorn, two bars of dark chocolate, and—God bless him—a caffeine eye cream for reducing bags. I smear some on, say a little prayer, and then fish out the last item in the box.

I may start crying again.

Simon has sent a teddy bear. A floppy, long-limbed, chestnut-brown teddy bear with a polka-dot bow around its neck. I hug it close and shut my eyes. No one has ever given me a stuffed animal, and I am struck by what a devastating realization that is. How unforgivable and insurmountable it feels. Honestly, I don't think it occurred to any of my foster families that I wouldn't have a stuffed animal. I used to fall asleep hugging pillows, and today I have a teddy bear. The smile on my face when I take a selfie of me with the bear is genuine, and I text it to Simon. He replies almost immediately: Every kid should have a teddy bear. You're too old for this, and you were too old when we met, but . . . a father has to give his daughter a teddy bear, so better late than never.

I close my eyes and hold the bear close. And I breathe. Better late than never, indeed.

Thirty minutes later, I am at the door to my Social Psych class. Stepping across the threshold feels like a monumental moment, but I remain calm as I take my usual seat and set my bag onto the seat next to mine. Intentionally, I am the first student to arrive, and I keep my eyes glued to the doorway, waiting for him. I do not put in my earbuds, and I do not bury myself in reading or pretend note taking.

Today, I just wait for him.

The room is nearly three-quarters full when he arrives.

I sit up taller in my seat.

Esben acts as if he cannot decide whether to look around the room or not, and I pray he'll look my way. He starts up the stairs to my right, and just when I think he's going to move into a row in front of me, he stops and very slowly raises his head. He's apprehensive, presumably waiting to see what I'll do.

I feel for him. I haven't exactly been predictable.

I give him a small smile, and his face relaxes. Other students are trickling in, and I'm sure we are being watched, but I don't mind. I take my bag from the seat beside mine and tip my head, asking him to sit with me. There's an adorable bounce in his walk as he makes his way up, while other students brush past him to get seats. Today, he doesn't respond when a few people greet him, and he has no reaction when his name is called from a few rows up. He just walks to me as if there is no one else in the room.

When he lowers himself into the seat beside mine, his arm grazes against me. "Hi," he says softly.

"Hi."

"How was the rest of your weekend?" he asks with a glint in his eye.

"Less drunk," I reply.

In the sweetest voice I've ever heard, he says, "You're cute drunk."

I bite my lip to keep from smiling too much, and I'm glad that the lights suddenly cut out when our professor flashes a PowerPoint display on the classroom screen. We don't speak or even look at each other again during class, and when the lights come back on, I fumble for an unnecessarily long time, packing up my things.

Esben stands. "Well . . . I'll see you Wednesday, I guess, yeah?"

He turns to go, and I feel my heart begin to pound.

"Esben, wait. Wait." I am panicked and frazzled and desperate. If I don't do this now, I will never do it. "Please, wait."

Fight or flight time.

"Do you . . ." I swallow hard. "Would you like to get a cup of coffee? Or something? Maybe you hate coffee. So we don't have to do that. We could do anything."

He's got this outrageously charming look on his face, but he still isn't saying anything.

"But if you want to, I love coffee," I continue. "Like, a lot. Probably too much. We could just go to the student union. It isn't exactly gourmet there, but . . . um . . ."

He takes my bag from my hand. "There's a really fun coffeehouse not far from here. Sofas and cushy chairs everywhere. And the coffee is much better than the union's."

"Sure. Yes. That sounds nice." I'm trying to sound casual, as though I may not faint at any moment. But then I again take in how kind he is, how easy he is to talk to. Just because I'm not fueled by gin doesn't mean that I should forget that. Although I am sort of wishing I had that teddy bear with me to cling to.

"My car is parked right behind the building."

"Okay." I seem to be having trouble moving.

Esben reaches out a hand. "I dare you not to like their mocha quad cappuccino." He gives me a reassuring smile.

So, I set my hand in his and let him pull me from my seat. My hand stays in his as he leads me through the crowded hall to the back exit of the building, and I have to force my legs not to buckle. When he lets go to open the door, my palm feels noticeably empty.

He looks at me. "I should warn you about something."

"You're not as nice as you seem, and you're going to stuff me in the trunk of your car and roll me off a cliff?"

"There aren't any cliffs around here." He gives me a playful pat on my arm. "I'm kidding!"

"I hope so, or I'm making a really big mistake."

"You're not." He flashes a perfect smile. "So, here's the deal. You thought my room was a mess? Prepare yourself for my car."

I rub my forehead. I'd forgotten that I'd called him a slob. "Oh God. Sorry about that."

"Don't be. You're right."

We walk to an older silver sedan, and he opens the passenger door. "See? You don't have to ride in the trunk!"

I laugh. "You're quite the gentleman."

Esben circles his hand in front of his waist, then bows. "I aim to please."

In the few seconds I have after he shuts my door and before he's in the driver's seat, I exhale loudly. *I am brave. I am brave. I am brave.*

The radio comes on when he starts the engine. "It's not far, but a little too long for a walk."

"It's nice that you have a car." I glance around the floor. "Even with the many empty cups, crumpled papers, books, and . . . I believe, forty pairs of sunglasses?" I smile to let him know that now I'm the one teasing.

"Ha! Right? I have a sunglasses problem. I keep thinking I've lost a pair, so I buy another cheap pair, then find the lost one. It's an endless cycle."

"It's not a problem. You're a collector."

"Reframing. I like it. Smart."

"'Reframing.' Nice sunglasses joke."

"Ha! And I wasn't even trying. Wait until I set my mind to doing something amusing!"

He pulls onto the main road, and I look out the window, unsure what to say now that we're officially en route and trapped in this car together. We're quiet for the drive, and I'm glad for the music that fills the silence. But the truth is our silence is not as strange as it could be. It's as though Esben is simply giving me space. My anxiety threatens to cripple me, but it's so weird and wonderful how he creates comfort when there shouldn't be any that my desire to take risks today remains strong.

I will fight for myself, really fight.

I have barely undone my seat belt before he has my door open. "The place is right here." He points to a deep-purple awning and a storefront with large glass panels framed in dark wood. He starts to walk, but I call his name, and he turns back.

"Yeah?" He comes to stand in front of me. "Hey? What is it?"

I'm grateful that the sun is blinding me, because I don't want to look at him when I say this. "I'm very nervous. I thought I should tell you that."

"I'm a little nervous, too."

"You are not."

"Of course I am."

"What do you have to be nervous about? I'm the one who is screwed up."

"Allison." He steps a bit to the side and blocks my face from the sun, so now I can see him clearly. "Are you kidding me? I'm *totally* nervous."

I focus on the buttons of his shirt. "Why?"

"Because I like you," he says. "Because I think there's something between us, and I'm very afraid that I'm going to do the wrong thing again and send you running. And I don't want that. If you're going to go running anywhere, I'd prefer that you come running to me. I understand that we don't know each other, not really, but . . . I'd just like to have coffee with you."

"I'm worried that *I'm* going to do the wrong thing again. And maybe I'm worried that when I buy you a coffee—yes, I'm buying—that I'll order for you, and maybe you have a dairy allergy, and I'll send you to the emergency room with some hideous anaphylactic reaction that will kill you. And that would really be the end of everything, and it's taking all I have to do this, because this is supposed to be when I *start* things, not end them." The wind sends a chill through me and blows my hair over my cheek. "Sorry for babbling."

Esben lifts a hand and tucks my hair behind my ear. "I don't have a dairy allergy. But I'll drink whatever you buy me, because you're totally worth a trip to the ER." He winks.

"Then let's go have coffee, and I'll try not to do anything that might kill you."

CHAPTER 13

BABY BLUE

The coffeehouse is indeed very comfortable, and the dark wood and mismatched furniture make me feel as though I'm in someone's living room. Acoustic music floats above us, but otherwise it's a fairly quiet spot. There is only one other customer, an older man, sitting in an armchair across the room. He's not reading or doing anything. Just sitting there. I am immediately struck by how lonely he seems, but I brush that off, because I know nothing about this man. I have no right to assume anything about him, just as no one has a right to assume anything about me. I probably look like a normal human.

Esben and I are seated on a couch. He has his body turned my way, looking open and relaxed. I, of course, am sitting stiffly, facing forward and clutching my steaming mug.

"You like your drink okay?" he asks.

I'm about to give myself third-degree burns, and then the emergency room deal might become a reality. I take a quick sip and set the mug on the glass table in front of us. "I do."

"You said you're from Massachusetts. That you'd lived all over. But you have a family there now?"

"Sort of. I mean, yes. Simon. He adopted me when I was a junior in high school. He has a house in Brookline."

"I love Brookline. Coolidge Corner is awesome. Such a fun area to walk around."

"You're from Massachusetts, too?" While I've explored some of Esben's online presence, I have presumably barely tapped the surface, and I still don't know basics about him.

"Framingham. Not as exciting as Brookline, and it was a drag to drive into Boston when I was a teenager, but it's all right." He sets down his drink and focuses on me. "So, you've got a single dad? And you like him?"

"I do like him. A lot. I don't think I'm . . ." I can't figure out how to say this or if I should. But I want to; I know that. I want to connect. Where's a motivational button when I need it, huh? So, I breathe, and I speak. "It doesn't make sense that Simon wanted to adopt me. I wasn't warm or . . . the typical teen girl. I didn't throw myself at the idea of adoption. I wasn't anything a potential parent should want. But he still went ahead. I don't get it. And Simon had a boyfriend when I first met him. Jacob."

I shift in my seat so that I'm facing him and hopefully looking less frigid and weird. I check to see if Esben has any iota of a negative reaction to the news that my adoptive father is gay, but he's simply waiting for me to continue. "They'd been together for four years, and once it became clear that Simon wanted me, that he *really* wanted to adopt me, his boyfriend bolted. I haven't asked Simon much about it, because it's got to be a sore subject."

Esben makes a face. "Kind of says volumes about that ex, huh?"

"Maybe. Simon wanted me . . ." I survey the room and take a second. "And he lost his boyfriend. Kind of proof positive that there's always a trade-off. You let one person in; the other goes out."

"I don't think that's true at all," Esben says. "I've got two parents who are pretty awesome. And my sister, Kerry, who you met. She and I are really tight. Plus, I've got close friends. Jason and Danny are my best friends here, but I'm still in touch with people from high school. There doesn't have to be a trade-off."

"Maybe not for you."

"Look, I imagine that spending most of your life in foster care didn't exactly instill the belief that the world is all magical and full of glittery unicorns and fluffy bunnies and such. How could it?" Esben looks down and brushes something imaginary off his jeans. "Did you live with a lot of different families or only a few?"

I fall in love with the fact that his question is not filled with pity.

"Yes," I say. "Too many."

I tell him about changing schools and families and rooms and . . . everything. About how there were never constants. Ever. About the cycle of hope and the rejection that became routine until I was left with only rejection. I tell him everything, because once I start talking, I cannot stop. This purge, this truth, is a flood that I cannot stop. I have never told anyone besides Steffi these details, and they have been secrets that jailed me.

Esben listens attentively and allows me to tell him way more than he probably expected. I want him to know these facts about me and my life because if he's going to bolt, I want him to do it now. I have a responsibility to make him aware of how fouled up my past is. It doesn't take a genius to see how that would screw someone up. He should have an out if he wants it.

"So, Steffi was your one bright spot," he points out.

"My savior," I say definitively. "Yes."

"I'm glad you had her. She probably made up for a lot."

"What's funny is that I didn't much like her when I first met her. She was tough and glamorous and feisty. She still is, but at the time . . . well, I kind of thought she was a snot," I say, laughing.

"So how did you become so close?"

"Oh. Well . . ." I reach for my coffee and take a drink. "Compared to other foster kids, I didn't have it so bad. I lived with plenty of nice people. Just no one who wanted me permanently. A few not-so-great people, but, overall, no one really crazy or mean." Despite a second of hesitation on my part, I notice how easy it is to continue with this story. "But the family who'd taken in Steffi and me had also taken in two boys, both of whom were a few years older than us. One day after school, I came home. I shared a room with Steffi . . ." I pause. *God, I haven't thought about this in ages.*

"You don't have to tell me anything you don't want to," Esben says quietly.

"I do want to." I know this as much as I know that I need to breathe. "I found her in our room with one of the guys, but I knew right away that I hadn't just walked in on them fooling around. He had her pinned to the bed, and her expression was . . . all wrong. Scared, paralyzed . . ."

Esben visibly tenses and is clearly very shaken by my words. "Jesus, Allison . . ."

I make my speech confident, reassuring. "It's okay. Really. Because when I saw the way her shirt was torn off her shoulder, when I understood that his weight was crushing her, I moved. Fast. It took me about two seconds to rip this guy off of her." I almost laugh. "Who knew I was so strong? But I slammed him into the dresser so hard that its mirror shattered. Then I punched him and gave him a massive black eye. The look on his face was priceless." Now, I'm actually grinning at the memory. "I still know exactly what I said to him. I won't repeat it, but there were a lot of threats of severe bodily harm to parts he did not want injured. Then I called up her caseworker and mine and screamed at both until my voice was raw. The guy was removed from the house about an hour later." I tuck my knees up and rest my head against the back of the sofa. "And that was that."

"And you were friends ever since?"

"Ever since," I confirm. "What's funny, though, is that she's rarely let me help her after that. I try, but she's pretty independent. Strong as anyone could be, really, and she's always doing more for me than she'll let me do for her." I smile. "She mothers me in a way, I guess, which I can't deny feels nice." I realize that I've just talked more to Esben than anyone besides Steffi. It's damn wonderful, but, still, I dig my fingers into my knees. But the good outweighs the bad, without a doubt. "Now that I've told you all my drama and trauma, tell me about you. I bet you have less garbage to share, and I would like to hear something happy."

"What do you want to know?"

"Anything . . . tell me about your sister."

"Kerry is amazing. I know she got you involved in the video, but I promise you'll like her."

"Don't worry. I don't have anything against her."

Esben throws an arm over the back of the couch and drops his head to the side. "Just me?"

"No. Not you either."

"I'm glad."

Neither of us says anything for a moment.

"So, anyway, Kerry . . . she's an art major here, and she's really talented. Drawing, painting, sculpture, she does it all. Oh, here's a fun fact. She calls me Baby Blue." He leans forward, his eyes sparkling. "Wanna know why?"

I laugh. "I do."

"I was born with a congenital heart defect called pulmonary valve stenosis. It wasn't a big deal, and it healed on its own over time, but I was unattractively blue at birth. When I was, like, twelve or so, and Kerry was eleven, she somehow found out about this, and for weeks, all she did was obsess over the fact that I'd been blue. She thought it was a riot, although my parents were not amused at how much she totally delighted in it, because they'd obviously been scared at the time. So, she started calling me Baby Blue and never stopped."

"I don't like that you were born with a heart condition, but I do really like her nickname for you. It's very cute." I am sinking into my spot on this sofa with more tranquility than I could have imagined. "Esben?"

"Yes, Miss Allison?"

"Thank you for making this easy on me."

"I'm not doing anything. This is all you."

I'm not sure if he's right. "Either way, talking with you . . . it's nice. It feels good. You're probably used to this. I mean, people must thank you all the time."

"Sometimes." He gives me an utterly disarming grin. "And sometimes they come to my room all drunk and cute and yell at me."

I hide my face in my hands for a second and laugh. "I'm serious. You obviously have an easy time being with people, listening to them, relating. All of it. I'm surprised you're not totally full of yourself. I . . . I will confess that I thought you'd be more . . . I don't know. Smug. Because you probably should be."

"I get a lot back from the people I meet. They give me more than I'm sure I give them. I love meeting strangers, learning about what's beyond first glance. Discovering everyone has a hidden story, a reason for their behavior." He's so thoughtful and earnest that he only enchants me more. "Sometimes simply getting someone to share frees them, maybe makes them examine who they are and change. I'm just planting seeds most of the time, offering opportunities. What's so special is watching people learn about themselves. I try to help out when I can. And do you know how many times I've been completely blown away by the kindness of others? The willingness of people to share or give or help out? I know tons of people out there suck, I do. But mostly, Allison, people are good. They really are. And I am lucky enough to get to witness so much of that good."

"You get a lot of attention for what you do. That can't feel shitty," I say, a bit challengingly.

His eyes sparkle a bit, and the half smile he delivers is too adorable for words. "Well, sure. To some degree. But my posts are not really about me. I actually try to avoid being in most, but there are invariably ones that I'm a part of. As you know." He slips in a quick wink before continuing. "Usually, though, I try to keep the focus on other people." He stops, and, just for a second, I see the nervousness he'd mentioned earlier. "I do not, however, go out to coffee with them. You're the first."

I look out the café window and watch a mother and daughter walk past. I feel a twinge of pain. I will never have a mother, and I'm lost in this dismay for a few minutes before I can return to Esben. As I'm coming to learn, he seems fine with me doing that. "Maybe you feel obligated to go out for coffee with me because of the kiss. Because your followers are all worked up about it."

"Allison," Esben says firmly. "Look at me."

So I do.

"I don't feel an obligation to do anything. I never do. It's not how I operate. I'm here because I want to be. *I'm* the one who didn't want that kiss to stop, so *I'm* the one wondering if you feel an obligation to be here. Maybe you're just making peace with what went down. Finding closure."

Intently, I look at him, falling into an already familiar sense of safety and wonder in those beautiful eyes. I think hard; I *feel* hard. I inhale and exhale, probably too loudly, probably too noticeably, but Esben does not flinch.

It takes another few deep breaths before I respond with deliberate and heartfelt words, and, with great intention, I open myself up to him. "I don't want closure. I don't want this to be done. Not with you."

Esben moves to sit a bit closer and lowers his hand from the back of the couch, lightly grazing my shoulder with his fingers. "I like hearing that."

"But I'm very fragile. And I don't know how to do this. Whatever this is."

"I know you're fragile. I get that." His touch lingers against me. "You're also tougher than you think. You're fighting right now, and fighters aren't weak. But you don't have to fight alone."

This is a hard idea to accept. "Why are you doing this? Why . . . why me? You have thousands of girls following you and adoring you, online and here at college, so I don't understand why you're here with me and being all awesome and cute and getting me to ramble and tell my life story when I could never do that with anyone else."

Now his hand rests solidly on my shoulder. "If you're asking me for a list of reasons, I can give you that. You're beautiful and sweet and feisty. You're intriguing and funny and quirky. You are a powerful force, and one I find myself remarkably drawn to. Not to mention, by the way, that you're the best damn kisser ever. Like, ever. But the simple truth is that . . ." Esben squirms in his seat in what I see as needless insecurity. "Can't I just like you without explanation? Just because I do?"

I'm dumbfounded. I let what he's said—what he apparently feels—sink in. He's handed me a certain freedom, which makes me feel so shockingly happy that I allow myself to give a truly flirtatious look. "So, the kiss was that good for you?"

Esben moves his hand beneath my hair, gently rubbing the nape of my neck. He speaks slowly. "The kiss was *that good* for me. No question."

"Well," I say as I reach for my coffee, "that's something *I* like hearing. And it definitely makes skipping my second class today worth it."

"I'll take it, very happily." Esben takes his mug and clinks it against mine.

When we leave, we walk to the car with our shoulders touching. He blasts music in the car, because we have spoken enough words for today, and we are both overtaken with a euphoria that leaves no room for anything else. After he parks, I go to the back passenger door to retrieve my bag. On the floor of the car, a paper bag has spilled open.

At least a hundred motivational buttons cover the floor.

A measure of exhilaration and wonder surges through me that I hope never leaves.

CHAPTER 14

WANTED

That night, I try to FaceTime Steffi, because I want her to see how flushed and idiotically glowy I am, but she doesn't pick up. Instead, she phones me right back. "Sorry. I look gnarly and am not subjecting you to my greasy hair and the bags under my eyes. It's as though I just flew back and forth across the country within a few days. Oh, wait. I did!"

"Then I am very grateful for your discretion." I throw the phone on speaker and check myself in the mirror while we talk. While I don't usually spend a lot of time examining myself, today is different. Today, I want to see myself happy. "How are you, eye bags and all aside? What do you have going on this week? Oh, and you never did tell me anything about that internship—"

"Ugh, that's boring. Who cares? I need to hear what's up with *you*. You're the one with the dramatically fun life." She does indeed sound exhausted, but I know she's trying to perk up for me.

"Um . . . will you walk me through how to curl my hair the way you did the other night? The night I went to Esben's room."

There's silence for a moment. Then I can hear the satisfaction in her voice as she understands what I'm really telling her. "You were *brave*, weren't you? Esben liked your hair, and then you were brave! You took a chance, and it paid off."

She begins hurling questions at me, and, because she insists, I walk her through my day, leaving out nothing. By the time we hang up, Steffi knows enough details that even she has run out of things to ask.

Then on Tuesday night, I am in the midst of studying when there is a knock on my door. "Hey, you. Can I come in?"

Esben is wearing a dark-green shirt under his leather jacket. He is all the colors of some magical forest that I want to get lost in. "Hi." I step back and try not to look as mesmerized as I feel.

"I'm on my way to go meet Kerry, and I'm already late, so I have, like, two minutes. She wants to show me what she's been working on in her painting class, but I had to come by here first."

"You did?" Even these two small words are shaky.

He nods. "I missed you today. Is that weird? It is, I guess. But it's true. I had a really good time yesterday, and today has pretty much whoppingly paled in comparison. So, I came to see you." Esben rocks on his toes a bit. "Is that okay?"

"Yeah. It is." It's so beyond okay that I want to start jumping up and down like a lunatic. Instead, I do something else that I really want to do. With less awkwardness than I would have anticipated, I step in and put my arms under his jacket and around his waist. I cannot believe that I'm doing this, and while I am absolutely trembling with nerves and insecurity, I want this intimacy so much.

Esben puts his arms over my shoulders and draws me close. "This is why I came by. This is what I needed."

I relax into his hold, and when he softly kisses the top of my head, I turn and rest my cheek against his chest. We stand as one for a few minutes, until he gives me a quick squeeze and says, "Damn, I gotta go. I wish I didn't."

My hands rub his back briefly. "I'll see you in class tomorrow?"

"Absolutely."

After he leaves, I inflate the unicorn Simon sent. Maybe it's because Esben mentioned unicorns yesterday; I don't know. But I set the pink monstrosity on top of the desk in the spare room.

On Wednesday, Esben sits next to me in psych class. His arm touches mine the entire time, and I take in probably 10 percent of the professor's lecture. He walks me to my next class, as though we're in some old-fashioned era and he's courting me. I could die over the sweetness and respect of this. We stand outside my classroom, only inches apart, and I'm too giddy to look up at him, so I busy myself, fussing with the zipper on his jacket.

He whispers in my ear, "So, can I get your cell number?"

"Yes," I say too breathily.

On Thursday evening, Esben blows up my phone with texts.

He sends a selfie he took wearing a shocking neon-orange bulky-knit sweater his mother just sent him. He's making an exaggerated frightened face. WTF? he texts. My mother has gone insane.

After that, he sends a picture of Chewbacca with the note: Because . . . Chewbacca.

Then a joke about a cow and a pretzel that I don't understand, and before I can reply, he writes, Yeah, I don't get it either. Some dude keeps posting it on my FB wall with a million LOLs. Help me! Help me!

Later, he sends a list of three important things he thinks I should know about him: 1. I often wear mismatched socks. 2. I loathe corn on the cob. I know I'm probably the only person in the world who does. So, I turn the ears on their ends and cut off the kernels, which always makes a huge mess, because they just fly all over the place, and only a few land on my plate. 3. I think you're incredible, and I'd love to run over to your room right now and tell you that in person and hug you and listen to the sound of your breathing, but I don't want you to get freaked.

I stare at number three and smile. Then I take a screenshot of it, because I want to keep this text forever.

I reply. 1. It's an interesting fashion choice. Maybe I could teach you how to do laundry. 2. Corn on the cob is annoying, and I support you 100 percent in this. We can research some sort of dome under which one cuts the corn and thereby contains the kernels. 3. I'm not freaked.

Then I think better of it and text him again. Okay, I'm trying not to be freaked.

A few minutes later, I add, Fine, maybe I'm freaked, but I'm also very happy.

I'll take it, he writes back. I'm way behind on writing a paper that's due on Monday, so I'm going to work tomorrow night (yay me!), but do you want to hang out on Saturday? Please say yes, because that's the only thing that will get me through writing about *The Brothers Karamazov*. I hate those brothers.

I reply, I'd be happy to help you survive Dostoyevsky by accepting. Sure.

See you in class tomorrow, he texts. Sleep tight, pretty girl.

I take another screenshot. I'm on the verge of texting the two images to Steffi, but I stop. I want to keep these just for myself.

And then I do sleep well, better than I can remember.

On Friday, Esben takes his now-usual seat next to me in class, and midway through, I watch as he slides his hand under mine, entwining our fingers. "Allowed?" he asks softly. I love when he smiles without actually smiling. It's all in his eyes.

"More than allowed," I say. "Wanted."

He lifts my hand to his mouth. I am entranced, seeing him lightly touch his lips to my skin, the way he closes his eyes for a moment as he does so, the shape of his mouth, his sweetness . . . it's enough to make me nearly pass out. My hand stays in his for the rest of class.

Later, I call Simon.

"Hi there, peaches. How are you?"

I am sitting on the edge of my bed, and I begin bouncing up and down. "Simon? I'm calling to tell you something."

"Oh. You . . . are? Okay, great." Simon stumbles a bit, probably because I haven't exactly been prone to randomly calling to chat. Today, though, is different. "Your roommate ditched the leopard seals and came back?"

"Better."

"The inflatable unicorn I sent is now officially your new roommate?"

I glance into the spare room and eye the ridiculous pink atrocity that has been sitting on the desk chair for the past few days. "I suppose that's true. But that's not it."

"Okay, so what's your news?"

I sit still, preparing to say this out loud. "I like someone."

"Liam Neeson?"

"No!"

"Flo from the Progressive commercials?"

"Simon!"

"Miley Cyrus? Was she wearing something kooky?"

"It's the boy I mentioned before. Here at school."

"Ah, okay, then. He's got your interest?" I can tell Simon is desperately trying to shield me from the surprise in his tone. "Well, wow. What's he like?"

"He held my hand and picked up ice cubes, and he has a carful of motivational buttons."

"Intriguing. But does he have an inflatable unicorn?"

I stop bouncing. "It's actually possible."

"Then I like him."

I fall onto my back and stare at the ceiling. "I really like him, too, Simon. His name is Esben Baylor. Google him."

"I will do that. It's my job to investigate my kid's suitors."

"You've been waiting for this moment for a while, haven't you?"

"I've been waiting for you to be ready. That's all." But I hear his keyboard clacking in the background.

"Okay. I have to get dinner, but I wanted to tell you this. I'll call you again soon."

I'm about to leave for the cafeteria, when I stop myself and check the student directory for Carmen's room number. Then, two floors up from mine, I stand outside her door and have an internal debate that ends with me knocking.

"Allison," she says with a smile. Carmen has dyed her hair baby pink, and it's whooshed off her face in a most dramatic manner. "What's up?"

"I was heading to the caf to get something to eat. Do you want to come with me?"

She pulls her student ID from her back pocket. "I was just on my way there. It's breakfast-for-dinner night, so I'm about to omelet myself silly."

"Then I will omelet myself silly, too."

She fist-bumps me and smiles.

We eat omelets, and nothing disastrous happens. She is from Wisconsin and has five brothers, and she's a biology major who wants to eventually become a conservation scientist. I learn that she has two pet chinchillas at home, won an egg-carrying contest when she was nine, and likes to read biographies about former child stars.

For dessert, we have waffle sundaes, and midway through the whipped cream and chocolate mess, I realize how much I like not eating alone. I'm resembling an actual integrated student. It's strange and wonderful.

And I like her.

Then, finally, it is Saturday.

I'd assumed Esben meant an evening date, but he wants to pick me up at noon. I'm not experienced enough to know if a lunch date shows less romantic intention than an evening date, but it's a possibility. It's nearly unbelievable that I'm even using words like "date" and "romantic" and applying them to myself, but the happiness I've felt over the past week is like nothing I've experienced before, and even I am not stupid enough to push that away.

That doesn't, however, mean that I am not feeling wobbly and nervous as I stand on the steps of my dorm, overlooking the tree-lined street. I wait for a bit, then check the time.

He's ten minutes late.

I take a seat. The leaves are in the process of turning red and orange under the October sky, and I look up as a breeze rustles the colors into a rich blur. I adjust the sheer pale-blue scarf around my neck and run my fingers through my bangs. Since I don't know where we're going, getting dressed was all the more stressful, but I went with jeans, ankle boots, and a shirt that matches my scarf. I twist the sweater I'm holding and scan the street for Esben's car.

I study the gray stone stairs and follow the lines of the cracks. Then I stare at the grassy area and count blades of grass. I get to ninety-eight before I shake myself out of my haze.

Now he's twenty minutes late.

I'm stricken by the possibility that he has stood me up, that this was all some cruel joke. *Oh God.* I stand and turn to walk up the steps, when I hear brakes squeal and a car door slam.

"Hey! Hey! Allison! Wait! Wait!"

With my back to him, I exhale a sound of relief. The patter of his footsteps as he runs up the stairs is practically musical, but I am unable to turn around. I feel his hand on my back as he rounds to my side. "Where are you going? You giving up on me so soon?"

"I thought maybe . . . I didn't know . . ." I pivot a bit and smile apologetically.

"Did you think I was blowing you off?" he says, noticeably upset. "Allison . . ."

I shrug with embarrassment. "You could've changed your mind."

"Not a chance. I'm sorry I'm late. My battery died and I had to get a jump."

"It's okay."

"Come on." Esben grabs my hand and leads me down to his car. He's about to open my door, when he stops. "I would never stand you up. One of these days, you'll trust me."

"It's not you I don't trust. It's me. And . . . the world. Everything. It's not you."

"Then one of these days, you'll trust the world and everything." He opens the door for me, and when I sit down, he leans in and kisses me quickly on the cheek. "But first, we eat. You up for a drive?"

"Sure. Where are we going?"

He starts the engine. "We're in Maine, yes? So what must we eat?"

"Mexican food."

He laughs. "Nooooo."

"Sushi? Parsnips? Frozen pizza?"

"You're nuts."

"Nuts? Okay. Pecans, cashews . . ."

His profile when he laughs again is hard to look away from, so I don't.

"You're not the best guesser," he teases. "We're in Maine, girl! We've got to get fried clams. Well, unless you're repulsed by seafood, in which case you and I are going to have to have a very serious talk."

"Actually, I love fried clams. All seafood, really. Simon and I go to a place in Boston that's so good. Down in Faneuil Hall. The Union—"

"Oyster House!" he finishes. "You do the raw bar?"

"Absolutely."

"God, I knew I liked you." He lets out what is indisputably a contented sigh and reaches for my hand as he pulls onto the highway. "Get ready, because this place will blow your mind. It's almost an hour to get there, but I promise it's worth it. And then, I thought we could go to this great orchard and pick apples and pumpkins. You know, a New England–themed day. Cool?"

I tighten my hand around his. Esben is not just taking me out for a quick lunch. He wants to spend the day with me. "Cool."

CHAPTER 15

GO FOR THE DREAM

Esben is right. The drive is worth it, and we haven't even eaten yet. We're at a traditional fish shack, complete with window service only and outdoor picnic tables, and I already know I'm going to love it.

I'm seated on one of the benches while he's getting our food from the window. Esben is leaning forward against the take-out counter, chatting with the girl at the register and occasionally calling back to the guy frying up our platters. He's so social and friendly that it's astounding. I can't ever recall starting random conversations with strangers. What undeniably has my attention more than Esben's outgoing nature, though, is his breathtakingly hot backside. I cannot help myself, because his jeans hug his shape with excruciating perfection. I'm starving, but I feel a certain disappointment when he stands up fully and turns to bring our food. Of course, the front of him isn't too shabby either . . .

I assumed he'd sit across from me, so my stomach flutters when he straddles the bench I'm on, facing me. Lord, this boy makes me so nervous and so comfortable at the same time, and I can't take my eyes off him.

"How's that look, huh?" he asks.

"So, so good." Then I realize that he is talking about the food.

He totally catches me ogling him, but before I can turn away, he's got a hand caressing the back of my neck. "It does look good. Best thing I've seen in ages."

His hand glides over my face, and he delicately moves his thumb across my lips. Esben slides nearer and slowly leans in. His mouth tantalizingly close, he whispers, "Best. Thing. In. Ages."

And then I shut my eyes and feel his lips on mine.

This is a gentle, tender kiss that lasts only a few heartbeats, but it only takes those few heartbeats for me to get blissfully lost.

Then he quickly kisses my cheek and sits back. "Hungry, gorgeous?"

Somehow, I am able to reply. "Ravenous." The smell is heavenly, and my now-grumbling stomach is probably the only thing preventing me from doing something stupid, like jumping into his arms and cramming my tongue down his throat.

"We've got it all here. Fried clams, oysters, scallops, shrimp, calamari, and haddock. Plus about five pounds of fresh French fries. Tartar sauce or ketchup?"

"Both. And, oh God, fried oysters? Most places don't have those."

Esben picks one up, dunks it in both sauces, and brings it to my mouth. "I'm about to upend your world."

I smile. "I think you already have."

He kisses my cheek again. "Eat."

I let him feed me the oyster, and while it doesn't hold a candle to the heated pleasure of his kiss, it's still damn satisfying. Between this juicy oyster that tastes of the sea and Esben's alluring presence, this is by far the best meal of my life.

We work our way through the mountain of seafood and wash it down with a large soda that we share. I don't ever want to leave this picnic table, but Esben is throwing away our trash and telling me about the orchard that's nearby as he leads me back to the car. It's a quick ten-minute drive that ends with a bumpy stretch on a dirt road, and after finding a spot in the packed lot, he bounds from the car excitedly.

His face lights up as he looks over the orchard. "This totally reminds me of being a kid. My parents used to take Kerry and me apple picking every year, and then my dad would make apple pie and apple coffee cake. I love my mother, but she can't cook to save her life. She is, though, a gifted pumpkin carver, and she'd spend forever assessing and rating pumpkins before buying any." He beckons and keeps his arm out, waiting for me. "Come on! This is going to be fun."

Very happily, I go to him. As though we have been doing this for years, his arm falls over my shoulder. "What kind of carvings did your mom do?" I ask as we walk.

"Everything. And not just traditional witches and ghosts and scary faces. Kerry and I would request weird stuff, too. Like, one time Kerry asked for a porcupine, and my mom nailed it. Last year, she texted me a picture of the pumpkin she did in my honor." He laughs. "It was a hashtag, and she said it took her ten minutes and that's all I was getting, because the year before she'd spent an unreasonable amount of time on the pair of flamingos I wanted." He stops short. "Oh God, Allison. I'm sorry."

I'm confused. "Sorry for what?"

"I'm going on and on about my family and childhood outings and stuff, and . . ." He shakes his head. "I'm really sorry."

"You don't have to apologize at all. It's not like I don't know that people can grow up with nice families."

"It was still dumb of me."

"Hey." I move to stand in front of him and get him to look at me. "I'm glad you had all that. Really. And I like hearing about it. Don't . . . look, Esben, you have to tell me about good stuff like this. If you don't, then it would mean you pity me or you're protecting me, and I don't want that. I don't need protection from *your* past. I need protection from mine."

He thinks on this. "Fair enough."

"Stop looking like you just ran over my dog." I grab his arm and pull him ahead. "So, let's go pick apples. And if you've inherited carving skills from your mother, then we may need a few pumpkins."

"I make some fierce triangle eyes . . ."

I laugh. "Good enough."

We begin walking. It's quite beautiful here, the rows and rows of trees spotted with red and green apples, the light smattering between leaves, and the smell of autumn rich in the air. I've never been apple picking before, and Esben seems to find how much fun I'm having amusing. We work our way up and down rows, and he soon stops picking any himself and just watches me as I peer through branches to find perfect apples.

"You're very selective," he notices. "Especially for a first timer."

"Maybe that's *why* I'm selective. I want to do this right. What if we come home with wormy, bruised apples? You'll thank me later." I'm eyeing a really big apple that I'm dying to get, but it's out of reach. "Can you get that one?"

"How about I help you get it?" He squats down a little. "Hop on. We'll piggyback you up to it."

If Esben wants me to plaster my body against his, I'm not about to refuse. As he stands, I tighten my legs around him and raise my hand. I'm at the perfect height, and I pluck the apple from the tree.

He starts to lower me, and I clutch on, stopping him. "Esben?"

"Yeah?"

"I'm going to tell you something, but I don't want you to get all weird and feel bad for me."

"Gotcha."

"This is my first piggyback ride."

He hikes me up higher, secures my legs in his arms, and starts walking. "Then I won't put you down yet."

We leave our apple bag under the tree, and for a while, Esben walks me through the orchard. I rest my head on my arm and watch

116

the trees go by; then I pull my fingers through his loose curls and see how the rays of sun pick up colors and highlights that I haven't noticed before. I am more relaxed and at peace in this moment than I could have imagined.

"You must be getting tired." I lean around a little. "Thank you."

"Anytime. You ready for pumpkins?"

"Absolutely."

"If you tell me you've never carved a pumpkin . . ."

I slide down his body. "Technically, no." I'm not sure why I find this funny, but I do, even though Esben clearly does not. This poor guy has no idea how many firsts I have never achieved.

He throws up his hands. "What? I'm going to make it my mission for you to do all the stuff you haven't. And why are you laughing?"

"I don't know! Maybe because you're so outraged over this. It's cute. I've helped scoop out the disgusting pumpkin guts. Does that count?"

"Nooooo! It does not count. Simon doesn't allow pumpkins at his house?"

"I'm not really . . . into holidays much. They were always a mixed bag growing up. Even when they were fun, that fun never lasted. I'd have, you know, a great Halloween, and then be out of that house before Thanksgiving. I kind of learned not to get invested. I'm sure Simon would like it if I were a huge Christmas fan or whatever, but . . . I don't know." Esben's face makes me laugh again. "It's not a big deal!"

"Come on. We're buying you a pumpkin. Or twenty."

While I was fussy about apples, it takes Esben thirty minutes to find a pumpkin that suits his carving needs. They all look the same to me, but I enjoy walking alongside him as he stops and starts, occasionally bending down to roll a pumpkin around.

At one point, he picks up what looks to me like a perfectly nice one and says sadly, "I'm so sorry. You are beautiful and perfectly round, but you do not have a stem, and, therefore, you are unfit for becoming a jack-o'-lantern. There are standards that have to be met. You can be a pie. Or bread."

"Or pumpkin bars? Those are really good. Simon makes them. Chocolate ganache, a layer of pumpkin cream, crushed cookies . . ."

"I like everything I've heard about this Simon fellow. He's a good dad, huh?"

"He is."

"But you don't call him Dad?"

"Oh." We walk down the path while Esben keeps looking. "I don't. I guess because he adopted me when I was so old."

"Does he mind?"

"He's never said if he does." I kick a stone. I haven't thought about this before.

Esben absolutely refuses to let me pay for the pumpkins and apples, even though he already paid for lunch, so I wander to look at display shelves set up with jams, a few baked goods, fudge, and locally made syrups. When I round back to the register, Esben is in a full-blown conversation with the man in line behind him. They're having a back-and-forth exchange about Maine attractions, and Esben is recommending our lunch spot.

"Oh, yeah, man! You have to go. We just ate there, and you won't find better seafood anywhere."

"That right? We'll drive on over then, if I can get my wife to leave the orchard. It's like she's never seen a tree before." He winks. "We've been on the road all day. Drove from New York City."

"Really?" Esben smiles and hands money to the cashier.

"Yes. But this was worth those hours in the car." The man looks around, then back at Esben, and leans in. "Want to know something?" he says a bit nervously. "After years working in the boring business world, we're going to do something fun and quirky. Finally. I've been a milk-shake addict all my life," he confesses with a laugh, "so we're starting a business around it. But not just regular milk shakes. Ones with skewers that stick out of the shake, loaded with extras. Brownie bites, fresh-baked cookies, candy bars. And in the colder months, we'll also do what we call 'hot milk shakes.' Coffee, tea, and cider drinks that'll come with doughnuts, pumpkin bread, and all that." He can barely contain his excitement.

Esben moves aside while the man pays for his pumpkin. "What a completely cool idea." He pauses, and suddenly I smile, because I know what he's about to do. He puts out an open hand. "My name is Esben Baylor. Any chance I could take a picture of you and your wife?"

Ten minutes later, Esben has posted a photo of this man and his wife, standing in the middle of the pumpkin patch, with a caption that tells their story and the hashtag *#goforthedream*.

After the car is loaded with apples and pumpkins and the four cornstalks that he's somehow squished into the backseat, we start the drive. I am glued to my phone, watching in awe as the comments pour in over this picture. I tap between his public Facebook, Instagram, and Twitter pages and his home page. It's impossible to keep up.

I drop the phone in my lap and stare at him.

"What?" he asks.

"*Who are you?* I mean . . . you have hundreds of comments in a matter of seconds about milk-shake man and his wife."

"What are people saying?"

I check again. The numbers are already way up. "Really nice things." I scroll and hardly know what to read aloud, because the sheer volume of comments is overwhelming. I read, "'I've always wanted to do something like this. Good for them. Hope they rock it out.' Lots like that. Someone wants to know the name of the store and when they'll be opening. Another person says . . ." I squint and then giggle. "She says that the milk-shake dude is crazy hot, and she's single, in case his wife ends up hating milk-shake life and runs off to Barbados with the ice-cream delivery boy."

"Well, that would be a sad ending to an otherwise inspiring story."

"How did you start doing all this? I mean, again, *who are you?*"

He laughs and pops on a pair of sunglasses. "This? This wasn't a big deal. But it's an interesting world, with interesting people. You just have to keep your eyes open." Suddenly, he pulls the car into the far right lane and takes an exit. "Speaking of ice cream, I totally forgot. There's a stand here that's insane."

"How do you know about all these places?"

"I like driving around, checking out little towns. Maine's got some quirky places. Campus can get a little claustrophobic."

I think about how much I love sequestering myself in my room. I may have to give that up.

Esben takes us to another window-service-only place, and we get in line. "Good. I was worried they'd already closed for the season." His arm goes over my shoulder again. "It's soft-serve ice cream, and they only have seven flavors or something, but it's so good. Trust me."

"I do trust you. And not just about the ice cream."

"I'm glad to hear that. And get the blueberry."

So, I do. And it's freaking outstanding, with bits of fresh berries swirled through the creamy blue ice cream. We sit under an umbrella at a small table, with our giant cones, and I can't resist checking his comments again. It's daunting. Then I stumble on more than one that makes me sit bolt upright.

Esben frowns. "What is it? God, did some jackass say something stupid? I'll block or ban or delete him. I don't put up with that stuff. Thank God it doesn't happen often."

"Um, no, actually. But you know how sometimes people comment on one thing but they're talking about another?"

"Yeah . . . I hate those. Like, I could put up a post of a chicken, and some dude will be all, 'Chickens are fine, but I once had a ferret who liked wearing knit hats,' and then forty-five people pipe in with their own ferret stories—"

"Esben." I wish I had a pair of sunglasses to hide behind. "It seems that people are still wondering what happened with us."

"Ahhh. Yes. That's been going on all week." He leans back. "Do you want to answer them?"

"Answer them? What do you mean?"

"You're not on Twitter or Facebook or anything, right?" he asks.

I shake my head, and he thinks for a minute.

"I could introduce you." His smile takes over.

"What do you mean?" It turns out that neither of us like eating the cone, so I take both and toss them. "How?"

"Come here." He scoots back his chair and pats his lap. "Sit."

I go to him and sit with my legs crossing his and my arm draped over his back. "Yes?"

"First," he says slowly, "first, though, there should be this."

For the second time today, he kisses me on the mouth. This one, though, lasts for way more than a few heartbeats. His mouth is cold, and he tastes like fresh blueberries, but the kiss is definitely hot. How anyone can be so sweet and tender, and also make me want to rip off his shirt right here at this ice-cream place, is beyond me. He's ignited my virtually forgotten thirst for romance and lust so easily.

I come up for air before I really do start tearing off his clothes. "I'm pretty sure that your second thing won't be as good."

He kisses me again, just for a few moments. "Probably not." He holds his phone in front of us, and I see our image reflected back. "What do you think?"

"We take a selfie?" I ask hesitantly. "And you post it?"

He nods and lifts his sunglasses. "Only if you want."

I lose myself in the amber of his eyes and think. The idea of taking this step is a bit intimidating, but it also feels exciting. I look down at the ground and keep thinking. And then I catch sight of something that makes me smile. Esben has on one blue sock and one white sock. I don't have to think anymore. "Yes, let's post a picture."

"You do know," he warns, "that we'll get some not-so-nice comments."

"From girls especially. I know." I don't say anything; I simply turn, touch the side of my face to his, and look to the lens.

Esben posts our picture.

Allison, meet everyone. Everyone, meet Allison.
#thiskissthiskiss #allison #180

I don't care about the comments, the reactions. Not right now. All I care about is that I was able to let him—let us—put this out there.

It's a damn milestone for me, and I will never forget this day. Or him.

CHAPTER 16

GRUDGE

A few weeks later, Esben, his sister, Kerry, and I are outside the bustling student union. It's the week before Halloween, and the chilly breeze is making us all shiver under the bleak gray sky. While we all have on thick sweaters or jackets, it feels like this might be the last tolerable day before true bitter temps set in. Northern Maine is not known for its easy winters. Steffi has been texting me sunshine pics for days, which maybe should annoy me, but the plethora of sunglass and cocktail emojis she attaches makes me giggle. I have been trying to get her on the phone for days and keep missing her, but the wacky texts are holding me over okay.

Esben is busy on his phone, and I'm holding Kerry's camera while she retrieves a small whiteboard and a bag of dry-erase markers from a bag. "Is this the first one you've done with him?" she asks.

"Yeah." I'm trying hard not to look like a nervous, insecure wreck. I'm not sure if it's going all that well.

Esben and Kerry are out here to ask students to share about their best friends, and I only somewhat reluctantly agreed to tag along. Part of me is dying to watch him in action again, and part of me is dying to cover my eyes and block this all out.

I want to run. I want to stay. I want to do both.

But I stay.

Kerry has as warm a smile as her brother. "You seem nervous. Don't be." She stands and trades the whiteboard for the camera in my hand. "I'm glad you came. I haven't seen you since that day." She doesn't have to spell it out any more than that. We both know which day she's talking about. "And you kind of left quickly."

"Just a bit," I agree. "I wasn't . . . prepared. You must think I'm out of my mind."

"No. Not at all. Those things can shake you up. You . . . were shaken up more than most, but it was . . . I don't know. I haven't seen that." Kerry scrapes her boot across the concrete. "Meaning, I haven't seen that in *him*, okay? He's not usually so affected."

"I guess . . . well, I wondered . . ." I am so far outside my comfort zone, but I have minimal defenses left. Esben has torn a lot of them down. "I didn't know if he was always so . . . reactive."

Kerry shakes her head. "That day . . . it was a first. I've been filming and photographing all of my brother's projects from the beginning. I've loved it, every minute." She stops and lets the breeze rush over us. "Esben has been talking about you so much that I feel like I know you. But I don't. Not yet." Kerry is as intense as her brother. "I'd like to, though, because it was all so beautiful, and you did something to my brother. You got to him. You *crazy* got to him."

"That day was all a little crazy."

"Crazy wonderful," she stresses. "But I owe you an apology. I just hauled you in without giving you a chance to get out of it. Sometimes I get as hyped up about Esben's stuff as he does, and I should have been paying more attention to the fact that you weren't into it. We needed someone else; you were there—"

I stop her cold. "I'm glad you got me in that chair." I can't help peeking over at Esben with affection. "It's probably the best thing that ever happened to me. So, thank you."

A gust of wind blows her honey hair across her face, and she grins when she brushes it back and holds her hand against her head. "You've got my brother all fired up, you know? But he's been hiding you away, so I'm happy we get to hang out today."

I feel an obligation to explain, to clarify that I'm at fault here. "Esben hasn't been hiding me. I think it's just because I'm a little shy, and . . ." This is so embarrassing, but I tell her the truth. "If it weren't for him, I'd probably still be locked in my dorm room. He's teaching me to loosen up and be social, I guess." I shrug. "Very patiently," I add with a laugh.

"Esben is certainly patient." Then she turns in his direction and yells, "And he's also completely unorganized and slow! Baby Blue, get off your phone! Time to move! It's not exactly eighty degrees here."

Esben looks up. "Sorry, sorry. I'm ready."

"Seriously, if it weren't for me, nothing would ever get done." Kerry bumps my arm. "Hey, I have an art show next month. Want to come?" she asks. "It's not that exciting, just a little evening thing over in the art building. Probably some bad hors d'oeuvres and stuff, but they actually have a nice gallery there. Maybe you'll come with Esben?"

"I would love to," I answer. And I mean it.

"The trick here," Esben explains as he walks toward us, "is to get the people who are not chomping at the bit to talk to me. See that group over there, watching us? It's a bunch of girls who want to squeal about the friend they met two weeks ago. I know that sounds mean, but it's true. So let's move away."

With the whiteboard in his hand, Esben approaches a student walking alone. I avert my eyes, because the idea of approaching a stranger like this is mind-blowingly weird to me, and the guy has a hat pulled halfway over his eyes. He is not exactly screaming to be spoken to.

"Hey, man. Can you help us out with something?" I hear Esben say.

I fill my head with rambling thoughts to block out the conversation, but when I finally peek back, I see the student facing Kerry's video camera. "My name is Chea, and my best friend is Andy."

"How did you meet Andy? What makes him so special?" Esben prompts.

"Well . . ." Chea glances off to the side. "I was born in Cambodia and moved to the States when I was eleven. I didn't speak any English, and school was really rough. I was in all these ESL classes, but also in the regular classroom, too. Nobody wanted to hang out with me. There weren't a lot of Cambodians at my school." He laughs, but it's a painful laugh. "The teasing was pretty awful. Kids can be vicious. I don't get why . . . I was alone all the time. I didn't catch on to English very quickly, and when I screwed up, it just made me not want to try. I missed home. I missed my friends. I hated the food here. Everything." He stops and stares at the ground. When he looks back up, he runs his sleeve over his nose. "What the hell? I'm getting all emotional, man. I haven't thought about that in ages."

"It's all right." Esben claps a hand on Chea's arm.

Chea sniffs and shakes his head. "But then this kid in my class . . . I don't know why, but he started sitting next to me at lunch. Andy. He gave me my first potato chip, and that was also the first American food I liked. He would point to things and name them in English, and I would repeat them. And, at some point, I understood that he wanted the Cambodian word, too. He was lousy, I tell you. Horrible accent, but he tried. Andy taught me to read better than the ESL teachers. He was my only friend that year. The other kids didn't understand why Andy would hang out with a loser like me, and they gave him a really hard time." Chea looks right at the camera. "But he didn't seem to care. He was my friend, and that was it. So, it was the two of us against the world."

"You're still friends?" Esben asks. He has been listening so intently. Not just interviewing someone, not just asking questions. He is present and connected and genuinely interested. It's beautiful.

"Yeah, yeah, for sure!" Chea nods adamantly. "He goes to Harvard. Can you believe that? I'm so proud." He claps a hand to his chest and smiles. "Harvard! Damn, I miss that kid."

Esben has written *#bestfriend #andy* on the whiteboard, and he gives it to Chea to hold up while Kerry takes a few pictures.

"Thank you for this," Chea says. "I should tell him more how much he did for me. And what he still does. There's nobody better." Suddenly, Chea throws his arms around Esben and claps him heartily on the back. "Thanks, dude." Then he adjusts his hat and takes off.

I'm rather slack jawed. *Holy. Crap.*

Esben whips around. "Not a bad start, huh?" Then he begins strolling in search of his next subject.

I walk with Kerry. "He's magic . . . ," I breathe out.

"I know, right? It gets me every time."

The next five interviews go well enough, but they're mostly girls cheering for the sake of the camera. Still, we hear some warm shout-outs, and Kerry gets some good shots. She calls it "filler," but I still think it's nice to hear about friendship, and I think about Steffi and how much I would have to say about her if I were a subject today.

Another four interviews in, Esben is getting visibly frustrated. He wants more intensity; I can tell.

"Allison? You want to pick someone out for me?" he asks.

"Me?" I have no idea how to do anything like this.

"Yeah. You'll be good, because you've got fresh eyes. A virgin consultant." He winks.

Oh, Lord. He has no idea how right he is. But I agree.

The three of us survey the options around us. There's such a blur of students out today, and it takes me a moment to start looking at them individually. Not far ahead, I see a white-haired older man in a long wool coat, with a plaid scarf tucked in neatly under the collar. He walks with an elaborately carved cane, although he doesn't appear to rely on it much. I suddenly very much want to know who this older gentleman's best friend is.

"Him." I point subtly.

"Professor Gaylon? Bold choice." Esben exhales. "Wish me luck." He throws back his shoulders and marches ahead.

"Who's Professor Gaylon?" I whisper to Kerry.

She's trying not to laugh as she holds up the camera. "He's an econ teacher not known for his affable nature. I'm soooooo glad you picked him!" Kerry scurries to catch up to her brother.

When I reach them, Esben is trying to cajole the professor into talking. "C'mon, you don't have a best friend? You'd really help me out here. Just a few words?"

"Wouldn't your time be better spent studying instead of engaging in this video nonsense?"

"How about we make a deal?" Esben is throwing out every bit of charm he has. "You do this really quick interview, and I'll put in two extra hours of studying tonight."

Professor Gaylon narrows his eyes and pokes his cane in Esben's direction. "Deal. Make it snappy."

Esben gestures to Kerry, and she moves in to film.

"So, tell us about your best friend."

"I don't have one. There. That's your interview!" snaps the professor.

He starts to leave, but Esben stops him.

"Hey, hey, wait! You don't have any friends? Who would you call in a crisis?"

"911."

"Are you married? Any family?"

"No. Never wanted to deal with a wife. Family's all dead."

Esben rubs his lips together. "Okay. Who do you call just to talk? When you need someone to lean on? When you want to go out to dinner?"

The professor is suddenly silent. For too long. Esben looks unusually uncomfortable.

I may not be as cranky as this man, but I do know bitter and hard. Without thinking, I step forward. "What about a former friend? Who did you used to call?"

The man jabs toward me with his cane. "That girl's smarter than you." He repositions his cane, then stands tall.

I step in closer. "What was his name?"

"Jerry DuBois. That son of a bitch."

Esben drops his head to hide his smile. "Oh my."

"You had a falling out?" I ask.

The professor's voice is sharp. "Falling out? I cut that man out of my life."

"Why?"

"I made a mistake. I got into business with DuBois. Went in on some real-estate deal he said would make us a fortune. I had my doubts, but Jerry was my good friend. I trusted him. And he screwed me over. Lost it all." He shakes his cane. "Never do business with a friend, kid."

"What happened? He took your money and never gave you your profit?"

"What? No, nothing like that." The professor searches for words. "It was a bad deal. The market didn't behave the way we thought it would. I was broke after. My fiancée left me."

"But it was just a bad deal. It wasn't intentional . . . ," I offer.

"I still lost everything," he snaps.

"What about when things were good?" I want to know. "Why was he your best friend?"

"We played cards, went drinking. Jerry liked a strong whiskey sour, and I always had a martini. Straight up with a twist." He makes a spinning motion with a finger. "Jerry was an English professor at the University of Maine, and he was always trying to get me to read

Shakespeare and whatnot. I tried, for him . . ." The professor smiles a bit. "He made me go to see *As You Like It* once. Guess what? I actually liked it! Jerry told really bad jokes and had terrible taste in women, but he . . . he was my friend. When my brother died, Jerry was in Chicago, and he drove across the country to be with me. Stood next to me when we buried him."

"So, Jerry wasn't all bad," I say.

Professor Gaylon looks at me. "No, he wasn't all bad."

"How long has it been since you've spoken?" I ask.

"Oh gosh . . . probably thirty-some years." He thinks for a long minute. "Thirty-six this June."

"Do you miss him?"

"Maybe I do. Maybe I do." He speaks more softly now, thoughtfully.

"Can you forgive him?"

"We were young. Not smart with money. And he was right when he said my fiancée was a money-grubber. He said she should have stayed no matter what. That was true. So, maybe I could forgive that bastard."

"Would you like to call him?" Esben asks.

"Kid, you are somethin' else." The professor clearly finds this idea amusing. "I wouldn't know how to find him. He could be anywhere now."

Esben can type on his phone faster than anyone I've seen, and it takes him all of ten seconds to hold up the screen to Professor Gaylon. "Jerry DuBois. Professor of English at Boston University. Phone number is 617—"

"He's in Boston? Well, damn, he always wanted to teach in Boston." The professor's face lights up, and he touches his hand to the screen. "Look at that. He's got more wrinkles than I do."

"Should we try his office?"

Professor Gaylon nods.

Esben calls the number and hands the phone over, while we all wait anxiously.

"Jerry DuBois?" the professor barks. "This is Carter Gaylon. So, you're in Boston now, you old bird. I called to say that if you buy me an expensive surf-and-turf dinner I will forgive you." He frowns and listens. "Fine . . . we can negotiate. Yes, fine. Saturday, it is . . . No, I don't need directions. I know how to Google Map." He thrusts the phone back at Esben. "Maybe you're not so dumb after all."

Kerry points at the whiteboard, and Esben hurriedly scribbles *#jerry #bestfriend* on it and snaps a picture.

Without another word, Professor Gaylon turns and leaves. There is, however, a slight jauntiness to his step.

CHAPTER 17

SPECTRUM

I'm stretched on my stomach on Esben's bed, with a textbook open to one of the most boring chapters in the history of textbook chapters, but I am forcing myself to pay attention. The November weekend weather is dreary and miserable, the sound of the rain pattering against the window, so it's a good day to snuggle up inside and work. Esben is sitting in his chair, with his feet kicked up on the desk. He has been engrossed in a book for one of his lit classes, and he's barely looked up in the past two hours since we came back from lunch. So, I'm startled when he suddenly drops the book and slides the chair the few feet it takes to reach the end of the bed.

"Allison?"

I can't tell if he's mad or what, but there's a somewhat confused look on his face that I'm not able to read. "Yeah?" I ask nervously.

"We have to talk about something," he blurts out.

Exasperated. That's what it is. Esben sounds exasperated.

Here it is. I knew whatever was going on between us wasn't going to last. "All right." I shut my book and stare at the cover rather than him.

"Are you seeing anyone else?" he asks.

It's a good thing I'm not prone to snorting, because this is the most ridiculous question ever. Now I look at him, because I have to know if he's swapped bodies with someone wearing a straitjacket. "Am I *what*?"

"We haven't . . . talked about that. Or about us. Or if there is an us. And . . ."

He's right. We haven't. And I haven't known how to bring this up. Or maybe I've been scared to.

"Esben, good Lord, if either of us is likely to be seeing anyone else, it's you. You're the one with half the planet dying to get a piece of you."

He laughs. "I think that's a slight exaggeration."

I move in front of him so that his legs rest between mine. "Maybe slight. But you know what I mean. You could be with a thousand people other than me. And probably girls who would be more . . . would be more . . ." I really don't want to have to say this aloud.

"More what?" he prompts.

Over the past weeks, I've spent hours and hours with Esben. We study, we talk, we have meals together. We do almost everything together. We kiss, we embrace—sometimes for longer than others—and then we say good night. And go to our own dorms.

If he is not already about to dump me, I'm very afraid that I'm about to blow this all apart. "When you walk me home, at night, you have never asked to stay over."

Esben smiles with a little embarrassment. "That's true."

"You've never . . . tried anything." The awkwardness of this unexpected conversation is nearly crippling.

"That's also true." Esben takes my hand. "Do you know why?"

"Because you're getting routine, nightly sex from Twitter followers who have stalked you to this very room, so you're not interested in me?"

He laughs. "No. Allison, I am crazy attracted to you, and I haven't so much as looked at another girl since I met you."

"So no Twitter lays?"

"Not a one." He takes my other hand in his. "It's not a secret that you've had a rough time, and I know how hard it's been for you to let me in at all. I don't want to push you into anything physical. I figure if you're ready for something more, you'll tell me."

I have to think about how to answer this. "Every time we kiss good-bye and you leave my room, I want to ask you to stay. But I also don't. I'm not sure if that makes sense."

"I think so. But keep talking."

"Look, I assume that you've got a lot more experience than I do, and you've probably had sex all over the place, and I don't know what the hell I'm doing. I'm pretty sure I haven't exactly blown you away with my risqué behavior, and I'm not getting why you're putting up with this. Why you haven't tried to . . . to take off my clothes or cop a feel or whatever." I free my hands from his and toss them up in the air. "I'm not exactly an expert on messing around, but I think it's kind of an all-or-nothing deal, yeah? And right now you're pretty much getting nothing. So, I'm kind of wondering if you're dating other people and we're just friends who kiss a little, but if that's the case, then we have to stop kissing, because I don't think of you as just my good friend Esben."

"You're really going to need to take a few breaths here." He looks very cute as he pushes my bangs back. "I thought *I* was the insecure one with the questions. But let's straighten out some things. First of all, I don't think of you as my 'good friend' Allison."

"Okay." That alone makes me feel a bit better.

"Second, I have not, as you wildly put it, had sex all over the place."

"So, you've had lots of sex in a limited number of defined and well-thought-out locations, then." It's jarring how much the idea of Esben with anyone else makes my chest hurt. "There's no way you're a virgin. You're too hot."

As he moves to sit on the bed next to me, he shakes his head. "What am I going to do with you?"

As a temporary answer to his own question, he turns my face to his and kisses me. It's a long kiss, but not a greedy one. It is also—I will allow—a loving one.

"In fact," he says. "I am a virgin."

"You are not."

"I am," he says very comfortably.

"How could you, famous Esben Baylor, not have had sex? You've got girls teeming all over you."

He shrugs. "I'm not saying I haven't done other stuff. I've dated and fooled around and all that. You know, everything but actual sex."

I'm very confused. "Why's that?"

"It's just never felt right. Sex is important, and I haven't been with someone who I've wanted to be that kind of close with. And, to be honest, I can't always tell if someone likes me for me or for what I do online. I've been burned a few times that way, so I'm cautious."

"I can understand that. But you know that's not me, so you just . . . don't want to sleep with me?"

It's hard for him to kiss me while he's smiling, but he manages to make it work. Then he says, "Quite the opposite, you nut. Let me be very clear. I want to sleep with you. Like, really, really want to sleep with you. And, by the way, you said before that it's an all-or-nothing deal? The physical stuff? There's a whole bunch to do between nothing and everything, a wide spectrum, in fact. Just as a side note." Now he's really smiling. "Allison, everything about you turns me on, and if the day comes when you're ready for us to have sex, I'm not going to complain. Like, seriously not complain. At all. But I don't think you're at that point. Am I wrong?"

"No," I say quietly. "But that doesn't mean that . . . I don't think about it. Or that I don't want to."

"But just not now, right? And that's fine. I get it. We only met a few months ago; you've got some understandable trust issues. There's no rush."

I take hold of his hands again. "You're a good guy, Esben. A really, really good guy. Remarkable, actually. I just need some time."

"I'm going to give you that, okay? Don't worry. And, one day, you'll stop looking for this—for us—to fall apart."

"But, still . . . Esben, you're a college junior whose girlfriend won't sleep with him. What if you explode?"

All of a sudden, Esben gets the most pleased look on his face.

"What?" I ask. "I just meant that—"

His hand goes to the back of my neck, just below my hairline. "You called yourself my *girlfriend*."

Ohmigod. I did. "That just slipped out. I didn't mean to assume, er, that we were . . . that you are my . . ." I try to breathe for his sake. "We haven't used that word, or even talked about it. I've just been rolling along, being all grateful that I haven't had some crazy meltdown and that you haven't figured out that you could probably have more fun with someone whose past isn't a battlefield of trauma. So, that word just slipped out. That's all."

"I want you to be my girlfriend. I don't want nameless, undefined, figuring-it-out stuff. We're past that. And you just proved it."

I ease in and whisper on his lips. "So, you're my boyfriend, then."

"Yes."

"Another first for me." I can almost taste him.

"How's it feel?" Esben's mouth barely touches mine, and, for just a second, his tongue runs over my lips.

"So, so good." I take him by the collar and pull him over me as I drop against the bed.

Esben props himself onto his elbows and holds his chest above me so that he's at the perfect height to sink his tongue into my mouth and kiss me with an intensity that nearly knocks the wind out of me. And I can't get enough. His fingers knot into my hair while our kissing continues, and I drink in the flavor of him—and of us. Intuitively, my leg goes over his, and I realize that I'm tightening our fit together, that I'm comfortable enough to do that. There's a full-body urge that sweeps through me, a heat and a longing that are new. For a moment, I am lost in our closeness and how the weight of his chest and waist pressed into mine is not nearly enough.

Except that it is. As much as I want so much more, he's right. I am not ready. Not at all.

Maybe I've tensed or otherwise signaled him—I don't know—but Esben rolls onto his side, his mouth never leaving mine, reassuring me. He paces our kissing, sometimes gentle and teasing and sometimes escalating the heat between us before bringing us back down again in a kind of blissful torture. Just because I haven't made out like this before doesn't mean that I don't know how good he is. He's got me in a safe place, one I believe, without a doubt, is enough for him. He's enjoying this as much as I am.

It occurs to me that this boy has not faltered once in the time that I've known him. Not on any level. I reach my hand up, touch his chest, feel the muscles in his shoulder, and then run my palm down his arm, over the bracelets he always has on, and then I set his hand on my hip. The truth is that I'm feeling a little drugged, a little out of my own head right now. I keep moving his hand until it's under the hem of my shirt.

Esben rubs his nose against mine. "Allison?"

I can't help but arch my back a little. "You said . . . you said there was a spectrum."

"There is, yes."

"Show me," I tell him.

"I didn't mean you had to investigate that spectrum two seconds after I mentioned it."

"I know you didn't." I slide his hand over my stomach, then up to just under my rib cage. "But the spectrum . . . it means we could do something and then not do other things . . ."

"It does."

"And you can . . . stop?"

He smiles. "Of course. Allison, *of course*. Any guy who's not a complete asshole would stop. We're not machines that get activated and then can't be shut down. I just want you to be comfortable, okay?"

"How can you be this . . ." I look into his eyes. "How can you be this everything?"

"Let's be clear here. I'm not saying that this is all a total breeze for me, because you're pretty damn hot, and I would love to be tearing your clothes off, and I'll probably have to take, like, forty cold showers later today." His grin is both mischievous and utterly sweet. "But you know what feels better than anything physical?" Esben looks at me for a long time. "How it feels to be falling for someone the way that I'm falling for you."

Esben could not possibly slay me more than this. He's making me want and hope for things I've never allowed myself to even dream about. "I was already so comfortable with you . . ."

"Yeah? Good."

"And now . . ." I want to feel his hand against my skin. "Now even more so."

"Again, good. But that doesn't mean we have to rush anything." Yet he lets me nudge his hand to make sure he moves higher. Which he does. And the moment that my breast is under his touch, his mouth goes to the side of my neck—

Both of us jolt at the pounding on the door. The pounding that very quickly becomes incessant.

"Esben! Esben!" A male voice booms through the door.

"Baby Blue, you better be in there!" Kerry says loudly.

"We've got a situation!" Another male voice.

Esben sighs and drops his head against me. "Really? *Now?*" he whispers. "Maybe they'll go away."

The hollering outside the room increases.

I laugh and reluctantly remove his hand from under my shirt. "I don't think so."

He grumbles, but climbs over me, kissing me quickly. "You ready to meet the boys?" he asks before going to see what's so urgent.

"I guess so." I sit and smooth down my hair.

He swings open the door and barks at the people behind it. "This better be goddamn important."

Kerry and two guys push past him. "Hey, Allison!" She sits on one side of me, and one of the boys plops down on the other.

He's a big guy, tall and very muscular, with black hair peeking out from under his baseball hat and a harmonica hanging around his neck. He grins at me and puts out a hand. "So you're the famous Allison, huh? Very nice to finally meet you. I'm Danny."

I smile back and shake his hand. "Hi, Danny."

He reaches out and delicately adjusts the top of my shirt, which was evidently hanging off my shoulder. "Sorry to interrupt." He winks before sticking the harmonica in his mouth and blowing out a few sultry notes.

"Hey, I'm Jason!" the second guy says and waves from his spot by the door. I try not to gape. While not quite as tall as Danny, Jason is even brawnier than his friend, and just as good-looking. The white T-shirt he's wearing contrasts strikingly with his dark skin, and his angular face makes me think he should be modeling and not studying liberal arts.

"Okay, what's so important?" This is the first time that I've seen Esben look truly irritated, and I can't help but be flattered.

"I've been calling and texting, but, for once in your life, you've apparently turned your phone off." Kerry holds out her own phone. "Read this. It's a Facebook post that's getting shared. The woman lives around here."

Esben takes the phone rather brusquely and reads aloud. "'Cassie's birthday party is supposed to start in three hours, and no one has RSVP'd. Not a single person. We invited the entire second-grade class. She's six, okay? Six.'" He lowers the phone for a moment and takes a sharp breath before he continues. "'What am I supposed to tell her when no one shows up? She has a strawberry birthmark over half her face, and one bratty girl in her class started bad-mouthing Cassie, saying she was ugly and contagious, and got everyone too afraid to talk to her. I can't stop crying. We've got a huge room with princess decorations reserved at Bounce Till Dawn, because that's what Cassie wanted. And she's so full of hope, and that hope is going to be crushed, because she has no idea what's about to happen. What in the hell am I going to do? Should I cancel the party and make up an excuse to Cassie? Sorry for the rant . . .'"

"Oh God," I murmur. I know about crushed hopes all too well. And I know about rejection all too well. I feel sick.

Esben passes the phone back to Kerry. "Jesus."

"She's six!" Kerry says angrily.

"I know." Esben's feet are tapping against the hard floor.

Danny still has the harmonica in his mouth, and Esben glares at him when he produces a long, sad note.

"This kid has to have people show up to her birthday party. You have to make that happen," Jason insists.

"I know!" Esben says sharply. He is visibly upset. "Sorry, sorry . . . just give me a minute. I don't know what to do."

He looks to me, and I give him a calm smile. "Yes, you do."

Esben spins in his chair and gets on the Internet while we all wait. The sound of his typing echoes throughout the room.

"Okay. The party is at one of those places with giant inflatable structures and slides and stuff. It's about twenty minutes from here. Here's what we're going to do. Kerry, comment on that post and tell her that a party is coming Cassie's way, and she is to take her beautiful daughter to Bounce Till Dawn and prepare her for the best princess party she could ever want. Don't let her argue with you; just tell her that the party is on. End of story. Share the post, and tag everyone you know." He glances at us. "Jason, find Professor Donahue. She's got trip- let girls who I think are around this age. Tell her what's going on, and see if she'll come. Ask her to tell other parents. Then call anyone you can think of who has a car, and round up as many people as possible to fill those cars. We'll need a caravan of sorts." He turns back to us. "Who do we know in the theater department?"

There's collective silence.

"Who do we know in the theater department?" he says with more urgency. "Think!"

"Oh, oh . . . Jennie Lisbon is a theater major," Danny says. "And she's megahot." He punctuates this with a whistle into his harmonica.

Esben claps his hands. "Good. Ask her to raid the costume department. Take anything that'll work. Princess dresses for everyone."

"Well, the girls," Jason corrects.

"No, *everyone*. This kid wants a princess party, then we're all going to be goddamn princesses. You'll love it."

"Dude, I'm not wearing—"

"Zip it!" Esben says gleefully. "You interrupted what was a very, very nice afternoon"—he pauses to wink at me—"even though it was for a good reason, and you put me in charge. So, you're going to be a princess, goddamn it. Allison, can you and Kerry find a toy store and grab whatever princessey things you can find? Glittery stuff, ribbons, whatnot. Oh, and some helium balloons. Lots." He opens a drawer and pulls out a small zipped bag and tosses it to me.

"What's this?"

"Petty cash," he answers with a smile. "You know, for emergencies."

I toss it back. "I got this." Simon keeps my bank account more than solid, and the only thing I ever spend money on is takeout.

"You sure?"

"Positive."

"Thanks, babe."

"Sure." I manage to say this without whimpering. No one has ever called me *babe*, and the way it naturally rolls off his tongue makes me melt.

He goes back to the computer and begins typing furiously as he talks. "I'm posting this. We're going to flood this place with people who understand that Cassie deserves the best birthday ever. This kid is going to know how many people are on her side." His face has such solid determination as he works on his post, and I am even more captivated by him. "There. Done." Esben stands up. "Okay, everybody, move. We're on the clock."

Danny stands and towers over us. "I'm gonna make a much better princess than you, Jase."

"Yeah, good luck with that. Just you wait. I am going to rock this out so hard."

Esben shoves them both playfully and pushes them to the door. "Go, go, guys." We hear their princess debate and screeching harmonica sounds continue down the hall.

Kerry gives him a quick hug and takes the car keys. "Love you, Baby Blue. We'll be fast, I promise." She goes to the door and coughs too loudly. "I'll give you two a second. Sorry for breaking things up."

Esben reaches for my hand and pulls me up. "I'm going to stay here and keep track of the comments. See what else we can come up with. I bet anything that someone will come up with something awesome. I'll also call this bounce place and let them know what's coming their way. See if they've got more rooms they can open up."

Everything about him is electrified right now. He's got an energy and a drive that has him totally on fire.

I put a hand on the side of his face, and I can't help but shake my head a little with disbelief. "You're like a goddamn superhero, aren't you?"

He laughs lightly. "Hardly. I just can't let this little girl be sad. At least not today."

The next five hours secure that I am falling for Esben the way he is falling for me. He creates much more than a birthday party. He creates a near festival. The bounce place opens every room they have, and people stream in—with the overflow crowd hanging out in the parking lot like tailgaters at a football game—and there are so many balloons and metallic streamers and dresses and crowns and presents that I can hardly see straight.

Best of all, there is a truly happy little girl who has the party of all parties and who is undeniably and totally delighted by it all, and a mother who's nearly speechless with gratitude.

When the party begins to wind down, I find Esben. He's pulling off his pale-blue dress with its poufy tulle skirt, and I take his hand.

"You're wonderful. You know that?" I say. "I could have used someone like you when I was a kid."

He looks at me so intently and with such care. "I'd have moved mountains for you, Allison."

"I believe that." I start for the door, then turn back. "Esben? No more push and pull. No more wariness. I'm completely in this with you. I think I have been from the minute you picked up my ice cubes, but I just didn't know it."

CHAPTER 18

SHATTER ME

It's the Wednesday after Thanksgiving, and I'm getting ready to go to Kerry's art show. Last week, I hitched a ride down to Massachusetts with Esben and Kerry, and although I could tell Esben wanted to meet Simon when they dropped me off at my house, and I know Simon wanted to meet Esben, I wasn't ready. That blending of worlds felt weird at the time, but I'm regretting it a little now. Maybe over winter break . . . and I cannot wait for Steffi to finally meet Esben when she comes for Christmas, as she does every year.

Back in my dorm room, Esben is at my desk and has been alternating between catching up on his social-media pages and sneaking glances at me. I've been fussing with my hair and trying to put on eyeliner the way Steffi taught me, and I'm not sure what's so interesting about that. But he keeps looking at me.

When I'm finally done, he spins to face me with a mischievous expression. "You look good," he says with a certain edge that I like.

"Thank you."

"That dress . . ." He eyes me up and down. "It's hot."

I wrinkle my brow. "It's not hot. It's a long-sleeve wrap dress."

He reaches out and strokes a hand over my waist. "One that hugs you in all the right places. You're oblivious to how gorgeous you are." His touch goes to my lower back, and he guides me closer until he's pulled me into his lap. Immediately, his mouth is buried against my neck, kisses covering my skin, grazing over the top of my chest.

I tilt my head back. "I should wear dresses more . . ."

"And purple. Purple looks great on you," he murmurs. "We still have thirty minutes until we have to leave. Think we could find something to do?" He pushes aside the top of my dress, and his mouth goes just above my bra line.

Esben wasn't kidding when he told me there was a spectrum. I haven't even taken my pants off with him yet, but he's somehow managed to keep us very busy these past few weeks. And given the way his tongue feels and the way he's periodically sucking on my skin, I'm pretty tempted to rip off my dress right this second.

"I know exactly what we could do," I say. Esben lifts his mouth to mine, but just before we kiss, I stop him with a smile. "I want to go on Facebook and Twitter and Instagram and all that."

He laughs. "You do?"

I nod. "I do. I'm ready. And I think it would be fun."

"It would be fun. We can send each other dirty tweets and drive our followers mad."

"Then I definitely want to do this. Will you help me?"

"Right now?" he asks and traces the line of my V-neck.

"Yup. And I'll thank you for it after the art show." I'm totally taking my dress off tonight.

"Deal." I nearly fall off his lap, because he's whipped us around to face the screen so damn fast.

I sit on the bed while he navigates social-media sites and fires questions at me. I didn't realize there was so much that went into these things, that it's more than just passwords and profile pictures. He knows all the ins and outs of privacy and posting settings, and he gives me a brief tutorial on the basics of how these sites work. Then he takes my phone, downloads the apps, and logs me in. Apparently, I motivated him to work at the speed of light.

"There. And I'm your first follower on Twitter," he says happily. "Since you have exactly zero pictures of you stored on your phone, I'll take one. Now, sit there, and keep being that sexy."

I blush, but face the camera.

"And while you're the only person I know who doesn't have a million selfies, I do like that you saved a screenshot of the text I sent you." Before I can say anything, there are a few clicks, then he lowers the phone. "God, you are so beautiful."

"Esben . . ."

"You are. Look." He crawls onto the bed and shows me the photo he's taken.

"You've got, like, a million filters on it."

He shakes his head. "Not a one. Now, let's get you some followers, okay?"

"Oh. I guess so."

Esben begins typing on his phone, and, a minute later, my own phone dings. It's some kind of Twitter alert.

"Apparently, I've been mentioned." I send him a fake-confused look. "I wonder who could have done that?" I tap the alert and am taken to my new Twitter page.

You all remember #allison, yes? Let me reintroduce you. Meet #girlfriendallison. She's new to Twitter, so let's give her a warm welcome. And coffee. She loves coffee.

I watch, stunned, as his tweet gets favorited and reposted over and over. And it takes only seconds for my followers to grow from this one tweet. I'm still blinking at my phone as Esben pulls me out the door.

"We gotta go," he says, laughing.

"Why are all these people following me? I haven't done anything."

He shrugs and zips my coat while I continue to stare at my feed. "Guilt by association, baby."

Esben guides me to the art gallery across campus, his hand at my elbow, because I cannot stop staring at my phone. "I have three hundred followers on Twitter. It's been ten minutes!" I tap the screen. "And . . . like, a zillion friend requests on Facebook! And lots of pictures of coffee . . . what do I do? Am I supposed to do something? Post?"

"God, you're cute." He catches me as I stumble over a curb. "Take some pictures tonight. I'll help you post some stuff later, if you want."

As we walk into the gallery, I put my phone away. It seems silly, but I'm kind of giddy over my newfound social-media presence.

The gallery is beautiful, and I had no idea this was here. Of course, if I'd left my room more, or done anything besides study for the past two years, I might have known about this. Floating stairs lead us up to the main floor, and we are met with spectacular lighting that manages to highlight the artwork but also make the space pretty sexy and romantic, although I'm not sure it's supposed to be. My interpretation could perhaps have something to do with my mood . . .

"There she is." Esben points at Kerry, across the room, talking to someone. "I'm so excited. I've only seen one of the pieces she's been working on, but she's really, really good. This is the juniors' and seniors' stuff only. It's a big piece of their grade for the semester."

He catches Kerry's attention and waves. She's in stiletto heels and a tight red sheath dress that shows her beautiful figure and plenty of cleavage, and she's got her hair pulled off her face. I would last two steps in those shoes, but she walks without the slightest wobble when she comes our way. "You came!" She throws out her arms and hugs me.

"Of course! Congratulations. This is a big night for you," I say as I hug her back. "And you look stunning."

Esben scowls. "You look barely clothed."

Kerry laughs and kisses his cheek. "Overprotective much?"

"Don't you have a scarf or something?" he asks with annoyance.

I loop my arm through his. "She does not need a scarf."

"Come on. Walk around, and see what you think," she says, beckoning us to follow her.

"I thought artists were supposed to wear, you know, big drapey shirts and billowy pants," he mutters. "A little more hippie, a little less lingerie model."

I laugh and whisper to him, "Your sister is a beautiful girl. You'll have to get used to it."

Kerry looks back. "Hey, is Jason coming? He said he might."

Esben scowls again. "What do you mean, 'Is Jason coming?'"

She whips away, calling, "Nothing!" over her shoulder.

Esben stops short. "Oh, I'm gonna kill him if—"

I drag him forward. "You're going to do nothing of the sort. This is Kerry's night, and you're going to behave."

"Fine. But just for tonight. Tomorrow, I'm going to kill him." But he's smiling now.

"Understood."

Kerry walks us through the gallery, pointing out not only her work but that of her fellow students. She has a number of wonderful artworks, including a black-and-white series of sketches that I love, but I wander to an abstract painting she's done that I particularly fall for. The colors are vibrant and cheery and smash across the canvas in wild wonder. I step in closer, entranced by the beauty, and I hear Kerry's heels click as she walks to stand beside me.

"You like?"

"I really do, Kerry. You're amazing. I can barely draw a stick figure, and you've got so many pieces here that have blown me away."

"Well, thank you! That's so sweet." She leans in. "So, seriously, do you know if Jason is coming?"

I grin. "Are you two . . ."

She shrugs. "Maybe. I don't know. We had so much fun at that birthday party, and he's really a sweet guy. I think there might be something happening. I mean, you saw him in his princess dress? And the way he carried that little Cassie around on his shoulders half the time?"

"He was awesome with her, yeah."

"I invited him. I thought maybe . . . I don't know." She crosses her arms and bites her lips. "He's not going to show up."

"He is going to show up." I spin her around. "He already has."

Jason is standing with Esben near an elaborate metal sculpture. It's obvious that Esben is working very hard to keep him talking and not let him get away. Poor Jason is scanning the room, then looking back at his friend briefly, but his attention is not on Esben right now.

"You better go break that up," I suggest. "Your brother is going to talk until he runs out of breath and passes out unless you intervene."

"Well, that might not be a bad thing. All right. I can do this." She throws back her shoulders in confidence. But then she doesn't move.

"Kerry! Go get him! If I had that hot body and a red dress painted on, I'd be strutting all over the place. Go. Get. Him."

She shakes her hands to relax. "Okay. I'm doing this. Why is there no alcohol at this gig? Ugh."

Jason's face immediately lights up when he sees her. When she reaches the pair, I'm amused to see that Esben gives absolutely no indication that he's going to leave them alone together, so I go over and insist that I'm starving and that we should hit the appetizer table in the other room. Begrudgingly, he agrees.

"Are you really hungry?" he asks as he hands me a plate.

"Starving. And I love these little . . ." I reach for a pair of mini tongs. "Well, whatever these are. Puffs of some sort. I might eat them all."

I stack my plate with them until they threaten to topple over, and Esben starts laughing.

"Okay, fine. I get it. We'll stay here and eat puffs and leave my sister alone."

"Oh! Wait." I set the plate on the end of the table and retrieve my phone, tasting one of these appetizers as I open my camera. "I should be taking pictures of this, right? Isn't that a thing? Posting food pics?"

Esben is trying to control his laughter. "Well, sure. If you want. I mean, we are in a beautiful gallery full of a million potential shots, but if you want to post greasy puffs, that's cool."

"Oh. You do have a point." I drop my hand. "Or I could take a picture of you. You're much better looking than a puff."

"I'm crazy flattered."

"You should be. The puffs are filled with Brie, and they're delicious." I put my arm around his neck and stand close. "You, however, still taste better." I kiss him quickly, then step back and make him pose for at least twenty pictures.

Then we spend a silly amount of time taking selfies, and he shows me how to post pictures and tag him on my new accounts. I also text some pictures to Steffi and proudly tell her that I am no longer a social-media virgin.

She texts back almost immediately. That's not the type of virginity I was hoping you'd lose next, but still cool.

We wander around the gallery a bit more, and I pull Kerry aside so that I can get an update on Jason.

"He asked to take me out to dinner this week. For Italian! That's a good sign. Romantic, right?"

"Definitely romantic."

"Hey, where'd Esben go?" she asks.

"I'm not sure."

We walk through the room and then check the other one. Then Kerry stops and stares into a small room off to one side we hadn't gone into. Her face falls. "Damn."

"What is it?" I ask. I step closer and see Esben looking at another painting.

It's a very large canvas that takes up at least a quarter of the wall, but I can't see it well from this angle. Kerry walks very slowly to her brother, and I start to follow and then decide to hang back at the entryway. Something is happening here, but I don't know what.

He turns to her, and there is nothing but distress coming from him. He looks so terribly sad. "Kerry . . ."

She stops next to him and faces the painting. "This isn't part of the show. This room is supposed to be closed off. I didn't mean for you to see this."

He puts one hand in his pocket and runs the other through his hair, undeniably agitated, shaking his head, seemingly at a loss. He turns to his sister. "Kerry," he says again. "I'm so sorry."

"Don't say that. Please, don't."

With what I can only see as deep tenderness, Esben embraces his sister, holding her close and rubbing her back. "I am. I'm so sorry."

I back away, feeling as though I'm witnessing something private. To distract myself, I head back to the main gallery, where I take pictures and post a few online; I even manage to successfully tag Kerry in the ones of her art. This does keep me busy, but it certainly does not make me forget that I have never seen Esben look so unhappy. This is beyond the upset of anything online that drives him to act. This is personal. For twenty minutes, I busy myself.

Then I feel Kerry's hand on my shoulder. She is calm but serious. "Hey."

"Are you all right?" I am very concerned about both her and Esben now.

"I am. But there's a painting I didn't realize would be hanging in that room. I should have checked. It's something that I did for myself, and I never meant for him to see it." She touches her hair and tries to smile. "I'd like Esben to talk to you. It's my story to tell in many ways, but I'd like him to tell you, because it's also very much his story."

"Okay, but . . . if this is private, if it's just between you two—"

"I want you to know. You'll understand Esben more, and . . . you're my friend, too, Allison, and I want you to hear this. But I'd like Esben to tell you. That will help him. You may need to push, but it's important to me. Can you do that?"

I nod, confused, and hug her. She squeezes me back harder than I expected, and even though she remains calm, she does take a number of long, intense breaths.

"I am okay, Allison. I really am," she says in my ear. "Please know that, and please get him to see that. So, make him talk to you. Promise me that you will."

My stomach drops, and I know something is very wrong. I pull back to look at her directly. "I promise."

"Now, I am going to enjoy the rest of my night." She puts on a real smile. "Is hunky Jason still here?"

I point to the front of the room, where Jason is awkwardly buttoning and unbuttoning his blazer. "I don't think he's leaving any time soon."

"God, he's so hot," she says.

"And tall," I point out.

"Way tall. I find that so sexy." She giggles and heads toward him. A few feet away, she looks back, more solemn again. "Hey, Allison? Thank you."

My heart hurts when I go to Esben. He's still in front of the painting, and I stand next to him.

I catch my breath when I take in what's in front of me. It's another abstract, but unlike the other Kerry produced, this one screams its colors, its anger. Harsh brushstrokes rip across the canvas, jagged edges create a border that unsettles me, and everything about her work is fueled by rage. Slowly, I let my eyes travel to the card underneath.

Title: *Shatter Me*
Artist: Kerry Baylor

Esben has not moved. His voice trembles when he finally speaks, and I can barely hear him. "Can we go? I want to go."

"Of course." But he stays where he is.

I take his hand. "Esben, look at me."

Slowly, slowly, he does. His eyes are sad. So tremendously sad.

"I've got you," I tell him. "I've got you. Let's go."

CHAPTER 19

―――――

RELIVING

I lead him out the back door, and he walks with me numbly. The wind is bitter tonight, and I pull his coat closed, because he doesn't seem to notice the cold. When we get back to my room, I sit him on the couch.

"Do you want a drink?" I ask.

He's slumped over, looking at the floor. "No."

"Okay."

Esben shakes off his coat and tosses it on the floor. "Actually, yes."

After some rummaging, I pour him a shot of what's left from Steffi's visit, and he waves away my offer of lime and salt and shoots the tequila straight. I sit next to him and wait. He takes two more shots and then leans forward and rubs his face.

"I spoke with Kerry," I offer gently.

He nods from behind his hands.

"She'd like you to tell me about the painting."

"No. I can't." His voice is level and sure. He's not messing around here. "I don't want you to hear this, Allison."

"You've heard all of my stories. All of my pain. Let me hold some of yours." I am overtaken by how I am only now considering that Esben's past may include anything but love and ease. It's only tonight that I realize that no one gets through life unscathed. Not even Esben. I was blinded by what I saw as his untainted life, his unfailing positivity. But even the best and the strongest are penetrable.

"I don't want you to hear this because I screwed up, okay? I screwed up so bad. So *unforgivably*." The break in his voice is gutting.

"I can't imagine that's true."

"It is." He clearly sees this as an indisputable truth—and he leaves little room for argument.

"I understand that this is impossibly difficult, but it would mean a lot to Kerry." Sobriety would probably be a smart idea, but I take the tequila and swig a shot straight from the bottle. "She was very clear about that."

He says nothing for the next few minutes, then takes another shot from the bottle before sitting back.

"When I was a junior in high school and Kerry was a sophomore, I dragged her to a party at some kid's house. His parents were away, so everyone was hyped up about it, and it was this big, drunken scenario. Kerry didn't really want to go, but I'd told my parents that we were going to a movie, and I convinced her to come. The girl I was dating, Jenny, was going to be there, and I wanted to see her someplace without parents around. So, we go to this party, and Kerry was clinging to me, because she didn't really know anyone there. And I didn't care that she was my sister who I'd thrown into a new and shitty situation." He sighs. "All I could think about was hooking up with Jenny. So, I called over a couple of seniors that I barely knew. I thought Kerry would be into talking to older guys, and they were good-looking and popular and all that. And she did seem to like them. They all got to talking and laughing, and she even . . . she even told me how cute one of them was. I saw her flirt. She seemed happy and into it. So I pawned her off on them. Because," he states assuredly, "I was selfish and dumb and thoughtless. Reckless. Later that night, Jenny and I found an empty room so we could fool around. I left Kerry alone with people I hardly knew. With booze everywhere and drunken idiots, in some stranger's house. Really goddamn smart, right? I did what no brother should ever do."

"Esben . . ." I want to take him in my arms, but I stay where I am. I think it's taking all he has to be able to speak these words, and I want to respect his space.

"Later, when I was ready to go home, I went looking for her. I searched the entire house, and I couldn't find her. So, I asked around and searched again. The only reason I finally found her is because I heard her crying. She'd shut herself in a closet in one of the bedrooms. When I got to her, she was on the floor." When he finally looks at me, his eyes are red, and his words are broken and full of pain when he forces them out.

"It took me all of two seconds to see how terrified she was. My sister could hardly breathe because of her fear and her panic. I had to help her stand. How awful is that? But I did. She couldn't move. Then? The minute I got her into the light, I could see . . . I could see blood. She had on pale pants, and there was no hiding it." He inhales sharply and reaches for my hand. "Christ, Allison, in the half hour that I'd left her alone, she'd been assaulted by *both* of them. They each . . . took a . . . turn." Esben's grip on my hand tightens. "Is that the right word? I don't know. *Turn.* It's so disgusting. Shows how little they thought about her. Like she didn't even matter. Like she meant nothing. Like she wasn't a human being. Like she wasn't my sister, the most vibrant, perfect, trusting girl in the world. One held her down and covered her mouth, while the other—" He can't say the words, and I don't blame him.

"Dear God." *Kerry,* I think. *Not Kerry. Not anybody.*

"Even then, even as young as I was, and as little as I could really comprehend what'd gone on, I knew how wrong it was. I'm not sure I knew enough to think 'rape,' though. How goddam stupid is that? I was just so terrified, and . . . I didn't want what happened to be real, so I think I blocked it out to a degree. All I wanted was to make it not true."

"Of course you did."

"As much as I wanted to beat the living hell out of these guys, I had to get her out of there immediately. I carried her to the car in my arms. I'm sure people thought I was just taking my dumb, drunk sister home . . . I wanted to take her to the hospital, to the police. Somewhere. But she wouldn't let me. The idea started uncontrollable crying, and she made me promise not to. She made me promise not to tell anyone. Not our parents, not the cops, nobody. My agreeing was the only thing that stopped her from losing it. So, I parked the car a mile from home, and I held her until just before our curfew, when we knew our parents would be in bed and we could get in unseen. She took a shower, and I threw her clothes in a trash bag."

He rubs his eyes. "I sat next to her bed all night, but I don't think she slept. The next week, I sent one of them to the emergency room. Broken cheekbone. I got suspended for five days, and I'm probably lucky that he didn't file charges. First and only time I've been in a fight. The other guy kept far away from Kerry and me after that. She and I didn't talk about what happened. Not for over a year. We were young, and I was too stupid to know that I should have taken her to the hospital right away. I was scared. I didn't know what to do. Oh God, Allison, I didn't know what to do, and so I did everything wrong."

There is such desperation and apology in his face, and I want nothing more than to take those away. To give him peace. But I know that I cannot do that. I cannot fix this. I can only be here.

"You were, what, sixteen? Basically a kid. Of course you didn't know what to do. You must have been overwhelmed and frightened to your core. I don't think anyone is prepared for what to do in that kind of crisis. Both of you were traumatized."

"I should have done better," he says forcefully before taking a long drink. "I love her. That was my baby sister. While I was fooling around with a girl for the first time, she was in the room next to me, being sexually assaulted."

The bluntness of his words—their truth—is not easy to hear. "Esben, you couldn't have known. If you'd thought anything was amiss, you wouldn't have left her. She was in a full house, with people all over the place. You were a kid," I say again. "I know how much she means to you. I know you would do anything for her. This was not your fault."

"I took her to that party! I took her to that party! If I hadn't . . ." His entire body is shaking hard. "That's the truth. It's undeniable. If I hadn't made her go to that party . . . but I didn't know. Allison, I didn't know that would happen! I would never have—"

"You didn't let these two guys rape her. They did what they did because they felt entitled. Because they wanted control. Because they were aggressive and awful. Because they wanted to feel some screwed-up sense of manhood. Because . . . I don't know. Because they had a million kinds of wrong running through them. You did not make them rapists. Kerry did not make them rapists. They were already sick, and Kerry got caught in their path."

He pulls my hand, and I move closer to him. Esben holds eye contact as though I am keeping him from falling apart, and I am fully aware of how reliant he is on me in this moment. It's another first for me. I've never been needed like this, but I can be strong for him.

"This was not your fault," I say again, more firmly. "This is the sole fault of two messed-up boys. That's it. Kerry also wanted you to understand something. She said that she is okay. She stressed that. I have the feeling that you don't believe her, but she needs you to believe that she is as healed as possible after this. She has to know that and that you trust in her."

"Okay." His whisper reminds me of a small child. So innocent, so fragile, so dependent on what I'm telling him. "When she got to Andrews, she found a really good counselor here. Scott. He's great. I've gone with her a bunch. He's helped."

"Good."

"She's done a lot of work."

"Also good. And she has a brother who adores her." I rub his arm. He nods. "Yes."

It hits me that Esben is also a survivor of this rape. We generally think about the effects on those who survive trauma—which, of course, we should—but we don't always think about the effects on the indirect victims. It's clear to me now that we should.

My phone has been blowing up with texts, which I've ignored, but Esben nudges me and even cracks a smile. "Better check those."

They're all from Kerry.

Are you with him? Is he okay? I assume he's told you everything by now.

I want him to know that I'm happy. I really am.

I could not ask for a better brother. Never. He is my world. Tell him that, okay?

Allison, where are you? Please answer me. I'm freaking out. I don't want Esben reliving this. It will always be a part of me, but it will not define me. It does not cage me. It DOES not.

Show him these messages, okay?

The painting? Yes, it's violent. But it helps express what happened. It gives me power. A visual way for me to expel that night. It's a positive thing.

I can't stand for him to be holding on to this.

I give Esben my phone. "Read."

Hesitantly, he goes through her texts. Then he types for a while on his own phone before tossing it on the couch. "I didn't want you to see me like this. I'm sorry. I should go. I'm so tired."

"No," I say. "Don't go. Stay here."

His smile is so sweet and so full of emotional and physical exhaustion. "If you'd said that any other night . . ."

I set a hand on his chest. "Not like that. Just stay here. Stay with me. I don't want you to be alone, and I don't want to be without you. So stay."

He looks at me for a long time, and his eyes grow wet again. "I'd really . . ." He struggles to speak. "I'd really like that."

"Then let's go to bed, okay?"

Without waiting for an answer, I pick up my phone and then help him walk to my room. Despondently, he sits on my bed, and I take off his shoes and socks. I push back the covers, then undo the top of his jeans. "Lie back." He watches me as I pull the zipper and ease down his pants. This is arguably not how I thought I might first take off his pants, but he can't sleep like this. I turn off the overhead light. Though it's dark, it's not pitch-black, and I know that he can see me as I get out of my dress and into a T-shirt.

"You really are so gorgeous," he says.

"I think you're a little drunk," I say with a laugh. I slip under the comforter and rest my head on the pillow.

Esben rolls into me, and I move my arm under him so that he's on his side, resting his head on my chest. "Yes. But tequila doesn't make me lie. It just lets the truth come out. And you are beautiful. Everything about you." He wraps an arm over my stomach and secures our closeness. "I hate that you know this. I hate that I'm a mess. I hate that Kerry was hurt so badly. I hate all of it."

"I know you do. But secrets will pull you under and drown you. You taught me that. We are beyond secrets. Way past them. You do not have to be infallible, Esben. You're allowed to be human and to have hurt and worry and . . . pain. And sharing those with me? It makes you stronger, in my eyes. That's how you've made me feel." I try to soothe him with my words, with my touch. When I run my hand over his shoulder and up and down his arm, I can feel him relax against me, so I don't stop.

He is indeed drunk, because as he begins to drift into the dark of the night, he says, "I love you, Allison. It happened when I wasn't looking for it, when I didn't know I needed it. But I fell in love with you so quickly and so smoothly. So without question." He shifts closer against me. "Don't say anything. I just wanted you to know."

Esben drifts off immediately, and I lie in the quiet, with his body glued to mine. I'm so floored by what he's said, and I wouldn't know how to respond if he were awake, but I keep him against me and soak in the feeling of this indescribable boy who has his body wrapped over mine.

When he is solidly asleep, I stretch for my phone and call Kerry.

"Hey," she says.

"Hey," I whisper back.

"He's okay?"

"Esben is asleep, and, yes, he's going to be fine. It was just a rough night because he loves you so much. But he understands what you need him to."

"Thank you. That makes me feel so much better."

"Thank you for trusting me." I pause. "Telling you that I'm sorry you went through this isn't enough. I don't know what to say except to let you know how much I care about you. I don't have many friends, but you're one of them, Kerry, and I'm proud of you for surviving with so much strength. And if you ever want to talk . . ."

"I'd like that, Allison. I don't keep this a secret, but I don't talk to everyone about it, obviously. But you're so great, and it means a lot that you didn't run from this screaming. I threw a lot at you tonight, unexpectedly, and you handled it with grace." She exhales loudly. "And now you understand why he does what he does, don't you?"

"Yes," I reply. It hurts to say what I do. "He wants to undo what he thinks he did. He wants to prove that the world is more than just brutal. To prove that there is good."

"Exactly," she says. "He's a warrior."

"He is," I agree. "And he's going to win this battle." I run my hand through his hair while he sleeps against me.

"Absolutely. But, still, you'll watch over him for me, yes? He only lets me get so close. It's why I wanted him to tell you about this. At this point, he has more healing to do than me. So, watch over him."

"Always," I assure her. "Always."

CHAPTER 20

BREAKFAST BLEND

When I wake the next morning, Esben is still curled over me, asleep. Despite the circumstances of how he ended up here, I can't help but admit how wonderful it feels to have him here. Lightly, so as not to wake him, I rub his back. I cannot believe that I have this handsome, dynamic, interesting, funny, caring boy in my arms right now. Three months ago, I would have totally rejected the idea that I could be as happy as I am today.

It's way before my alarm will go off, but I can't get back to sleep. I'm not crazy about extricating myself from Esben, but nature calls. And, more strongly, coffee calls. Simon sent me back to school after Thanksgiving with a pound of a breakfast blend, and I'm craving a cup. And after the tequila shots my boyfriend downed, he'll probably be even more in need of coffee than me. While I'm sorry that he's probably going to wake with a hangover, I do rather love the impending opportunity to take care of him and make him feel better. There's a novelty in this that swells me. Gently, I touch my lips to the top of his head and then ease my body out from his hold. I slip on my robe before tiptoeing out of the room and quietly shutting the door.

While a pot of strong coffee is brewing and sending off steam and an awakening aroma, I check my phone.

There's a text from Steffi that came in the middle of the night. Yo, social-media user! Nice pics. You look beautiful, and Esben gets sexier every minute. I mean that in a nonlascivious manner. Mostly.

I smile and start to text back, but the phone rings in my hands.

"Steff, what are you doing up? It's three thirty in the morning there!"

"I don't know. Can't sleep. Saw your text bubbles and decided to call."

"How is erotic Esben?"

"Oh my God, Steff!" I cover my mouth to muffle my giggling. "You are not to start calling him that!"

She gasps. "You're whispering! You're whispering! He's there, isn't he? Naked and strapping and passed out in your bed from the hours of hot sex!" She is way too joyful about this idea.

"He is not naked!" I go into the Jenga/inflatable-unicorn room but still keep my voice down. "But he is here."

"Because he stayed the night?"

"Yes, but not like that. We just slept in the same bed, that's all."

"Ugh, so there were clothes on and stuff?"

"Well, yes."

"That's disappointing," she says with exaggerated distress. "But at least it's progress."

"Goodness, I'm so sorry you're so sad about this."

"Did you just say 'goodness'?"

"Apparently. I don't know why."

"How quaint of you. Perhaps I shall start exclaiming 'Goodness!' from now on. It has an old-fashioned ring to it. There's no reason to get a bee in your bonnet, missy! Egad and fiddlesticks and dang it all! God save the queen!"

"God save the queen? Really? How does that fit in here?"

"I think it's a nice substitution for swearing. I'm going to start using it, like, all the time, so get ready."

"Stop it, or you're going to make me laugh too loudly and wake erotic Esben!"

"Well, it is morning, so then we'd have to call him erec—"

"Enough!" It is very hard to suppress my laughter, so she has got to knock this off. "Listen, we have to make plans for Christmas. Simon asked what dates you want to fly in and out." Ever since I've lived with Simon, he's made sure that I get to see Steffi over the holidays. Even when she was with Joan and Cal, the couple who basically kicked her out when she turned eighteen, Simon drove me the hour it took to reach her on Christmas Day. For the past few years, he's flown her into Boston for two weeks, and she's spent Christmas and New Year's with us.

"Oh. Listen . . . about that," she says more seriously now.

"What? What do you mean 'about that'? I don't like the sound of this."

"Okay, please don't get mad, but . . . I'm going on a cruise!" she says excitedly.

"You're going on a what? What are you talking about?"

"A bunch of the people I hang out with here are doing a three-week cruise, and one of the girls had to drop out. She's selling me her spot for dirt cheap, and I can't pass it up. I'm heading to Hawaii! And . . . and . . . other places! I don't even know the itinerary, but it's a cruise! To top things off, I have a major crush on one of the guys who's going. His body is enough to make me burst into flames."

This is not making any sense whatsoever. "So you're not coming to Boston at all? Oh."

"Don't be sad. You hate Christmas anyway, and if you saw this guy, you'd probably dump Esben and go on a cruise with him, too."

"If you say so."

She pauses. "There will be other trips."

"Spring break, maybe?"

"Sure! And definitely this summer, okay?"

165

"Okay. This trip does sound like it could be really fun, but you have to promise to send me a million pictures. Especially of this hot guy."

"Deal!"

I'm happy for her, really, but I can't help being a little bummed out that we won't be together over the holidays. "I'll have Simon mail your presents to you."

"No, no. He really doesn't need to get me anything."

"Of course he does. He loves spoiling you."

"Seriously, it's not necessary."

I laugh. "If you think for two seconds that Simon will not be shipping out large boxes to you, then you are forgetting who he is."

"Ha! Well, that's true."

"I'll miss you," I say. "But raid the buffets for me."

"And I will miss you terribly while I'm pigging out at the dessert bar. Now, tell me how things are going with Esben."

I lie back on the bed and smile. "Good, Steffi. Really, really good."

"Yeah? Tell me everything. We haven't talked in a week, so I want all the dirt."

I gush for twenty minutes until her yawning tells me that she's finally exhausted enough to sleep. "I think you should get to bed, sweets. You sound totally wiped."

"Okay. But, Allison? I'm so happy for you. You deserve a great guy like Esben, and, goodness, he's just as lucky to have you."

"Thanks, Steffi." I can't help sighing contentedly. "I miss you so much, even with your new, idiotic expression, and I miss seeing you every day, so we at least need to talk more, okay? It used to be every day, and now it's once a week or so."

"Okay, we'll work on it. We've both got a ton going on, but that doesn't mean we're not as close as ever."

"I know. It's just . . . I've never had . . . I've never had an Esben before. I just want to make sure that you know I'm still here for you."

"Always. You are my bestie," she says. "I don't forget that for a second."

After we hang up, I finally pour my cup of coffee and peek in on Esben. God, asleep he looks even more like a damn angel.

I check the time and then call Simon.

"Good morning, sweetheart," he answers, all chipper. "You enjoying the coffee I got you?"

I slurp loudly into the phone. "Right now, in fact."

"So I hear. Excellent! What's going on?"

I explain about Steffi's cruise.

"I see. Well, Steffi has always been one to seize the day, so let's be happy for her that she's taking this wild adventure. I know it will be strange not to have her with us, but we'll make do."

I clear my throat. "I was thinking that this year, we could . . . you know . . . do more Christmas stuff."

He pauses, and I know he's trying not to sound too excited. "Really?"

"Yeah. Like, we should get a tree and hang stockings."

"Lights? Wreaths? Extra presents? Ninety kinds of garish cookies?"

The idea makes me anxious, but it's time for me to get over my holiday phobia. I am not a kid without security anymore. *I am not.* "I think it would be nice."

"I think it would be nice, too."

I'm quite sure that Simon is jumping up and down right now, but I appreciate his effort to remain calm in the face of this exciting news.

"And how is young Esben?" he asks.

"He's good." Then I stop for a second. "But he just had a tough night. He's a little sad." I run a finger over the rim of my coffee cup.

"I'm sure he's glad to have you for support."

"I hope so. I think so . . . I'm not used to seeing him unhappy." I fidget with the sash on my robe. "I care about him so much."

"I know you do, and, from what you tell me, it's obvious he cares about you just as much. Allison, it's all right to be sad sometimes. Even though he's generally upbeat, he can still have low points, too. It means he's human."

"You're right." I drop the sash. "Thank you."

"Tell him that I said nice job on that last video. The one with the sketch pads."

Esben spent the day after Thanksgiving in downtown Boston, fighting Black Friday crowds, handing people sketch pads and asking them to write or draw whatever makes them happy. The video compilation of people holding up words and pictures is yet another beautiful piece of his, complete with music, lots of smiles, and a few tears. Surprisingly, few people responded by drawing anything material, despite being in the midst of all that shopping chaos and greed.

"It was really nice, wasn't it?"

"I'm on Twitter, you know," Simon admits a bit shyly. "I didn't know if I should follow you or not."

I laugh. "But I gather you follow Esben? Of course you should follow me. You're my father."

There is a long silence, and I think both of us are slightly taken aback. While I may refer to Simon as my adoptive father when I speak about him to other people, I have never directly addressed him as *my father.*

"Yes, I am," he finally says softly. "I am. So, I'll follow you as soon as we hang up. And I'll be sure to tweet reminders about calling home, eating your veggies, and getting plenty of rest."

"Esben taught me how to block people," I inform him with a giggle, "so you'd better be careful."

"I will behave! I will behave!"

"Okay. I'll see you online. Bye, Simon."

"Bye, kiddo."

I check Twitter, and, within only a few minutes, Simon has followed me. So, I follow him back and then go check out what exactly Simon tweets about. Gardening, cooking, lots of tweets to Bravo about various reality shows . . . then I see something from last week that stops my scrolling.

Simon has retweeted Esben's video, and he also replied with his own short video. I click on it. Simon, dressed in a formal shirt and tie, is sitting at the kitchen table. "Hi, everyone," he says nervously. "My name is Simon, and, uh . . . what makes me happy is . . ." He reaches for a piece of paper and holds it up. *Allison,* it says. "My daughter, Allison. I waited a long time for her to come into my life, and it was worth it. She," he says, swallowing hard, "she lights up my life." He sets down the paper and stops the video.

I poise my finger over the heart symbol below his video. It takes me a few seconds, but I tap it. Then I retweet his video and caption it with, How awesome is my father?

I text Simon. Would it be okay if we had Esben over for dinner during break?

He's never texted back so quickly. Any night or every night.

Every night might be excessive, I reply.

I'm a very good cook, Simon points out. He may never want to leave.

I laugh. Fair enough.

Esben's gravelly morning voice booms from my bedroom. "Where is my human pillow? Where are my clothes? Why am I alone in this bed? Do I smell coffee? Do I have a headache because I drank too much tequila or because someone hit me over the head while I was sleeping when I got frisky?"

His morning voice is even cuter than his fully awake voice. I go into my bedroom and stand on the mattress. "So, I take it you don't want me to jump up and down?"

He groans. "Oh God, please don't." Then he moves his head a bit. "Although I could see up your robe if you did . . ."

I drop to sit. "We'd skip a step on the spectrum if that happened."

He tugs me down to his chest and hugs me. "And I am quite enjoying the spectrum."

I stay against him, enjoying the heat that emanates from his body and the way he holds me so firmly and yet so tenderly at the same time.

"Want coffee?" I murmur.

"In a minute. Let's just stay like this for a little while." He lifts the covers. "Don't worry. I ate, like, forty mints I pulled out of my pants pocket because I don't have a toothbrush here."

"Thank you for your thoughtfulness." Because it seems idiotic to keep my robe on after I didn't have it on all of last night, I take it off and tuck myself under the sheets, and he rolls over so that he's spooning me.

"How are you feeling?" I ask.

"A little rough, but I'll be okay." Esben runs a hand through my hair, and we lie together quietly for a while. "Especially with you here like this."

As difficult as it was to see Esben so upset, I do feel that our relationship has better balance now that I have been able to do something for him. From the day we met, I have been the fragile one, the one leaning on him constantly. Now, I understand that I am capable of letting him lean on me. I'm stronger than I knew.

Later, I bring him a cup of coffee, then another, and I wait until he's awake enough to talk.

"Esben?"

"Yeah, baby?"

"What happened to Kerry . . . it's why you haven't had sex yet. And why you're so careful with me."

"Partly, yes. Look . . . I know that what happened to her was rape, not sex. Two very, very different things. Drastically different." He drinks a little more coffee and gathers his thoughts. "I may be dying for us to have sex, sure, but I am going to be very attentive about what we're doing together. It's easy for girls, especially, to feel pressure to move faster than they want, because they think the guy will leave otherwise. I'm not that guy." He sets down his cup and puts an arm around me.

"I know that. I really do. You've been so good and made me so comfortable. What Kerry went through? It's horrible, Esben. It's horrible. But, as you said, what happened to her and what's happening with us are two entirely different things. I'm asking you, very directly, for something. I'm asking you for intimacy." I turn in to face him, and I place my hand over his and move it under my top, guiding him across my stomach so that his touch radiates over my skin.

Esben begins kissing my shoulder, and I know he's smiling when he says, "You *are* comfortable, aren't you?"

I inch his hand a little higher. "I am." So much so that I push him back onto the bed and tease my hand up his chest. "I want you out of this shirt."

"You do?" he asks hesitantly.

I begin to lift up the fabric. My breathing has picked up, and I want to stop talking now. "Waist up, okay?" I manage to say. "No fabric between us. Just you and me."

Immediately, Esben rolls me onto my back, his hand now caressing my skin. "Yes," he says with heat and promise. "Yes."

I tug up on his shirt. Hard. "Take this off. I want to see you."

So, he does. And, later, mine comes off.

And then, even later, when Esben's bare chest is pressed against mine and when his mouth is still exploring my skin, he whispers to me. "Allison," he says, "you're wonderful. You know that? Everything about you is wonderful."

I ease his hand to my underwear, and, before he can say anything, I nod. "Yes, I'm sure."

Despite our move up the spectrum, we both manage to make it to class. Somehow.

CHAPTER 21

CHRISTMAS WONDER

After being in a car for hours yesterday and then running errands all day today with Simon, it's very nice to be curled up on the couch in Simon's house in Brookline. *My* house. I have to start saying that. This is *my* house, too. The ride I got from Esben and Kerry took absolutely forever, because it was snowing and the roads were a mess. Simon texted me every fifteen minutes to make sure that I wasn't dead, but I understand that he was nervous, especially once he found out that Esben's car is not exactly new, nor equipped with all the safety features Simon would like. Even though the drive was a long one, I had fun with Esben and Kerry, and I'd been so looking forward to seeing Simon.

Our shopping trips today included filling two carts at the supermarket, because Simon has gourmet meals and plenty of baking planned. He's promised to teach me some basics, and I'm just hoping to learn to make something edible. Then he took me to the mall and insisted on buying me new clothes, including a few special outfits for Christmas and New Year's. Not only did I not protest, I enjoyed it. I enjoyed being treated to such nice things, and I enjoyed being with him. And I particularly enjoyed sneaking off and buying him a reindeer statue that he'd been admiring but didn't buy for himself. His look of delight when I gave it to him made me smile, because I knew he would add this to his collection of holiday decorations that had taken over the house.

The constant Christmas music that played over the mall speakers didn't bother me, the bustling crowds didn't make me insane, and the peppermint hot chocolate we tried that tasted like liquid holiday didn't conjure up childhood trauma. All new and welcome experiences. Simon did try very hard to get me to take my picture with Santa, but I drew the line there.

Right now, I am wrapped in a mahogany-colored chenille throw in the plush living room, while Simon swears in a most colorful manner as he tries to unknot strings of lights for the tree. Even though I know she's unreachable, I text a selfie of me pouting to Steffi, because she's not here, and then a picture of a frustrated-but-amusing Simon. Damn cruises and their unreliable Wi-Fi! This spell where we can't talk or text is killing me, but I am happy for her high-seas dating adventure.

"Would you please let me help?" I have repeatedly offered to assist in this monstrous light-detangling task, but Simon keeps insisting I sit here with my cocoa and relax. "And I feel bad that you waited for me to decorate the tree. It's already December nineteenth!"

"Of course I waited for you, silly. And I should have just bought some new lights while we were out today. But, at this point, I am in a battle that I have to win on my own." Furiously, he shakes the bundle in his hands, and, suddenly, the tight ball comes apart. "Huh. That was weird." He looks at me. "It's a Christmas miracle!"

Playfully, I stick out my tongue at him. "It is not."

"You being in the holiday spirit brought Christmas luck, then. How's that?" The Santa hat he's got on, paired with his bright-green shirt and red tie, is ridiculous in the most wonderful way. "Speaking of which, it's nice to see you so happy about the holidays this year. Esben have anything to do with that?" he asks with a smile.

"Maybe," I admit. "It's not just about having a boyfriend, though. He's made me see how much good is actually out there. How to move on from my past, I guess." I pull the blanket around me more tightly. "I was kind of stuck there."

"I know you were. It's understandable. You've had a rough go of it."

I watch him undo one of the last knots. "I'm sorry, Simon."

He stops and looks up. "For what?"

"For not . . . for not being better."

"Better? Better at what?"

"For not being a better daughter."

He drops the lights and sits next to me on the couch. "Allison, don't ever say that again."

"Do you ever regret adopting me? Your boyfriend left you because of me. He wanted to adopt a cute little baby, not some pissy teenager." Then I ask him something that I have never asked him before. "How did you even know about me? One day, I just heard that there was a potential adoptive father who wanted to meet me. Then you and I talked for an hour—I was probably boring and miserable to be around—but then I was told that you wanted me. I've never understood why."

"Oh, Allison. Honey . . ." He waves a hand. "First off, Jacob was an ass. I'd probably known that for a while, but it was one of those relationships . . . you know, the ones you get trapped in and stupidly don't bother to get out of? So, I'm glad he left. Best thing to happen to me, next to you." He smiles warmly. "Listen, yes, the plan was that we were going to adopt a baby, but there was this wall of pictures at the adoption office—tons of them—all kids who were in need of families."

"Like old-timey wanted posters in a sheriff's office." I pull the blanket in tighter. "Only we were unwanted posters."

Simon nods. "Yes, actually. That's how it felt. So totally unfair and upsetting. Anyway, I was looking at the pictures, and I had a few thoughts. The first was that I was horribly naive about how many older kids were in foster care. And the second, stronger thought, was that one of these kids belonged with me. You. It was only then that I realized I wasn't someone who needed an infant. It wasn't important to me to make bottles or see first steps or hear first words. Kindergarten, grade school . . ." He leans back and crosses his legs. "I didn't need to do any of that. I wanted to be a father, but being a father is about a lifetime of parenting, not just little-kid stuff."

I hang my head and play with the fringe on the blanket. "My picture was there?"

"It was," he says. "Every picture had some basics about the kids, including how long they'd been in foster care. When I got to yours, I read that you'd been in the system for over sixteen years. I also read that you loved to read, that you were a great student. I don't know, a few other things. It wasn't so much the facts about you as it was . . ." He thinks for a moment. "It was about how I felt when I saw your picture. One of those things you can't explain. I just felt a connection, and I knew right then that I wanted to be your father. I stood in that hall with your picture for so long that Jacob eventually came looking for me."

I look at him now. "And he hated the idea."

"He did. And so I hated him." Simon says this defiantly and then smiles.

I crack a smile. "No, you didn't."

"Okay, fine. I didn't hate him, but I did know right then that something was horribly off between the two of us. He didn't feel at all what I felt. So, I would have to make a choice. And I chose *you*. And I chose myself. It was the opportunity I'd needed to see that Jacob and I were truly a terrible fit. Wanting to adopt you? It was the easiest understanding I'd ever come to. Of course, I was terrified that you wouldn't like me or that you wouldn't want to live with a gay man. The day I met you, I must have changed my outfit ten times. I had a stack of things I'd bought for you, but then they all seemed stupid, so I left them at home. If you thought they were awful, you might decide I would make the worst dad ever." He looks embarrassed. "I was very nervous, because I knew so definitively that I was your father. Sometimes you just know things, right? Without reason or fact. You just know them."

Four months ago, I might have disagreed, but not today. "Yes. I'm sorry that I didn't know then. I'm sorry I didn't see right away that you were my dad."

"Sweetheart, it's okay. That would be expecting a lot."

My eyes begin to burn a little. "But I know now. I really do." He puts an arm around me, and, instinctively, I turn into him and hug him tightly. "I love you, Simon."

His hug back is so secure and so fatherly and safe. "And I love you, too, Allison. Very much."

"Just so you know," I say, "I really liked you when I met you. We talked about how perfect Jane Austen is and why we both despise zoos. And you told me that you hate all dried fruits except dried cranberries."

"That's still true. Why would you take a perfectly nice piece of fruit and ruin it like that? But dried cranberries in an arugula salad? With a hit of blue cheese? Can't beat that." He rests his chin on top of my head. "And we shared a love of eighties movies, sunsets that look like postcards, and the sound waves make when they crash onto shore. We clicked. That's all there is to it. You were my daughter, from that first moment."

Without thinking, I rest my head on his shoulder. "You got me things to entice me to live with you?"

He chuckles. "It's so embarrassing, but I did."

"Like what?"

"I actually still have the stuff, if you'd like to see."

"Really?" I sit up and face him. It's so Simon to keep this stuff. "I would."

It only takes him a few minutes to go to his study, and he certainly doesn't have to dig for the box.

He watches me nervously as I open it, and I laugh. "You don't have to worry. I'm not going to ditch you if there's something weird in here."

"Still, be kind. I was very anxious back then. And I guess now, too."

In the box is, of course, a collection of things I would have loved. A trio of jangly silver bracelets from Tiffany's, a gift set of Calvin Klein perfume, a cashmere hat and scarf, and a zippered makeup bag full of lip glosses. Then I pull out a Wonder Woman retrospective book and a set of Wonder Woman cuff bracelets.

"They're dumb, aren't they?" he says.

"No, Simon. They're not dumb at all. Not even close." I keep looking at the cuffs. "How did you know I would like Wonder Woman?"

"I figured you'd deflected a few bullets in your time and that you were probably tough as steel."

"I wasn't so tough," I say quietly. "I could've used these cuffs."

"Of course you were tough. You still are. You're just happier now."

He's right. "These are wonderful gifts." I am touched and at a loss for what else to say.

Simon rubs my back and pulls me in for a quick hug. "Ready to get these lights on the tree, kiddo?" He claps his hands. "Let's get her all gussied up, shall we?"

He stands on a stepladder and begins to hang the lights, while I hold the rest of the string and feed it to him as needed. "So, since you won't let me buy you a car"—he stops and waits for me to roll my eyes, which I do—"how about a Christmas list?"

This feels like a tremendously big deal, because I'm not one to ask him for anything. But for his sake, I think for a bit. "Those sheets you got me at the beginning of the year? I really like those, and I wouldn't mind more."

"'Wouldn't mind more.' Noted. What else?"

"Maybe a new phone case."

"Also noted. What else?"

We finish hanging the lights before I reply. "Maybe we could take a vacation this summer?"

"Sure. You, Steffi, and me? What did you have in mind?"

"Just you and me," I correct him.

He lands a row of lights across branches before he responds. "I'd like that. Where are we going? Martha's Vineyard? Cape Cod? Nantucket? The Hamptons?"

I can't help but laugh. "It doesn't have to be so high-end. A beach trip would be nice. But maybe a small house. Nothing too fancy, okay?"

"A luxury cottage, then," he says with a smile. "We'll boil up lobsters every night and track sand all over the rental house from our days by the ocean."

"There's something else," I say with a touch of anxiety. I adjust some lights and fidget too much with their placement. "I mentioned this before, but . . . could Esben come over for dinner?"

"That's not a Christmas present, but absolutely." His eagerness is palpable. "Any night is fine. Oh, I could do an appetizer tray with smoked salmon, deviled eggs . . . and then beef Wellington for an entrée and a trifle for dessert!"

"I . . . I was thinking something less formal."

"Well, sure. Box spaghetti and a jar of sauce it is," he says with mock pouting.

"Okay, okay. Upscale and show off your cooking it is. And wine. There better be wine."

"Why? You nervous for dear old dad to meet the boyfriend?"

"A little," I confess.

"Don't be. I adore him already. Anyone who makes you this happy is clearly someone I'm going to like."

"Okay."

"Then we'd better get this house in Christmas order to impress him!" Simon crosses the room to retrieve one of three ornament boxes. "Let's do this!"

CHAPTER 22

DANCING

Simon reties his apron yet again and surveys the kitchen. "Okay, I think we're in pretty good shape. Does Esben like cheese? I hope he likes cheese!"

I can't help laughing. "Why are you more nervous than I am? He's going to love you. And the cheese. *All* the cheeses." I glance at the tray. "All nine of them."

"Did I go overboard?"

"I would expect nothing less." I go to the sink to wash my hands after shaking my head over the plate of rather gloppy deviled eggs I just made. Obviously, I don't have Simon's cooking gene, but it seems his best effort to teach me today has failed wildly. "So, Simon," I start a little cautiously, "now that even I am dating, I was wondering about you."

"Wondering about me what?" Simon is leaning over the cheese platter for a bird's-eye view while he obsessively rearranges the positioning of the cheeses.

"Wondering about you dating. I mean, are you? You haven't mentioned anyone." I dry my hands and then pause. "Oh. But maybe you wouldn't have. Because I've been such a closed-off shrew."

"Allison!" He stops fussing with the cheeses and glares at me. "Don't talk about yourself like that. I do not have a boyfriend, nor have I been dating. I don't know how to meet people, really. What am I going to do? Go cruising a gay club at my age?"

"You're only forty-three! But I'm not sure a club is the best idea. What about online dating—"

I am interrupted by the doorbell.

"He's here! He's here!" Simon shouts. "Where are the grapes? Oh, never mind. I'll add those later." He tears off his apron and beams at me. "Are you ready? Do I look okay? Should I answer the door? Do you want to make an entrance?"

Simon has gone bananas. "You look very handsome. How about I answer the door, and you finish your wine."

"Yes. Good thinking. I will be right out." He takes a big drink. "You look very pretty in red, by the way."

I've got on one of the things Simon bought me yesterday, and I must confess that I'm enjoying wearing the fluffy red mohair pullover. Paired with the black leather pants he insisted I buy, it's an outfit Steffi would approve of. I make my way to the door, and I'm actually delighting in the lights and garlands and endless decorations that grace the house. When Simon goes all out, he really goes all out. And I pretty much love it.

I've barely opened the door when Esben starts talking. "I know it's ridiculous. I'm sorry. My mother made me wear a suit. I told her it was crazy, and no one goes to dinner at their girlfriend's house wearing a suit, but at a certain point it became easier just to put it on than to convince her it was not 1940."

The last thing he should be doing is apologizing, because he looks absolutely . . . well, dashing. He's wearing a black suit with a red button-down shirt and swirly multicolored tie, and I am so taken aback that I cannot speak. Or move. Or do anything.

"Oh God, it's that bad? I'm sorry. I should have thrown some clothes in the car and changed in a McDonald's or something. Allison?

Please say something before I strip down here on the front step out of sheer humiliation."

"Sorry, sorry." I smile. "Although, that does sound pretty tempting . . . you look gorgeous. Seriously. I think I love your mother." I swing the door open wide and shiver from the chill.

"And I think I love those pants that are painted on you." Esben's hands go to my waist, and his mouth goes to the spot just below my ear that he knows drives me crazy.

The gift bag in his hand crinkles against my lower back while he snuggles against me. I'm used to seeing him every single day, so even the very short time that we've been apart has left me wanting. But there's Simon and his beef Wellingtons to consider, so instead of plastering Esben up against the front door, I take his hand and lead him into the main room. My father is desperately trying to look casual while setting a smoked-salmon tray on the coffee table next to the insane cheese festival and my mangled eggs.

Simon stands up and smiles warmly. "Based on the way Allison is now glowing more than that hideous inflatable Santa across the street, you must be Esben."

"Simon!" But I laugh.

Esben steps forward and shakes his hand. "It's really great to meet you, sir. I've heard so many nice things about you." Esben indicates the gift bag he's holding. "So, my mother sent this with me. I think it's an ornament."

"What a very kind thought. And that bag over there," he says, gesturing to a velvet bag on the sideboard, "is for your parents. It's a bottle of red from a California vineyard I'm crazy about."

California. I think of Steffi immediately. This cruise she's on better be stupendous, because I would love to have her here with us right now.

Esben glances at the coffee table as he starts to sit. "Oh, a cheese platter! Look at that bad boy." Then, to Simon's delight, Esben leans over and examines it from above. "Nice placement. I'm hesitant to disrupt your artwork, but, if I'm not mistaken, that's a Saint André, right?"

Simon is beaming rather smugly at me. "It is! Please, help yourself." He hands Esben a plate, and I sit back and smile as the two begin an in-depth discussion about cheese. I knew I had nothing to worry about.

Simon's dinner proves to be another culinary success, but, even better, Esben, Simon, and I talk nonstop. The conversation flows easily, and there is more laughter than there's been at this table before.

We do run into a small hitch during dessert, however. With Simon's guidance, I'd been responsible for the trifle and its layers of whipped confections, sugared berries, chestnut mousse, and chocolate shavings, and it certainly looks gorgeous. As I sit back to watch the two men in my life take their first bites of my labor of love, it only takes one bite for me to realize something is very wrong. Both make valiant efforts to conceal that there's a problem, but it's of no use.

"What?" I demand. "What is wrong? I did everything you said, Simon!"

Simon wipes his mouth and holds the napkin against his lips for a moment while he composes himself. "There is a slight issue. With salt."

"Salt? There's no salt?"

I taste the trifle. It's horrible, and I immediately spit out my bite into my napkin. "Oh God!" I look at them apologetically, but they're both too busy giggling.

Esben takes a big drink of water. "It was . . . it was a really *beautiful* trifle, though."

"Yes," Simon agrees kindly. "Aesthetically, you were right on target. But since we are now without a dessert, why don't we venture into the North End. It'll be very festive there this time of year."

Esben perks up. "I bet I know what you're thinking! Mike's?"

"This kid is good," Simon says, looking at me. "Exactly! A little chocolate cheesecake!"

Simon drives us to the North End, Boston's Little Italy. This area of the city is tremendously charming, and the old-world feel of the neighborhood has me enchanted tonight. Wreaths hang from arches above the streets, white lights twirl up and down lampposts, and we pass a Santa Claus standing on a corner, collecting donations.

When we are all seated at a small table inside Mike's Pastry, I stare at my plate, taken aback by the size of my slice of the chocolate mousse cake that dares me to tackle it. "Both of you pose with your desserts made for giants. I need to post this important moment."

"I've created a social-networking monster," Esben explains to Simon. "Sorry."

"Quiet! Hold up your plates!" I take at least ten pictures of them and then go on Twitter, Instagram, and Facebook to post and check in at Mike's Pastry. I tag the picture *#singledadtakesusout*, *#boyfriendesben*, and *#dessertporn*. After my picture goes live on Facebook, some weird window pops up. "Wait, Esben, what is this? It wants me to use something called Nearby Friends?" I show him my phone.

"Here." He takes out his own phone, and, within a few seconds, he's showing me his screen. "See? If you enable this feature, then when you're out and about, you check in places and can see who on your friends list is close by. I don't use it much, because the majority of people on my personal page aren't really people I actually know." Esben taps his screen, and a list of six people show up. "See? A few people are around. This person is pretty close." He looks again. "Actually, more than close. He checked in to Mike's!"

"Who is it?" I ask.

He frowns. "Christian Arturo. He comments on my stuff sometimes." He clicks on Christian's profile and taps through a few pictures.

"He's kinda hot," I whisper.

Esben yanks away the phone. "Hey!"

"Well, he is! But don't worry. He looks a tad young."

"Yeah, it says he's in high school." Esben looks around the room and then smiles. "There he is."

But his smile falls away as he takes in the boy on the opposite end of the café. Christian is even more handsome than his photos indicate, with dark hair and dark skin that stand out against his white shirt. And on second glance, I see that it's a tuxedo shirt and that his jacket rests on the back of his chair. He's slumped in his chair, his cannoli untouched, and he radiates a sadness that makes me want to scoop him up in a hug.

"Go back to his page," I say quietly.

The three of us lean over Esben's phone and read through the posts near the top of Christian's page.

"He was . . . going to his winter formal," Esben reads. "Rented a tux . . . it was going to be a big night . . . and his date got food poisoning."

"Oh no. That's too bad." Simon glances furtively at Christian. "He looks so depressed."

Esben is still glued to his phone, but I can tell he is thinking, deciding what to do. Because this is Esben, and he can't do nothing. I suspect he's hesitating because we're with Simon, so I prompt him.

"Esben?" I touch his shoulder. "Go. Go get him."

Without even looking at me, Esben smiles. "You know me well, don't you?"

Simon appears confused for a moment, but when Esben gets up and crosses the room, understanding passes over Simon. "This boyfriend of yours? He's quite extraordinary."

We watch as Esben gets to Christian's table, shakes his hand, and sits down for a moment. Simon and I keep eating, our eyes glued to the table across the room. In only a few minutes, Esben and Christian stand and come to our table.

"Allison and Simon, this is Christian. I invited him to sit with us."

"Of course. We'd love to have you." Simon pulls out the chair next to him, and a clearly flabbergasted Christian sits.

"Hi," he says shyly. "Thank you. It's nice to meet you. I, uh"—he looks nervously at Esben—"I follow Esben. This is so weird. Dude, you're so cool. I can't believe you just came over to me. And now I'm sitting at your table." He looks at me. "You're Girlfriend Allison. And you're Girlfriend Allison's father, right? I know my hashtags."

I'm all kinds of crazy flattered, but Esben is as embarrassed as he always is when someone compliments him. "I was sorry to hear about your dance tonight."

I nod. "Yes. That's disappointing. Your date got sick?"

"Gosh, Allison," he says shyly. "You're even prettier in person. You guys are my favorite couple ever." Then he giggles a little nervously. "Yeah. I got a call ten minutes after I left my house. I didn't want to disappoint my mother, because she was so excited about me being in a tux and going to a dance and stuff, so I just came here instead. A little cannoli comfort." Christian sighs. "This night isn't exactly going as planned."

"You didn't want to go alone?" Simon asks.

"Well, no . . ." Christian shifts uncomfortably in his seat. "My date? It's . . . well, it's a boy." He braces for us to freak out and almost seems more flustered when we don't have a reaction. "So, yeah. Okay, I guess you're all cool with that. His name is Doug, and I really like him, and he seems to like me, and . . . this was going to be our big night, because, well . . ." Christian glances around the table. "Is anyone drinking that water?"

Esben smiles and pushes the glass his way. "Go on."

"Look, I assume everyone at school knows I'm gay, and everyone seems fine with it, but I haven't exactly officially come out, you know? Tonight was going to be that official night. Mostly for myself, I guess, but my parents didn't know that I wasn't going with a girl. It was going to be a big night, you know? I just wanted to go to the winter formal and dance with a boy and stand under twinkle lights, and . . . I don't know. It's dumb probably. It's just a dance."

"It's not dumb," Simon says immediately. "It was important to you. It's also important that you had a fun and safe way to come out. God, I wish I'd had that," he says with a laugh. "You kids have it so much easier than I did at your age."

Christian visibly relaxes. "Yeah? I guess you're right. The kids at my school are really nice. It's still just nerve-racking, though. In a good way, I guess, but I was all amped up to go with Doug and finally be up-front about it. I'd really like to do that. For myself."

"You could still do that tonight," Esben offers. "Or something like that. If you want."

"What do you mean?" Christian sits up straight, his interest piqued.

I'm smiling, because I suspect what Esben has in mind. "Let's get this bow tie back on you," I say. "And your tuxedo jacket." Meanwhile, Christian starts redoing the top buttons he'd loosened.

When our winter-formal boy is ready, Esben takes Christian's hand. "Let's go."

"Where are we going?"

"To a dance. Of sorts."

Esben leads him from the pastry shop, with Simon and me following closely.

"What's he doing?" Simon asks excitedly.

"Something awesome. Just watch."

Christian's face registers a mix of doubt and anticipation, but he lets Esben lead him down the block and back to a trio of musicians we'd passed earlier. A light snow has started to fall, and, although it's certainly chilly tonight, the cold is more than tolerable, and fifteen or so people are gathered, listening to some very romantic-sounding Italian music. I loop my arm through Simon's and take in the scene.

Esben stands directly in front of Christian. "It's not your winter formal, but we have music, we have twinkle lights, and I'm in a suit. I would be honored to be your first dance."

It feels like forever until Christian replies, but when he does, it's worth the wait, because of the sweet crack in his voice. "I would really like that. Oh God, I would *really* like that." He moves into Esben's arms. "Is anyone going to care?" He quickly peeks at the crowd, but no one has pulled out a pitchfork. "Can we . . . can we take a picture? I could . . ." Christian is having trouble speaking. "Maybe you could post it. I can come out in a really big way," he says with a bravery I admire.

"Whatever you want. This is your night. Pics and video, and then you choose." Esben gives me a quick nod and then begins moving slowly.

I whip out my phone and take a few stills before recording this dance, this pivotal moment in Christian's life. Again, I am struck by Esben's ability to be so caring and so genuine with a stranger. I am mesmerized by him and by this dance. The woman who is singing gives them a smile, and then another couple begins dancing. As the minutes tick by, Christian relaxes more and more, coming to rest his cheek on Esben's shoulder. There are a few tears on his face, but the smile he wears makes those tears beautiful. Esben meets my eyes, and if he didn't already have the entirety of my heart and my trust, he has them now. They dance for three songs, and when Christian slowly lifts his head, there are six other couples, all dancing closely on the crowded sidewalk. The musicians stop for a break, and as we clap, the vocalist also asks the crowd for a round of applause for the dancers. The clapping goes wild. Esben spins Christian from his hold, raising his hand in the air in a celebratory move. The applause increases, and Christian's smile outshines anything I've seen before.

Simon tightens my arm in his. "What a guy. I could've used an Esben when I was younger."

His words mirror what I've said myself. Probably everyone could use an Esben.

Christian looks up at my sweet boyfriend, shaking his head in apparent disbelief. "Thank you. Thank you so much. I will never forget this. Or you."

"Thank *you*. That was my first dance with a boy, too." Esben grins and gives him a big hug. "Listen, I'm really happy for you. Now, let's go post your coming out. Tell me what you want me to say."

Under his breath, Simon whispers, "Where did you find this creature? He is one of a kind."

"He found me," I answer. "He found me."

On Christmas morning, Simon spoils me with presents, but the last one I open quickly becomes my favorite. The gift bag is stuffed with blue tissue paper covered in white stars, and I start smiling as soon as I lift out the gold Wonder Woman tiara. "Oh my God, Simon! It matches my cuff bracelets! I love this!"

"Do you? Really?"

I nod sincerely and put on the tiara.

"Good," he says happily, "because . . . hold on . . ." He rummages behind him and gets another bag from behind the tree. "I got one for myself, too!"

Then we eat waffles with hand-whipped cream and fresh strawberries while we wear our Wonder Woman tiaras. And over breakfast, I hand him a box with a small final present, one I hope makes him happy.

Simon removes the top of the box to find the framed picture. "Allison . . ." There is such joy on his face, and he sets a hand over his heart. "My sweet, generous girl. You got your picture taken with Santa for me."

"I did."

"This . . . this means a lot to me. Thank you, kiddo."

"I'm having the best Christmas ever. You kind of rock the holidays, Simon," I tell him truthfully.

"Just for that, you get a second glass of champagne."

We clink glasses, and the bubbles fizz loudly.

That night, when Simon has gone to bed and the house is quiet, Esben and I are on the sofa, looking out the window at the heavy flakes swirling as if we're in a snow globe.

"I got you something," I tell him hesitantly. My hand shakes a little when I reach behind me and take hold of the bag.

He smiles and puts the bag between us. "Why do you look so scared?"

I shrug. "I don't know. Just open it, and end my torture."

Esben laughs and digs into the tissue paper. "Oh, Allison . . ." His voice softens when he holds up the silver sand timer. Engraved on the top are the words *It only takes 180 seconds.* He flips it upside down, and we watch the sand pour from one side of the glass to the other. "This is so perfect." He kisses me until the sand has finished pouring out.

Then he winks, flips it again, and keeps kissing me.

After a few more flips of the timer, he sits against the back cushion, and I lie with my head in his lap as he strokes my hair while I watch the winter sky. The wind howls, then calms, intermittently.

Esben puts a small box in my hand. "This is for you."

"But you already gave me—"

"Shhhh. Just open it."

Inside is a wide silver bracelet with brilliant stones, and Esben clasps it on me. It takes me a minute to understand what I'm looking at—what the orange, turquoise, citron, red, pink, and deep-blue stones pattern into—but then I see the shape that wraps around my wrist. And I know why he's given this to me.

"It's a phoenix," I say breathlessly.

"Yes," he says. "Because, just as the story goes, you have risen from the ashes."

I sit so that I can gaze into his eyes. "You helped me do that. Esben, you helped me so much." Looking at this gift that has so much heart and meaning, I am at a loss. "This is beautiful. Esben . . . I don't know what to say."

He looks at me for a long time, and there is a new level of emotion and intensity that emanates from him. "Just say that you love me. Please. Because I am so goddamn in love with you that I can hardly breathe when we're apart. I know I said it when I was drunk, and I shouldn't have, even though I meant it. But I'm telling you now that I love you."

There's no need for me to think over how to respond. "I do love you. I don't remember what not being in love with you feels like."

"Good. Because you don't have to."

Six days later, we ring in the New Year in downtown Boston. Amid horns and cheering and bitter temperatures, Esben tells me he loves me over and over again. Even in all the chaos of the celebration, I hear him as clearly as if we were the only two people there. And I tell him the same thing.

CHAPTER 23

YOU HAVE MY HEART

We might as well be in Alaska, given how cold January on campus is. We're on day two of a heavy ice and snow storm, and they're predicting that classes will be canceled tomorrow, something almost unheard of. Carmen and I decide that we are tough enough to brave the weather this afternoon, and we head to the union for hot chocolate, though, after, as I'm bundling up again to go back to the dorm, I look at her. "I really don't want to go back out there. Maybe we can just sleep here?"

She yanks a thick hat down to just above her eyes. The giant pom-pom sticking off the top somehow suits her to a tee. "No way. Esben's friend, that hottie Danny that you set me up with, is coming over in half an hour, and I need to be defrosted by then."

"Fair enough." My parka feels a million inches thick, and my gloves make my hands look like a giant's, but I still froze on the way here. "Things are going well with Danny?"

I'm not sure what propelled me to set up Carmen and Danny, but they've both got their quirks, which I thought might match up well. Danny with his harmonica, Carmen with her ever-changing hair . . . and it's only been a few weeks, but, apparently, I was right. There's something about connecting these two that makes me crazy happy.

"Things are going so well that I shaved my legs today." She tosses her giant fuzzy hood over her hat and grins.

I cover my face with my scarf and brace myself. "Let's do this!" My voice is muffled in a Darth Vader sound that makes us both giggle. "Esben is still in my room, because he hasn't wanted to go outside. You and I are the tough ones."

She nods. "You know it!"

We barrel through the icy mix that pelts us relentlessly across campus, and we crash into the warmth of the dorm entryway. Both of us start laughing, somehow invigorated from the rush of braving the weather, and I shake out my coat and scarf and stomp my feet before making my way down the hall. Esben is in my room, typing on the computer, but he tilts his head my way as soon as I walk in.

"Hey, Popsicle," he says before kissing me.

"What're you doing?" I hang up my coat and sit on the bed. It's starting to get dark, and the screen is casting a glow on his face in a way I find endearing, so I don't bother to turn on other lights.

"Just going through comments and clearing out a few jerks. Kerry does most of this for me, but she's been busy, so I'm trying to catch up."

"Got it."

I lie back and call Steffi, but it goes to voice mail. I've barely spoken to her in weeks, because she didn't have cell reception on the cruise. Now, she's having to move to a new apartment, because the building's owner is selling it and kicking everyone out. My phone dings, and I have a text from her.

Sorry, can't talk. At the salon, getting my hair colored. You around tomorrow? she writes.

Yes. Any luck on a new apartment? Want help moving?

All good. Just annoying, but I've got it. Talk to you soon.

Suddenly, Esben makes a disgusted sound.

"Is something wrong?" I ask.

"With Kerry so taken up in her love life, I'm really seeing how many idiots there are out there. It's starting to really piss me off. I just spent two hours cleaning out garbage." He scowls. "And have you seen the pictures Kerry has been posting?"

"Oh. Those. Well, yes . . ."

Kerry's social-media feeds have recently been cluttered with pictures of her and Jason.

"It's creepy," he complains. "My sister and my best friend! It's gross."

I laugh. "It's not gross. They're very sweet together."

"Ew! Look at this one! They're kissing!" Esben enlarges an image and then claps his hands over his face. "My eyes! My eyes!"

I scoot over and swivel the chair so that he's facing me. "Then don't look at them."

He rests his elbows on his knees and smiles flirtatiously. "Can I just sit here and look at you, then?"

"If it will distract you, then yes."

I move in a little more, and he puts a hand on the side of my face. "Still a little cold, huh?"

"A little." But the touch of his palm makes me anything but cold.

I inch in closer and touch my lips to his. I intended nothing more than a simple kiss, but once I slip my tongue into his mouth, I know my intention means nothing. Within seconds, I am kissing him with a new level of passion and need, and Esben is responding smoothly, matching my pace.

But then he slows us down, kisses me on the cheek, and sits up. "There's, uh, a party on the third floor tonight, if you want to go." Esben is flushed and trying to control his breathing. "An ice-storm party, they're calling it. Apparently, there'll be a lot of slushy drinks. We could go get tipsy on weird blue cocktails and stuff."

While we have been hitting parties together, and I've been having fun meeting more people and spending time with his friends and my new ones, I do not want to leave this room tonight. And, based on the way Esben is running his eyes over me, I don't think he particularly wants to leave either.

"I don't like slushy drinks. I do, however, like other things," I inform him mischievously.

I grab a fistful of his shirt and pull him from the chair, bringing both of us down against the bed. He starts to roll to lie next to me while we kiss, but I push hard to keep him on top of me, parting my legs so that his fall between them and getting his body tight against mine. Our kissing intensifies, and my hands travel over his arms, then to the bottom of his shirt, then to his lower back. I press my hands into his skin and bring his waist against mine. Esben makes a sound and moves his mouth to my neck, his breathing quickening as his lips move more roughly against me. He only takes his mouth away when I loop a leg over his and then peel his shirt up over his head. I get my own shirt off and yank him back down. My desire and ache for him are nearly too much, and when his tongue strokes over my stomach, it's my turn to make a sound. We've been very heated before, but not quite like this.

After he's worked his way up to my neck again, I set my hands over the front of his pants and undo the top button of his jeans.

Esben stops and lifts himself up more to look at me. "Allison?"

I smile. "Esben?"

"Whatcha doing there?"

I don't say anything when I unzip his pants.

He closes his eyes for a second before speaking again. "Allison?"

My hands round to his back and tuck under the top of his jeans. "Yes, Esben?"

"Whatcha doing there?" he asks again with a smile.

"I'm done moving through the spectrum. I'm ready."

He searches my face. "You're ready?"

"I am. I want to be with you."

"There's still other stuff we can do. I want you to be sure—"

"I am totally sure." I kiss him softly. "I love you, and I trust you. And I trust *us*. Do you have any idea what it means to me to be able to say that? And feel that? God, I am so happy, Esben. I never thought I

194

could be this happy. I am so ready." I kiss him again and tease my fingers over his skin more. "Are *you* ready?"

"I was ready about two seconds after I met you."

My hand slips lower over the front of his pants. I smile at him. "Allowed?"

He smiles back. "More than allowed. Wanted."

"So, make love to me."

I'm pretty sure he stops breathing for a second.

"And let me make love to you," I continue. "I want to show you how much I love you. I *need* that," I tell him.

Esben smiles softly and nods. "I need that, too."

I lift my hips and push into him. "Good."

We start back at the beginning of our spectrum and work our way through, slowly, lovingly, sometimes nervously, but with every stage, I am secure in his love, his touch, in the care he takes with me. Even when I'm not sure about what I'm doing, he makes it okay. My hands go where they haven't before, I want things I haven't before, and I experience things I haven't before. We figure each other out together; we learn together.

Later, when we are as close as we can be, and he's moving very gently against me, he looks into my eyes. He tells me how much he loves me, how beautiful I am, how his world is complete because of me. "You have my heart, Allison." His voice trembles. "You have my heart."

"And you have mine," I whisper back.

We kiss, and I wrap my arms around him, raising my hips more assertively to meet his and then digging my nails into his skin.

He lifts his chest a bit and stops moving, his breathing ragged and hot. "Are you okay?"

"Yes. I'm so okay," I manage to say. "Please don't stop."

He doesn't.

After, when I am curled into him and his arm has fallen over me, I am overcome with how peaceful and complete I feel. It's true that in my head I am also jumping around, screaming about how I just lost my virginity, and I'm sort of desperate to tell Steff, but mostly I feel as though moving my naked body from his would be devastating.

"So." Esben all but clears his throat. "How was . . . or, was that . . ."

I start smiling, listening to him figure out how to ask this. Esben is the least insecure person I've ever known, and there's something rather cute about how nervous he sounds right now. "Yeah?"

"I'm just trying to figure out or, you know, make sure that you're good with this. And that *it* was good. Or at least not awful or anything." I can feel him tense. "Oh God, it wasn't awful, was it?"

I turn and face him. "Are you out of your mind?"

"Truthfully, right now, a little, yes."

"If it was awful, why do I want to do it again already?"

He laughs softly. "Yeah?"

"Yeah."

"Give me a few minutes, and you have yourself a deal." He props himself up on his elbow and lowers the sheet, running his hand across my stomach and letting his eyes travel over my body in the hint of light we have. "God, you are stunning." He lowers the sheet even more.

I don't worry that my breasts are too small or that I don't work out as much as I should. I don't worry about anything, because as much as what we've done tonight is about the physical, it's also about so much more.

"You feel all right?" he asks me.

"I feel wonderful," I tell him truthfully. "And you? Was it . . ." Now it's my turn to feel slightly nervous. "Was I . . . I mean, obviously I haven't done this before, so . . . how was it . . . for you?"

Esben's kiss could be enough of an answer, but when he finally stops, I see how his eyes twinkle. "Don't forget that I hadn't done this before either, but I have to say that I think we did pretty damn well."

"Okay," I reply with less conviction than I'd like. Now that it's all said and done, I'm starting to second-guess myself.

"Allison? Listen to me," he says. "That was beautiful. No one could ask for a better first time." His fingertips start to glide up and down my inner thigh, and my body slowly ignites again. Then he settles his hand between my legs. "And I already know that no one could ask for a better second time."

I don't argue with him. I can't.

At midnight, we microwave soup and eat the last of the Parmesan crackers from Simon. In the hopes there is more food in the care package that arrived today, I tear it open. God bless Simon. There are still-fresh fudgy brownies with cream-cheese frosting, some kind of upscale microwaveable cheese risotto thing that tastes like heaven, high-end bottled water, Advil, individual brown-sugar oatmeal containers, and my favorite junk food ever, stove-top Alfredo noodles. "Jackpot!" I call out.

I remember that another box arrived today, and I haven't looked at the return address until now. I grin, because while it's addressed to me, I know that it's from Simon for Esben. "You have a package here," I inform him with a big smile.

"I do?"

I bring the box into the living area and hand it to him.

His look of delight warms my heart for so many reasons. "Simon sent me cannoli from Mike's!" he exclaims as he reads the printed note. "Dude, that Simon is so cool."

Esben, as I expect, takes a hundred pictures and immediately posts them, tagging Simon and noting that this fabulous cannoli giver is my father. He also posts a picture from our night at Mike's, and it's one in which Simon looks particularly handsome. We go to the small kitchen in the dorm and eat the risotto and hydrate while the Alfredo bubbles in a beat-up pot. I didn't know that sex could make me so ravenous for food, and I couldn't be more grateful for all of this. I need to figure out how to thank Simon properly.

When we are totally full and cannot stay awake any longer, Esben and I curl up back in bed. I am exhausted and nearly unable to think because I am so flooded with euphoria.

Yet, just as I start to drift off, there's a slight sense of heightened awareness that something is off. Not with me, not with Esben. I'm missing something. A moment of discomfort tries to work its way in, as though the ice storm may not be the only thing crashing down on me. I shake it off. Tonight is not for falling into my old patterns of worry and negativity. I'm still learning to accept the good, so I stop myself and refocus on tonight.

Because tonight has been everything I have *never* dreamed of.

CHAPTER 24

LOSING AIR

When I wake the next morning, it takes me a while to understand that I am not dreaming. That this is *actually* my life. It's astonishing and wonderful. And when Esben wakes, my life only improves when we make love again. My entire body may be sore in some ways, but I also feel better than I knew possible.

As expected, classes are canceled today, and I couldn't wish for a better day to stay locked in my room.

I text Steffi, begging her to call me when she wakes up. Clearly, I have got to tell her all the details of the past day, but this has to be done over the phone and not text. I know that she's been an advocate for my happiness more than I have for years, and it would mean the world for me to show her how far I've come. To share the proof that I am taking charge of my life.

Late afternoon arrives, and I'm still unshowered and in my robe. The feel and smell and taste of Esben are all over me, and I love it. Esben is currently reading a book on his phone while languishing in bed half-dressed, and I'm flitting around the suite, tidying up and grinning stupidly while I do various unnecessary cleaning projects. I'm just so goddamn happy that I don't know what to do with myself.

My phone finally rings, and I practically fling myself across the bedroom to reach it.

"Steff!"

"Hey, honey."

"Oh my God, I've missed you so much! What is up with your phone situation? Why haven't you hooked up the new one from Simon? I want to see your sweet face!" I gush. "I have news. I'm so glad you called." I move into the second bedroom and half shut the door. "How have your crazy trips been? I want to know everything!"

"Allison, I need to talk to you." She sounds strange, but I can't tell how exactly.

"Okay. Yeah, of course. Anything. What's going on?"

There's a long silence that unnerves me. "Esben is with you?" she asks.

"Yes. Why?"

"Good. I want you to have him with you for this." Her voice has an unfamiliar monotone, a weakness to it, and my chest tightens. "This is going to hurt."

"Steffi." I sit down on the bed. "Tell me."

"Allison, you are my best friend. You always have been, and you always will be. And I know that you love me, so I'm going to ask you to listen and let me get through this."

"What are you talking about?" A panic begins to rise, and my heart is pounding with a beat I cannot keep up with. I suddenly know where this is going. The actual content doesn't process yet; the words don't permeate my thoughts yet, but I know.

"This is going to be rough for me to get out. Tell me that you will listen and let me finish. As my best friend, you need to do this for me."

I inhale and exhale so roughly, and I already feel the pain that is coming. "Yes."

"I've been lying to you, Allison. I haven't been on a cruise. I'm not moving to a new apartment."

I'm so confused. "Okay, so what—"

"You know that when I was a kid, I had cancer. I haven't told you everything about that, though. There was a tumor in my shoulder. I had surgery to remove it, then really nasty radiation and chemo. The chemo was awful, but it helped treat the cancer. After that, I got tons of scans and lab work and heart testing done for years, and everything was clean for a long time."

I can hear her gather her words, and I clasp a hand over my mouth to muffle my need to cry out.

"With the kind of chemo I had, once-normal cells are triggered to overproliferate, and people can end up with too many white cells. It saved me at the time, but there's always a risk that it can cause other cancers down the line. And that's what's happening."

"No," I say. "No!" I am calm but forceful. I will not allow this. Not now, not ever.

"This cancer I have now is deadly. It's called AML leukemia, which stands for acute myeloid leukemia. It's as serious as it gets."

I rally, and I do not panic. And I hyperfocus on the facts, because that's all I can do. "Okay. So what's the plan?"

"There is no plan. There is nothing to do."

"What do you mean?" My vision grows blurry, so I shut my eyes.

"The only option is the sort of chemo I had before, and, even though I was young, I remember that hell enough to know that I won't do it again. No one likes any kind of chemo, but this particular kind that I had and that I'd need again? Never. I won't do it. It's not an option." The finite quality of her tone scares me to my core. "I'm taking some medication, but it's not going to do much."

I won't accept this. We will not allow this cancer to take her down. Not after everything she's been through and everything she's triumphed over. I begin to pace the room. "You have to do the chemo. I'll come out there. I'll stay with you, and I'll get you through this. I know it'll suck—I get that—but we can do this." I've got moments left before I fall apart, so she needs to take me up on this.

She's too quiet and soft when she answers. "Allison, no. I'm not doing the chemo. And I would never let you watch me go through it. Even if I could put up with how awful it is, it would only buy me an additional month or two on top of the limited time I have. There's no point."

A month or two.

My arm stretches out to grab the desk. I'm going to collapse. This is not happening. I have got to be in the midst of a vivid and graphic nightmare. I will wake up. I will wake up, and this will not be happening.

"Steffi . . . Steffi . . ." I am losing air. I cannot breathe.

"So, listen to me, Allison. Listen to every word I say to you." I know that she's tearing up, and the break in her words guts me, because I have never heard her be anything but stoic and tough as nails. "I hate doing this to you. I hate that more than anything that's happening to me. I wanted to tell you sooner, but I couldn't."

"When you came out here." I stand now and begin furiously pacing from the bedroom to the living area and back, as if I can outrun this. "Honey, you knew you were sick then?"

"Yes. I'd just found out. I didn't want to see how you'd look at me, so I put off telling you until I had to. I couldn't take seeing your face. How you were going to hurt. But I'm tired all the time now, I feel awful, and you need to know what's happening."

I control my voice and my words. "Steffi, what can I do? There must be something. I can fly out there immediately. I'll do anything for you. Let me help. We can find another doctor, another treatment center. We will fix this, okay?"

"Shit, Allison, there is no fixing this!" The force of her response slams against me. "There is *no* fixing this. This is the end. I'm going to die."

The entirety of what she's saying begins to wash over me, and I cannot do anything but freeze in place. Time stops, my heart stops, life stops. "How long?"

The roar of the silence is excruciating. Steffi finally answers. "A few months. Maybe more, maybe less."

The sound that rips from my chest must be loud and alarming, because Esben is at my side. Without knowing how I got there, I find myself on the floor, with my head pressed into the carpet, my fingers gripping the phone hard. Esben's hands are on my waist, trying to pull me up. But I cannot move.

"So, don't talk, Allison," she continues all too calmly. "Here's the deal, and I'm so sorry for this, but it's what has to happen. It's what I need." Now her words are shrouded in heartache. "This is going to be the last time that we talk to each other."

"No! No!" I slam my hand against the floor. "Steffi, no!"

"Yes. It's going to get really bad, and I don't want you to see me deteriorate that way. And, no, don't try to talk . . . stop it. Don't talk," she warns me when I cannot control myself. "More than you having to see how this disease is going to take me down, I cannot worry about you and what this is doing to you. I can't." She's wrecked—I know this—but she continues in a straightforward tone. "This is my choice, and I get to have that. I haven't been able to make many choices in my life, but I at least get to choose how I handle my death. And you're going to respect what I'm asking of you. I love you, and I will always love you, but we are saying good-bye right now."

My world goes black.

"No!" I scream. "No! Don't shut me out! I can help! I can help!"

There are sounds behind me, a touch on my back, maybe. I think that Esben's hands are on me, trying to pull me into him, but I'm not sure.

"I love you so much, Allison," I hear her say. "Don't forget that. But I need to do this alone. Don't call me, don't text. Don't try to be in touch at all. It'll just make it harder on me, okay? Every call or text would be about cancer. About how I'm feeling. Or there'd be a freakin' dance around cancer that I don't have the energy for. I already feel like shit all the time, and it's going to get a lot goddamn worse, and I do not want to feel like I have to tell you all about it. Because you love me, you'd want to help, and you can't. You can't do anything. No one can. I have great doctors and great nurses, and . . . everyone is taking care of me as best they can. I'm in good hands. It's just this disease. It's nobody's fault, but there's no saving me. There's not." Steffi is so blunt, and a knife through my chest would hurt less. "Please. I love you. I couldn't have asked for a better friend. A sister, really. And I'm so glad you've found Esben and that you're in love and have someone to get you through this. And you have Carmen, right? And other friends? You can do this. Do you hear me? You can do this. You have to."

It's hard to hear myself over my devastation. "Stop saying good-bye! Don't you do this. Jesus, Steffi, don't! I love you. God, I love you so much. Don't you dare say good-bye! This isn't right—"

"Esben is with you?" She asks this again with too much serenity.

I'm not sure. I'm not sure of anything. Where I am, what I'm hearing. "Esben?" It's hard to talk though my thready breathing. "You're here?"

"I am," he says firmly.

Finally, I notice how tight his hold is on me. I stop fighting it and let him lift me from the floor so that I'm resting against his chest. "Yes," I tell Steffi. "He's here."

"Good. Hold on to him. He's going to get you through this. That makes it better for me." Steffi is so calm and takes so long before she speaks again that it panics me more. "This hurts. I told you it would. I wish there was some better way to prepare you, but there isn't." Steffi's voice grows raw, and she gets assertive in a way that sends ice down my spine. "I'm going to hang up now. I need to. Please know that I hate this as much as you do. If I thought I could tolerate not cutting you out, I would. But it will make this all easier on me. Tell me that you understand this."

"No!" I am in pieces. "It's not right. Let me be with you! You have always done everything alone. Don't do this alone," I beg.

"I especially need to do this alone, so, stop. I'm asking you to stop," she says sternly. "Tell me that you understand. Tell me that you'll live your life with everything you've got and that you will not let this stop you. You will be happy, okay? You'll do that for me?" She's begging me, but there's so much control in how she does so. "Give me that, Allison. Please. And promise me that you'll let me go."

There is infinite desperation in what she asks of me, and I know that I have to give her what she needs. If I flew out, she'd refuse to see me. I know her. I realize now that Steffi has always stubbornly refused my help, anyone's help. If I'd understood that years ago, maybe I could have pushed more for her to let me in. But her walls are clearly a thousand times thicker than mine ever were. After everything my friend has done for me, there is no choice now but to give her what she wants, no matter how much I hate it. "Okay," I say through tears. "Yes. I understand. I promise. I will do everything you want. I love you. I love you, Steffi."

"Be brave. Be brave. Be brave. You can do this."

She hangs up, and I begin to truly lose my ability to breathe. My ability to scream, however, is in full force.

Esben holds me with my back against his bare chest as I sob, and he's the only reason I can sit up. I cannot do anything but heave sobs and succumb to searing pain.

This is the first time that I understand the term "blinding pain," because the agony I'm in has cut off my vision, and I break free from Esben and crawl forward, groping for anything to break. I hear the couch thump hard against the floor several times, and I must be doing this, but I don't know for sure. Then there's the sound of glass shattering, then rattling and a crash as I careen around the room, my howling piercing my own ears.

"Allison, no. Baby, no." Esben grabs me and pulls me in, taking something from my hand before he has me fully in his arms.

I want to cling to him, but my legs give out before I can. As I drop to the floor, Esben catches me in his arms and carries me to my bed. Gently, he sets me down and lies, facing me. My hands claw at him, and I'm crying and pleading. "Make this stop! You have to make this stop!" I call out Steffi's name over and over. Suddenly, I stop and wipe my eyes and look up at Esben. "Wait. You can fix this. You fix everything. So do it. You have to do something."

He shakes his head in confusion. "What is going on? Steffi?"

I shove my hands hard against him. "She's sick again. Just tell me that you'll fix this, goddamn it! Do something! Someone will know how to help her."

Esben exhales loudly.

"She says it's terminal, but that can't be right. We can't let it be right. Fix it. Change things back to the way they were. You can do anything, so do this for me. Please, oh please, Esben . . ."

He pulls me in, and I try to fight him, but I'm too spent now. "I wish I could . . . ," he says.

"No, no, no. Don't say that! Don't say that! Please, just this one thing! You're magic; you can find a way." Now I am crying again, because I know that I'm being crazy and asking the impossible.

"I would do anything for you. I would. This just isn't something I can fix. God, I'm so sorry."

I fall apart. For hours, I cry and choke on anguish while Esben holds me. Eventually, my tears give out, my voice goes, and my throat is so raw that my body battles against my mind and shuts down my crying. There is nothing left in me now.

CHAPTER 25

RESCUE

It takes three weeks before I become emotionally functional again. Though I've been going to class and getting my work done, outside of that, I've alternated between being numb and grief-stricken. The wind has been knocked out of me, and it's taking forever to breathe again, but I'm trying. I know it's what Steffi wants. She would hate knowing the impact her illness is having on me, so I've got to pull myself out of this despondency however I can. Kerry and Carmen have both been great, being patient with me and letting me cry when I need to. It's so important that I have these new friends, but I am constantly reminding myself that I'm not replacing her with either of them. That thought does try to push through more often than I'd like, though. And Esben's friends Jason and Danny are bear-hugging me so often that I'm surprised I'm not bruised. And with each bit of comfort I'm offered, I think how Steffi has no one comforting her. Just because that's her own doing and her conscious choice doesn't make her isolation any easier to swallow.

Three days after Steffi called me, I told Simon. He's been wanting to come up, but I've been putting him off. It almost feels as though seeing him would make me break down again, because our shared love for her is so great.

I wake up this Saturday morning in February, and I'm determined to treat it like any normal day. I must.

The spare room is again full of unopened packages from Simon, and the scene reeks of emotional backlog. It's time to clear out some of my pain, so I start with something simple and open the biggest box first.

A few days after Steffi's call, I learned I'd smashed the coffeemaker and glass pot and also overturned the minifridge, shattering bottles inside. I don't remember this, and Esben cleaned everything up before I saw the shambles I'd created. I think I broke more than I know, but I really don't care. The coffeemaker, however, I have actually missed, and every time I automatically look for it and it's not there, I am hit with yet another reminder and another hit of pain.

Methodically, I now unbox the new coffeemaker and mugs and set them up. Everything looks as it did before, but that's just a trick of the eye, because nothing is the same.

I will be brave. I will be brave. I will be brave.

I will keep going.

It's still early enough in the day for me to feel as though it's salvageable. That maybe I can try for one day in which I don't break down every minute. Esben left while I was still sleeping, and I'm not sure where he's gone. I spend an hour cleaning up my space, changing the sheets, taking a shower, and drying my hair, and then I make a pot of coffee, as though my entire soul is not shredded.

It's a little after eleven when Esben lets himself into my room, still shaking snow from his hair.

He brightens when he gets a look at me. "Hey, baby. You look good."

"I showered and put on something besides sweatpants." I try to smile. "I figure it had to happen sometime."

Esben hangs up his coat and then takes me in his arms. "I know this is a nightmare." He rubs my back for a bit. "Still nothing?"

He checks in all the time, even though we both know that I won't hear from Steffi.

I lean against him and shake my head. "No."

Every day, I call her. Every single day. I've been hoping that she'll change her mind, that she'll let me in, but she won't pick up my calls, and I always go right to voice mail. Half the time, I leave messages, and half the time, I don't, because none of my words so far have changed her mind. I've had Esben and Simon try to call her, too, but she's simply cut herself off from the world. Her social-media accounts are all shut down, and e-mails bounce back as undeliverable.

I take a very long breath. "I think it's time to stop. This is what she wants. I have to accept it."

"Yes, I think so," he says gently.

"But I imagine what she's going through, how she's feeling. I wonder if she's in pain, who is taking care of her." It hurts to breathe when I say this. "How bad things are now. How . . ." I start to choke up. "How long she has. Is she scared? Is she lonely, sad, angry? Will . . ."

God, I can't believe I'm saying this out loud. That I have to prepare myself this way.

"Do you think someone will call me when . . . when she's gone?"

"Yes. I'm positive. Steffi will make sure of that." The confidence in Esben's voice helps to reassure me some.

"Steffi has always been like a selfless mother who would do anything to take care of her child. She has always worried about me, watched over me, more than she would let me worry about and watch over her. Always. It's not right. I got to save her from pain once before, when I ripped that guy off of her. I want to do the same now. Rip the cancer out of her. Rip the hurt away. Esben, I would trade places with her in a heartbeat, I would."

"I know you would. But this is who she is, and you can't change that, especially not now. How she's handling this is her choice. If pushing you away and taking this on alone gives her some kind of comfort, then you need to allow her that."

I nod and focus on staying calm. "I need distraction. I need to think about something besides this. Just for a while."

"Okay. What do you want to do?"

The feel of being in his arms, the now-familiar safety, makes me want more. More of him. So, I lift my mouth to his and kiss him. "This. I want to do this." My hands rub over the front of his shirt, up to his shoulders, and then I untuck his shirt.

Esben catches his breath when I move my hand to the front of his pants. "Allison, you sure? We haven't since . . . since that morning."

I touch my lips and tongue to his neck, and, in one quick movement, Esben picks me up, and I clamp my legs around his waist while he carries me to the bedroom. His touch, his sound, the way he moves and breathes and makes me feel so alive are exactly what I need. Instead of losing myself in him and in making love, I do the opposite. I find myself again.

After, while I rest on his chest and my body is still racing, he asks, "You doing okay?"

"I think so. As much as I can be." I roll onto my stomach and hold myself up on my arms. "I feel better than I did earlier today."

"I like seeing your smile back," he says, but I know he's still worried about me.

"I'm trying." I kiss him quickly. "So, where were you this morning?"

"Oh, yeah . . ." He laughs and stretches over me to get his phone.

He shows me his home page, and I read for a few minutes, my smile now broad. "That's the older man who was at the coffeehouse you took me to. I remember him. You got him a puppy?"

He shrugs. "He's there every time I go in, and he always looks so lonely and sad. It was bothering me. So, I started talking to him, and he's got no family nearby. Only a daughter halfway across the country, who can't be bothered to call him more than once a year. He just seemed so bummed out and depressed, and . . . I don't know. What's more fun than a puppy? I drove him to the shelter and hooked him up with that little black Lab. Cute, huh?"

I zoom in on the image, and the puppy is certainly an adorable ball of fluff, but that's not what's most important here. "God, that man has the best expression ever! Look how happy he is!"

"Right? And he's retired and home all day, so he's a perfect puppy owner."

"Was the shelter depressing, though? All those dogs who need homes?"

"A little, I can't lie."

"I always feel so bad for the older dogs that nobody wants. Everyone wants a puppy or at least a young dog, but the older ones can stay in shelters for years. The dog versions of me," I say with a small laugh.

Esben grazes his fingers across my bare shoulder. "People don't know what they're missing."

"One day, I'm going to adopt a really ugly older dog. Like, so ugly that only I will think he's cute. The most seemingly unadoptable dog possible."

"I like that idea. A lot."

Esben must be rubbing off on me, because my wheels start turning. I Google ugly dogs and older dogs and unwanted dogs. Esben is quiet while I scour the Internet. Then I look down at the phoenix bracelet that cuffs my wrist. "I . . . I have an idea," I tell him.

His grin is infectious when he exuberantly pulls me on top of him and tickles my waist. "I was waiting for this. I'm all in."

I laugh. "You don't even know what my idea is!"

"Yes, I do!"

I roll my eyes. "Of course you do. You practically invented all this stuff. So, you'll help me?"

"Absolutely. Let's go."

"Now?"

"Now."

He grabs a handful of our clothes, and I giggle when he covers us in a mess of the jeans and shirts that we'd ripped off.

My spirits are already lifted in a way they haven't been since before the phone call, and I'm almost self-conscious over how I cannot stop smiling. "I'm excited."

"There's my girl." Esben sits and tangles his hands in my hair. "I'm proud of you."

"You think we can do this? They won't mind?"

"They'll be ecstatic."

My phone rings, and I jump. There's always the hope that Steffi might call.

"Hey, Simon." I make bug eyes at Esben and try to cover myself with the shirt that he's tossed on the bed. I can't talk to Simon while I'm naked and straddling my boyfriend!

"Okay, don't get mad," he starts. "But I've been worried about you. Really worried. So, I'm driving up to see you."

"I'm not mad at all, but you didn't have to do that." I slip off the bed and scrunch in funny positions as I try to get dressed with one hand. Esben starts to laugh, and I glare at him to be quiet. "When will you be here?"

He clears his throat. "In about six minutes."

"Six minutes!"

Esben leaps out of bed and yanks on his underwear and jeans.

"Wow. Okay." My hair probably looks like sex hair, and I start pulling a brush through it while Esben hooks my bra for me. "Do you mind coming out with Esben and me? We've got a little something planned."

"Anything. I just want to see you. I'll pull up where I parked when I took you to school this fall."

God, that seems like ages ago. "Okay, see you in a minute."

We scramble to pull ourselves together, then rush outside. I scan the street for Simon's car, but he doesn't seem to be here yet. We stand on the steps, getting colder by the second, and Esben sneaks a steamy kiss while we wait. Just as his tongue is really starting to heat me up, a fierce horn blow makes me jump. I look to the street again, but Simon still isn't here. I'm about to go back in for another kiss when the horn blows more violently. I pull back and look again.

"Wait a second. Is that Simon?" I go down a few steps and peer at the sleek silver car. "Oh my God, it is." I rush to the passenger window to find a smiling Simon waving at me.

He rolls down the window. "Hello, kids!"

"Slick ride!" Esben exclaims.

"When the hell did you buy a Porsche?" I demand. "This is insane!"

"That other car had almost two hundred thousand miles on it," he says with a shrug. "I figured, why not? Get in. You must be freezing. Want to drive?"

"No way." I shake my head. "I'd be too scared I'd wreck it."

Simon sticks out his tongue. "Esben? You up for it?"

"Seriously? Totally! Are you sure?"

In answer, Simon gets out and heads for the passenger seat.

"Woo-hoo!" Esben bounds to take the wheel.

Before Simon gets in, he gives me a huge hug, and I feel my chest well with emotion.

"I'm so glad you're here," I manage. "Thank you."

"I will always be here. You're going to get through this. You are."

Twenty minutes later, we're at the dog shelter and walking down a long hall lined with metal cages full of dogs. We've let Simon in on our plan, and now he's even happier that he came up. The barking sounds jubilant to my ears, and I can hardly hear Faith, the woman who stops periodically to tell us about some of the dogs. She's the one who helped Esben earlier today with the puppy, and she was immediately receptive to my idea. We're going to take pictures of the dogs and post them with information about how special each one is, in hopes of encouraging adoption. My goal is to get people to think outside the box and look past what may not initially be the cutest pet possibility. While Faith is gushing over how fabulous Esben is, I give him a wink and move down the hall to look in the pens.

I stop in front of a giant dog with shaggy gray fur. His legs are too long, his coat is a weird color, and his snout is awfully long and out of proportion to his face. This is not an attractive dog, and I love him immediately. The beast sits in the corner of his pen, and behind wisps of fur, I see dark, sad eyes. I see dejection. When I bend down and call for him, he doesn't even come over to me. Worse, he looks away. I read the printout that hangs from the fencing.

"Esben." I stand and call more loudly over the barking. "This one. Let's start with this guy."

He nods, and Faith comes over with a leash. "You guys can take them outside if you like. Better lighting probably. So, this is Bruce Wayne," she says with a wistful look. "We give the dogs fun names in hopes of attracting adopters. It sounds silly, but it helps. He's very shy. Been with us for two years and, before that, at another shelter for four. He's nine now, and . . ." Faith stops for a second. "No one has ever asked to take him out. It breaks my heart. I love this guy, and I'd take him if I could, but I already have five dogs at home. He needs a break."

"Can I take him out?" I ask.

"Sure. He's very nervous, so give him a few minutes, but he's really gentle."

I look at Simon for encouragement, and he nods. "You know how to do this. I know you do."

He's right. I understand this dog too much. It's almost heartbreakingly pathetic how much.

Out of the corner of my eye, I see Esben raise his phone to capture whatever will happen.

The door to Bruce's area swings open, and I lower my body slowly and then inch in, keeping close to the entrance. "Hey, Bruce," I say softly. "Hi, buddy." He doesn't respond, so I sit down and lean against the concrete wall. "That's okay. I'll just wait for you."

And I do. For a long time. Every few minutes, Bruce glances at me briefly, then turns away. But then I inch a tiny bit closer, say a few soft words, and wait some more. I will do this all day if necessary. When I am about two feet from him, the dog finally turns his body slightly my way. Then, without warning, Bruce lurches toward me. For a moment, I'm afraid this giant is going to bite my face off, but instead he tries to climb into my lap. He's so huge that I can barely accommodate his size, but I do what I can. Bruce leans his weight against me, and I start to laugh while petting him. He's smelly and ungainly and utterly sweet. I rest my face against his stinky fur and will this sweet dog to feel how loved he is, how worthy he is. Bruce starts wagging his tail.

"I can't believe this," Faith says, and she slowly comes in and hands me the leash. "He hasn't wagged his tail since he's been here. Not once. You've got a magic touch."

I rub Bruce's ears and slip the leash around his neck. His wagging intensifies when I stand and start to lead him out. I look at Simon with disbelief, and his face mirrors my feelings.

"Well, let's go for a walk, shall we?" he says.

Bruce practically drags me down the hall as we follow Faith outside, and I'm laughing with delight as we enter the shelter's good-sized penned area. I wish the leash was a little longer, because crazy Bruce is now hopping around in some kind of celebration. I pet him again, and then he drops onto his back for a belly rub. This is all so odd, the parallels between Bruce's sad life and mine. Though I really can't imagine I wasn't adopted because of my looks, Bruce and I do share something in common: nobody wanted us. Truly, and for no good reason, nobody wanted us. Both of us started out so eager and hungry, and over the years, we grew more and more dejected. It was hard for people to look past that. I get it.

But I have learned from their mistakes, and I know this dog has heart underneath his outward damage.

"Simon? He's a sweet guy, huh? He's not a dog that most people would look at, but he's kinda special, right?"

Simon kneels down. "He is. Check him out. There was a really happy pup hidden in there, huh? Aren't you a sweet thing? Just a big boy who was a little down, huh? You feeling better now? Yeah?" He begins cooing and scratching Bruce's stomach. "Allison reminded you that you get to be loved, just like everyone else, huh? Did she?"

For the next ten minutes, we goof around with Bruce, and both Simon and I pose for pictures, hoping to show Esben's followers how wonderful this dog is.

"Posted!" Esben says happily. "Between that video and the pictures, this dog will be adopted in a heartbeat. I put up a shot of his fact sheet, too. Okay, we've got a ton more dogs to photograph, so, want to keep—"

"Esben?" Simon says with a tone I can't figure out. "I think you're going to need to edit that post."

"What do you mean?" I ask him.

But then I know. And I shake my head over how fantastic Simon is.

"Because," Simon says as he stands proudly, his eyes still glued on Bruce, "Mr. Bruce Wayne has already been adopted. If the shelter approves me, that is."

Faith grins. "I'll start the paperwork."

I kneel down and pet Bruce more. "Simon, are you sure? You don't have to do this. You really want a big old dog? One you have to drive home in your new Porsche?"

"I do. There's no way I'm letting this guy go after what I saw. He'll look very cool riding next to me. And who knows? Maybe he'll turn out to be a man magnet, and I'll be flooded with dates." He bends down next to me and touches my shoulder. "And we need some cheer. Things are rough now, but they're going to get rougher."

He's right. I know that Simon is hurting over Steffi, too.

"Our family just got a little bigger." He tries to give me a reassuring smile. "Strength in numbers."

Simon poses for a picture with a drooling Bruce, and Esben shares the photo online: #brucegoeshome #girlfriendallisonsfather #victoryissweet

Later, when I am making a silly face while holding a rat terrier that looks more rat than terrier, Esben takes a bunch of pictures and then checks to see the comments on his feed. "People are loving these!"

"Yeah?" Simon is throwing a ball that Bruce has no interest in chasing.

"Uh, Simon?" Esben is grinning. "You seem to be gaining quite the fan club."

"I am?"

"Check Facebook."

Simon pulls out his phone. "I have fifty-eight friend requests! And . . . ten messages."

"You've been tagged *hotdad* a whole bunch," Esben says with a laugh.

"Great. A bunch of women, probably." Simon fake pouts.

"Um . . . I don't think so." Esben waves his phone around. "A lot of comments from guys. And some cute ones, too."

"Really?" For the first time in an hour, Simon steps away from our new dog. "I'm going to have to do a little investigating, it seems."

I sit with more dogs than I can count, I smile more than I have in the past three weeks, and I am overcome with the feeling that I might do some good for all of these deserving animals. This process makes me understand Esben even more. Helping others can help me heal myself.

While Esben is posting the last photo, one of me with an outstandingly cute yellow Labrador—one who has not been adopted without any discernible reason—I lean against him. "That Lab? That dog is a sweetheart. I hate this. I hate that she's been so alone. But I know that we're going to find her a family because of this. She's going to be loved, and she'll feel that love, and she will forget her past. I know that." I breathe him in. "I feel so much better. Thank you."

"This was your deal, my sweets. This is all you." He swings his arm over me and keeps me close.

"There. One day down," I state with as much pride and courage as I can muster. "Now I just have to get through the rest of them."

"We'll do this every day if you want," Esben promises. "For as long as you need to."

We might have to. I cannot fathom how I will survive the days that lead to the call.

The call in which I'll be told that Steffi has died.

CHAPTER 26

SOCIAL DESTRUCTION

By the second week in March, the weather begins to lift, and it's a good way to kick off spring break. Simon and I were going to take a trip to Washington, DC, and do touristy stuff together, but there's a massive airline strike involving most of the major airlines, and we lost our flights. Although I'm disappointed, I'm also exhausted from late nights of research and paper writing, so I don't mind some downtime here at school. Simon wanted me to come home and stay with him, but I think he understands that I just want to lie around here and sleep for a week.

Esben and Kerry are driving home tomorrow, and I'm going to be in the minority staying on campus during break, but I'm actually looking forward to the quiet. This is a desire for *healthy* alone time, unlike it would have been last year, and I'm proud of my progress.

Esben has been furiously clicking away on his laptop, and I glance up from my collapsed spot on the bed to see what he's doing. He's leaning against the wall, with my legs over his, and by the stern face he's making, I know he's in a mood of sorts. I shut my eyes and take a few more minutes to recover from this week. Both of us have been stressed out, although I'm not sure exactly what's been going on with him. He seemed to sail through the two big tests he had this week, yet something has been getting under his skin over the past month. Just traces here and there, but enough for me to notice. I've tried asking him, but he's assured me up and down that nothing is wrong.

I'm not convinced.

Apparently, I've fallen asleep, because I'm jolted awake when Kerry simultaneously knocks and bursts through the door. "Hello, my darlings! What's shakin'?"

It takes a minute for me to respond. "Hey, Kerry." I rub my eyes and yawn. "You look happy."

She gives a twirl. "I am. I'm all in love and swoony and feeling full of life and all that corny stuff." She throws a sidelong peek at Esben, who has not looked up from his screen, and then raises her eyebrows at me. "I was hoping for some girl talk."

"Sure," I say with a stretch. "Give me a minute."

"What's up with grumpy there?" she asks.

It takes a few nudges to draw his attention away. "Yeah? What? Oh, hi, Kerry. Sorry."

"Hiya, Baby Blue." Kerry puts a hand on her hip. "Why so pissy?"

"It's just . . . I didn't understand how much crap you filtered out online."

"What do you mean?" She sits in my desk chair and frowns.

His neck cracks as he rolls his head. "You haven't been deleting comments and banning and blocking people the way you used to."

"Oh." Her face drops. "I didn't realize. God, Esben, I'm sorry."

"Don't be sorry. I knew that you've been pulling back, and that's fine. You're . . . preoccupied or whatever with Jason. And I get it. It's cool. I'm just getting up to speed on a lot of posts from the past few months, and . . . I'm seeing so much more now," he says with little expression. "I didn't realize the scale . . . the level of vitriol." He shakes his head with an awful sense of understanding. "The absolute expanse of it. It's too much. It's really just too much."

Kerry's flush of exuberance is fading. "They're just idiots, Esben."

"You have to ignore them," I say with less conviction than I'd like.

"How am I supposed to ignore this guy? I just went way back to Cassie's party and the pictures. Some moron wrote . . ." He shakes his head and breathes before he reads this aloud. "He wrote, 'Dude, that kid is weird looking. No wonder no one wanted to go, lol.' And under the picture of that little schnauzer? How's this for crummy? 'That dog is fricking disgusting. Shoulda been shot years ago.'" He hits the wall behind him. "Tons of crap about our professor and his former friend. Way too much about Allison and me. Horrible, disgusting, offensive stuff that I will not read out loud. That I've already deleted. But why?" He gives us both a hopeless face. "Why? I don't get it. I'll never get it. And I don't want to. I don't want to understand these people."

"Oh, hell." Kerry runs her hands through her hair. "This is my fault. Look, it's always been like this, but I'm usually on top of removing the crap. I'm really sorry. You shouldn't have to see this kind of stuff."

Esben raises his voice sharply. "No. I *should*. I should see every word. You've been protecting me from too much. I've been stupidly naive. I've seen plenty of BS online before this, but it's getting to be too much. It's way too much. I've hit my limit." He scoffs and rubs his eyes. "God, I'm so dumb. All I want to see is the good, decent people who support and rally and shout out the awesome stuff. I've had blinders on. Not to mention, why can no one spell properly? Does nobody go to school, like, ever?"

Kerry is gentle in her response. "You just can't give much credence to these jerks. They don't get it. Their comments say a whole lot about them and not much else. You've got to look away. In order to do what you do, you have to be willing to accept that part of the population isn't going to understand or respond the way you want. The way they *should*."

"I don't know." He lets his laptop slide off his legs. "Maybe I don't accept it. What's the point, really? I can't get anyone to change, can I? That's probably what I thought. That I'd create change. How stupid does that sound? Look at Cassie. Jesus, who would pick on a kid with a comment like that? I can't . . . I can't begin to understand. And that's the tip of the iceberg of this garbage. Who knows what else I've missed?"

"Esben." Kerry looks uncomfortable. "It doesn't matter. The voices of the supporters are louder."

He shakes his head. "I'm not sure I believe that anymore."

"Did you not see how many of those dogs got adopted? Have you forgotten about the message you got from Faith and how freakin' thrilled she is? How the shelter got flooded with so many applications, not to mention donations from all over the country, that they could barely keep up?"

"That's true," he admits.

"And Cassie's mom messaged you just last week to thank you for the thousandth time," Kerry points out.

I push his laptop in front of him. "Have you checked in with Christian, the boy you danced with? You should. I bet he's doing really well, and it'll make you feel better."

He hesitates, but then cracks a smile when I lift his hands and plunk them onto the keyboard. "Okay, okay. Maybe you're right."

"While you do that," Kerry starts, "maybe Allison will feed me some of Simon's gourmet food? It's past lunchtime, and I'm starving."

She raises her eyebrows and rubs her hands together with such pretend greed that I have to laugh.

"Of course." I rub Esben's shoulder and then scoot off the bed. "This week," I announce formally, "we have marinated artichoke hearts, three kinds of olives, rosemary crackers, mousse pâté, roasted red pepper dip, and Sweety Drop peppers. Simon has gone all appetizer crazy, it seems."

Kerry clasps her hands to her chest. "Oh, I so love him!"

I feel ridiculous setting out this fancy slew of food while in a dingy dorm room, but Kerry is delighted and eating up everything.

We are halfway through the pâté when Esben explodes in the next room.

"Goddamn it! *Goddamn it!*"

Both of us freeze.

"That's it! Screw it! I'm done!" he shouts with more anger than I've ever heard from him.

"Baby Blue? What is it?" Kerry tries to stay calm.

He appears in the doorway, his open laptop in one hand. "You wanted me to check on Christian? I'm so glad I did, because now I know that it will always be one step forward and an infinite number back."

"What? What happened?" I ask.

Esben looks near tears. "The post we put up? All the people cheering for him and throwing out support? That meant nothing. Because there were two people who didn't support him. At all. His parents, who claimed they had no idea at all that he is gay. And they find it so disgusting and intolerable that they kicked him out of the house. Totally cut him off in every sense." The laptop shakes in his hand. "He's staying with friends most nights now, but he's also slept in a park a bunch of times, and he's trying to figure out what to do next year without a college fund and if it's too late to try for financial aid."

"Oh God," I say under my breath.

"He had no idea his parents would react like this. None." Without warning, Esben hurls his laptop against the wall, and Kerry and I both flinch sharply. "Who does that, huh? To anyone, not to mention their kid? What freaking year is it that anyone would do that? Tell me! This is my fault. This is *my* fault. I should never have approached him. If I'd left him alone, he'd still have a family." He's frantic now, his voice growing louder with every word. "Who knows what other damage I've done? Those dogs? For all I know, they're off living with people who beat them or don't feed them! There's no way to protect or help anyone. Not without repercussions. Never." He's pacing the floor. "I'm out. I'm done. I'm going to shut it all down. Close my accounts, delete everything. Screw it. Know what, Allison? You were probably right. People can't be trusted. They suck. I mean, when it comes down to it, by and large? People suck."

"That's enough," Kerry says sharply.

"It's true!" he shouts. "Nothing I do will disprove that. And nothing will reverse time, will it, Kerry? For you, for anyone else. There is no way to make up for anyone's past."

"No one expects you to reverse time, Esben." Kerry speaks softly but with a confidence that I've learned is genuine. "That's impossible. And no one is asking that of you. You have made my life so much better, and you've helped me heal in immeasurable ways. You know that. Come on, you know that!" she says adamantly.

It's obvious that he isn't listening to her. "I'm probably just adding to the problem," he whips out. "Creating a place for people to spew their hatred and ignorance. God, that ultimately ends up as the heart of what I do, doesn't it? I offer up opportunities for the masses to crap on any moment of hope or positivity or love, right? I can't win at their game."

"Don't say that, please." I stand up. "You cannot lose sight of the thousands of people who have been moved and uplifted. Those are the voices who scream the loudest. Look at me! Look what you've done for me. Look how you've changed me and made me stronger and more alive than I've ever been."

He tries to soften his demeanor. "You're different, Allison. You are different. That's one-on-one. That's because of what's between you and me, and because you're such a wonderful person. Online? With the hordes of followers? Totally different."

Before I can get to him, he throws open the door and leaves.

"Should I go after him?" I ask Kerry.

"No. It's okay. I'll go. I think I can calm him down." She pauses by the open door. "And, Allison? Don't listen to what he said. Even I know that people are mostly good. My brother is just passionate, that's all. And passion has its upsides as well as its downsides. It . . ." She taps her hand on the open door. "It evokes tremendous generosity and tremendous hurt. Esben is in the hurt right now. It's a momentary price to pay when his payoffs are so big. Give me a few, okay? He'll be fine. This is not the first time he's exploded over this stuff, and it won't be the last."

His laptop is on the floor, and I pick it up to see how badly he's damaged it. When I grab the base, the screen falls off at the hinges, and glass shards spill onto the floor. After I've gone over the carpet at least four times with the dorm vacuum, I put away the food that Kerry and I'd been eating. Then I sit on the ugly orange couch and wait.

And wait. For much longer than I would have thought.

I miss Simon. Maybe I should catch a ride with Esben and Kerry and go see Simon this week after all. I allow myself to be distracted by these thoughts because I am so discomforted and unsettled by everything else going on. I hate that the boy I love so deeply is in the midst of a clear crisis.

Forty-five minutes after they left my room, Esben and Kerry return, with Esben looking much more together. My body sheds its tension.

Esben is barely through the door when he says, "Allison, I am really sorry. I was being crazy—"

"Stop. It's okay. Don't apologize. Don't." I touch the place next to me on the couch, and he sits. "I can't imagine what it's like to do what you do, on the scale you do. That's really intense, and I'm sure it can feel . . . useless. That you're fighting against too much."

"It does."

"One negative thing seems like it overrides a thousand positives. In a sea of love, all you see is the one person drowning."

His defeated face is unfamiliar. "Yes."

Kerry seats herself on the floor and looks up at him. "If you don't want to do this anymore, or if you want to take a break, that's all right."

His body language, the way he emotes his internal struggle . . . it's brutal to watch. Esben is at a loss; that's clear.

He's thoughtful before he says anything. "I think I should. I'm not sure I have a choice. This has all gotten out of hand, and I can't control it. I guess I've never been able to, but with all of these followers now . . ."

"I know," Kerry agrees. "Since the fall, your following has grown so fast. You're at over seven hundred thousand on Twitter. That's insane. And no one can have that kind of online presence and not take on a whole bunch of assholes in the process. It's not fair, it's not cool, and it's discouraging."

Sorrow and pain are visible in him. "The BS is all louder than anything else right now. That's the opposite of what I intended." He grabs his sister's hand. "And, Kerry, that's not your fault. You were doing too much before. Shielding me. I see that."

"So get off-line," she offers. "Just get off-line."

"Allison, are you okay with this?" He turns to me with so much more worry than he should have.

"Absolutely," I tell him. "I don't want you to be unhappy. This is supposed to be fun and . . . it's supposed to spread love. And make you feel good, too. If it doesn't—then get out."

He clasps my hand in his and takes a hard breath. "Okay. Okay."

My phone rings, and the melody of the particular tone sends chills through me. I tense and throw my free hand against Esben's arm, pulling at his shirt and fumbling for speech. "No. God, no." Every part of me is shaking and screaming, yet I am barely able to get these words out.

"What?" he asks.

"Allison?" Kerry is by my side.

Before my eyes fill with tears and I can't see straight, I look at the caller ID and confirm what I know to be true. "It's Steffi's number. Esben? It means someone . . ." Christ, I cannot breathe. "Someone is calling to . . . tell me . . ." There is no way to finish the sentence. And I cannot pick up this call.

The room starts to spin, and I hand him the phone.

"You want me to answer for you? You sure?" he asks gently.

I nod.

"Hello?"

His voice sounds funny, muffled by the deluge of panic swirling through my head, and I can't hear anything else he says. I'm just trying to breathe. It's not until he shakes me by the shoulders, saying my name sharply, that I refocus.

Esben is on his knees, in front of me now. "It's Steffi on the phone," he says.

I stare at him, unable to process those simple words.

"She's called. She wants to talk to you."

I shake my head, confused.

"Allison? Steffi is on the phone, and she's asking for you. This is real. Talk to her."

"What? What?" I clap a hand over my mouth to stifle the sob that threatens to break through. I look at Esben with desperation and hope and fear.

He makes me take the phone and whispers, "It's all right. But she needs you."

"Steffi?"

"Allison."

Oh God, she sounds so weak.

"I'm here, and I love you," I tell her instinctively.

"I love you, too. So much." It's an effort for her to speak, I can tell. "I made a mistake."

It's so hard not to cry. "What do you mean?"

227

"I thought I wanted . . . to do this alone, but I don't."

"Okay. Okay." Because I must force myself to cope as I never have before, I stand up and walk the room, running my hand through my hair. "Tell me what you need. Anything." Then I stop and look at Esben.

He is on high alert and nods confidently at me. Whatever I have to do, he'll help.

"I don't have long, Allison. I can feel it. The nurses know it, too." Steffi's crying breaks my heart, yet again. "I don't want to go without you. I really need you."

"I'm coming. I'll get a flight. I'm coming, I promise." But as I say this, I realize the problem I'm about to run into, and Esben's stricken expression tells me that he agrees. "I will be there," I tell her anyway. "You just hang on, okay? Just hang on."

"Thank you."

"I'll call you when I get a flight."

"My nurses . . . are Rebecca and Jamie." Her breathiness carries through the phone. "I'm sleeping a lot. So, they may answer. I'll have one of them text you their numbers. I'm at Cedars-Sinai."

"Okay, honey. I'm leaving now. I'll get to you. I *will* get to you." It takes all my willpower to hang up and even more willpower not to fall apart. "Steffi wants me there. It's almost over."

"I heard." Esben takes me in his arms and rubs my back. "The airline strike. *And* it's spring break. We have a problem."

I push away and look at him, panicked. "There's no way I can reach her. What am I going to do?"

He smiles sweetly at me. "I said we have a problem, not that we can't do this. Kerry?"

She's next to us in a flash. "I'm ready. Tell me what you need."

"Start checking flights out of Bangor and out of Boston. Try Manchester, New Hampshire. Anything. We're getting to LA. One way or another."

"You're coming with me?" I drop my head against him in appreciation.

"I think we're going to have to finagle one hell of a trip, and it'll be easier if I'm there. That is, if you want me to come, of course."

"I do. I don't think I can do this without you."

"You could, but you don't have to," he says as he hugs me. "I need a picture of her. Do you have one on your computer that you can send me?"

"Yes. Why?"

"Just do that, then throw a few things in a backpack, and let's go. I'm driving us . . . somewhere. Kerry? How are things looking?"

"Gimme a minute, gimme a minute . . . I'm trying to find something . . ." She's shaking her head, though.

"Is Danny around?" he asks.

"No, he left for home already."

"Then get Jason. We need him. I'll do a post, and you monitor Twitter, and Jason can stay on Facebook."

Kerry gives him a friendly shove. "You're not messing around if you're bringing in Jason."

"Shut up. You know I love him."

"Wait, what's happening?" I'm nearly speechless. "What are you doing? You're posting this?"

"If you're okay with it, it's the best way." His arm goes around my shoulders, and he kisses the top of my head. "There are hundreds of thousands of people out there who are going to hear about this. And they are going to help us reach Steffi."

"Two minutes ago, you were going to get off-line. You can't possibly think this will work. God, Esben, it's one thing to get help for a kid's party. Or to adopt a dog. But there's no way even you can do this."

"Yes, there is." He squeezes me tightly. "Watch me."

"What about . . . you two are supposed to go home tomorrow."

"Our parents will understand," Kerry says. "They know us. They know Esben."

"Thank you. Thank you both, so much." I look between these amazing people. "I don't know what else to say. You guys are—"

"We love you," Kerry says firmly. "And we're going to get you to Steffi."

"We will," Esben agrees. "Send me that picture; then we're leaving."

My emotions are trying to take over. "What if . . ." Dammit, this hurts. "What if we don't make it in time? What if—"

"Don't talk like that," he insists. "We will get there. Listen to me. We will."

I hope he's right about that. He has to be.

CHAPTER 27

#ALLISONANDSTEFFI

Esben's post has exploded. He had to break it into a ton of tweets to get it all up on Twitter, but that's probably good for exposure anyway.

My friends, I need to ask for your help. #girlfriendallison has a best friend, Steffi. A best friend who has been Allison's support through hell and back, especially while growing up in the rocky and often scary and unstable foster-care system. Many of us understand what it means to be lucky enough to have a true, hard-core friend, and Steffi has been Allison's saving grace over and over.

With a heavy heart, I am asking for your help.

Steffi is in the final stages of a brutal cancer, AML. It's imperative that we get Allison to her as soon as possible so that these friends can be together when Steffi leaves this world. We need to make it to Cedars-Sinai in Los Angeles as quickly as possible. Between the airline strikes and spring break, we need your help. Starting this journey now from Landon, Maine. Please use the hashtag #allisonandsteffi if you can help. Thank you in advance, and love you all.

He's attached a beautiful picture of Steffi and me, and I'm torn between looking at it constantly and never wanting to see it again. She is healthy and vibrant in the photo, and I know she won't look anything like this when I get to her. *If* I get to her.

An hour into the drive, I've accepted that I cannot keep up with the three of them. Esben, Kerry, and Jason are alternately silent and rapid-firing back and forth as they track comments and try to make a plan. There's talk of too many airports, too many cities, too many time slots. Mention of trains and rental cars and overnight stays that will never get us there while there is any life still running through my friend and hero. I'm terrified that I won't be able to give Steffi what she needs in her final hours.

Final hours. I want to vomit at those words.

"Stop jumping so far ahead!" Esben shouts. "I don't want to hear about what could happen if we randomly got to Orlando, okay? Or about that person in Phoenix who will throw us in a wheelbarrow and run us to a bus station. Subway schedules in random cities do nothing! That's not helping! We've got seats on a flight from Bangor to Chicago. That's cutting it close, but let's assume that will work. So get us from O'Hare to a second location, preferably directly to Los Angeles. Give me two steps at a time, max."

I take a break from staring out the window and set my hand on his shoulder. "Esben, they're trying their best."

"I know, I know." He looks into the rearview mirror. "I'm sorry, guys."

"Chicago is a huge start," I remind him. Steffi sent me ten heart icons when I messaged her this news.

Two generous, incredible sisters from Colby College, on their way home for break, are meeting us at the Maine airport to give us their seats. They've already arranged this with an airline agent, and I have tweeted them five times already to thank them.

I call Simon, and he picks up immediately. "I'm up to speed. What can I do? You have the credit card I gave you for emergencies. Use it for whatever you need."

"Okay. Thank you so much." Something about hearing his voice weakens my resolve not to cry. "But I'm not sure that will help."

"I know," he says sympathetically. "But it's there. Don't worry about the expense. This is Steffi we're talking about."

"Thank you. I had to call you . . . I just . . ."

"It's all okay. I love you, and I love Steffi. I know you're going to be rushed and crazed, but don't forget that I'm here. You tell me if you need anything at all."

"I will." I'm back to looking out the window.

"I'm texting her, and she's writing back," he tells me. "Just so you know."

"Simon? I love you."

I have to hang up before I crack.

The flurry of talk in the car is more than I can absorb, and I check out Twitter and Facebook to see if I can help out at all. It only takes a few minutes of scrolling to understand how difficult this will be. There are tons and tons of replies and hashtag comments, including a substantial portion that send love out to Steffi and me. Ones from people who have been in similar situations, on the brink of losing a best friend. The outpouring of support in such a short time is mind-boggling and incredibly touching. Excruciating, but touching, still. The problem, though, is that right now what we need is practical help.

"Do a new post," I say, but they're so busy talking and trying to plan that they don't hear me. "Guys, we need a new post!" I say more loudly.

"Why?" Esben asks.

"Because this last one is clogged with . . . with good wishes. It's all so sweet, but we need a post for solely practical offers of help."

"You're right. Dammit, I should have thought of that. Kerry, log on as me and post again. Thank everyone for their kind words, but ask that this thread be only for logistics and stuff. Tell people that we'll do a new post for each leg of this trip. Letting people know where we are, and if we have a next step planned."

"Gotcha."

Jason's hand rests on my shoulder. "You holding up okay?"

I nod. "For now, yes."

"Atta girl."

There is some quiet while the new posts go up, and I flip off the radio, because every song sounds like a funeral to me right now.

"Oh hell," Esben suddenly says.

"What?"

But the sputtering noise from the car answers, and Esben pulls off to the side of the road. We're out of gas. He hits the steering wheel hard three times. "I cannot believe I did this."

"We left so fast . . . ," I offer. "None of us thought to check."

We all sit, unmoving and unspeaking, for a few minutes, and I know that we're all thinking the same thing: we're on a single-lane road, and there hasn't been much traffic.

As Steffi would say, God save the queen; we've got a problem.

Jason is the first to talk. "AAA will take too long. Let's see how far a gas station is from here. I'm a fast runner."

"Nine miles," Kerry says a minute later. "Near the airport."

"Post this." My fingers are nervously strumming against the windowsill. "Esben, post our location."

"Allison, we're kind of in the middle of nowhere. I don't know if—"

"Post it," I say more assertively.

"Okay, okay." Esben takes his phone from Kerry.

"Do you have paper or something for a sign that says we need gas?" Kerry asks as she opens her door.

Esben pops the trunk. "I think there's a cardboard box in the back. I don't know about a pen, though."

"Lipstick," she answers. "I have five lipsticks in my purse."

Kerry and Jason stand outside with their rudimentary sign, while Esben and I both stare at our phones. My stomach flies into knots every time a car passes, and after ten cars go by with no help, I start to shake my head. This isn't going to work.

Suddenly, Esben lights up. "Boom!" He turns to me and smiles. "Someone is coming." He hops out of the car, and I follow.

"Seriously?" I'm in disbelief. "Someone is bringing us gas?"

"Red pickup truck. A teenager and his dad. From that direction." He points behind us.

My heart pounds while we wait. We're cutting this really close, and I hope to God we can make it to the Bangor airport in time. Then, like a rescue beacon, a rusty red truck emerges from behind the slight hill of the road, and we all erupt in cheers. It flies toward us so fast that I'm afraid they're not going to stop, but the driver whips in front of Esben's car, revealing a teen boy in the truck bed, who triumphantly raises two plastic gas containers.

"Hey!" The boy's face is flushed as he holds out one of the containers. "This enough for you?"

Esben takes one of the gas containers and then shakes the teen's hand. "You must be Finn. Dude, you're amazing. Yeah, this is more than enough to get us to a gas station. I'd love to talk, but . . ."

"Fill 'er up, kid!" the father calls from his driver's seat.

Esben and Kerry begin to refuel us, and I go to shake Finn's hand. To my surprise, he leans over the truck bed and hugs me. "I saw the tweet. I couldn't believe we were nearby, and we'd literally just been getting gas for lawn equipment." He's holding me so tightly. "My mom died from cancer nine years ago. I hope you make it to your friend. I can't imagine if I couldn't have been with my mother."

Now I squeeze him back. "I don't know how to thank you."

"You don't have to."

"I do." I pat his back and pull away. "I'm going to thank your father, too."

"Don't," he says seriously. "He's having a hard time right now. It's a reminder . . . just . . ." Finn tries to smile. "Just be with Steffi. That will make my dad happy."

I nod and touch his arm. "I'm going to do everything I can."

"Ready!" Jason calls. "Let's go!"

We get back in the car. In front of us, the red truck beeps four long honks, and the father holds his muscular left arm out the window and pumps a fist at the air, wishing us luck. Then he blasts away, smoke and dust billowing behind him.

"Floor it, Esben," Kerry says. "Floor it. We can make it to the airport on what's in the tank."

The car screeches as we pull from our spot on the side of the road, and I look at the clock. We won't make this flight. An extra fifteen minutes and maybe we'd be okay. Esben is driving as fast as is responsibly possible, but it won't be enough.

"The flight's going to leave," I say flatly.

"Just hold on." Kerry is on her phone again, typing away. "I'm writing Caroline and Deb, the girls with the tickets . . . okay, they're with a ticket agent. They have to print new tickets with your names and all that. Security is moving really fast, but they're ready to put you at the front anyway."

"Don't think. Just drive," Jason says calmly to Esben. "Just drive."

We say nothing more until Esben pulls up at the small airport and slams on the brakes. We all get out, and he tosses the keys to Kerry as he rounds the front of the car to take my hand. "We'll be in touch. I love you guys."

I start toward my friends, but Esben pulls my hand. "No time. Come on. The flight is supposed to leave in four minutes."

As we rush to the glass doors, I look back to see Jason and Kerry waving. As if I didn't already know how wonderful they are, today has cemented my understanding of that.

We both scan the terminal, and I yank Esben toward the airline's ticket counter.

"Caroline? Deb?" he yells ahead.

Two girls, both with long red hair, wave wildly. "Esben! Allison!" they scream.

We reach them, and one says, "No time to talk. Show the agent your licenses."

We do, and she prints out our tickets in record time. "I'll walk you to security," the agent says. "They're holding the flight for you."

"What?" I could cry. "Oh God, thank you. I'll pay you two back for the tickets. Message me."

"No. It's on us. Just go." The two girls run with us to security, and I try to say something, but they both shake their heads.

"We're sisters, and we were in foster care until we were five. We get the bond," Caroline says.

"Your friend Steffi needs you more than we need anything." Deb's voice cracks.

"I'll never forget this," I call out as I stand in the scanning booth.

"You two rock!" Esben shouts.

We're still holding our shoes as we run to the gate, which is thankfully right outside the security checkpoint. God bless little airports.

There's a flight attendant standing there. "Esben and Allison?"

We nod.

"Welcome to flight six forty-two." She scans our tickets and then motions for us to quickly enter the corridor to the plane. The door slams behind us, and we all walk briskly. "I'm Michelle. Let me know if you need anything."

I assume that our fellow fliers are going to shoot us seething looks for holding them up, but the moment that we are in view of the other passengers, applause erupts. I look to Michelle and Esben with confusion.

"We explained what's going on. They're all behind you," Michelle says. "Let's take off."

I can't believe this, but as we walk down the aisle, people touch my arm, give me friendly nods, and continue clapping. One woman even has tears in her eyes. In a fog, I make it to our row and drop into the middle seat, next to a serious man in a business suit. Part of me is waiting for him to yell at us for delaying the flight, but he gives me a very brief smile before going back to his book.

We buckle our seat belts, and I lean against the headrest as the plane begins to taxi. Esben is rustling in the seat pocket.

"What are you looking for?"

"Damn," he says under his breath, as he flips the plane's info card in his hand.

"What?"

"No Wi-Fi."

"Oh God."

Quickly, he sends Kerry a voice text. "We're going radio silent for almost two and a half hours until we hit our layover in Detroit. Get us from O'Hare to Los Angeles. Do anything you have to, Sis. Anything. I know you can do this. And send Steffi a text and let her know that we're off-line. Stay in touch with her and her nurses, okay, Sis?"

Seconds later, she replies, and it's already soothing to hear how steady she is. "Got it all. I will get you two a flight. Calling Steffi now. Hold tight. Try to sleep, okay?"

The noise from the plane increases, and we quickly pick up speed. The landing gear lifts, and I know that we are officially airborne, legitimately on our way. I'd celebrate, except that our ultimate destination holds no reason to celebrate. I will have to block that out. But I don't know how. I've got too much time, with nothing to do but sit and think. White noise has always been my friend, so I try to focus on the bland sounds that envelop the cabin.

This scenario though? Steffi in a hospital bed? A hospital bed where—I am barely able to think this—she is dying?

Memories of our early days flood my entire being. From my initial dislike to the time I stopped the attack on her to our subsequent sisterhood. I remember so much.

The fact that every single time that I've seen her, she's always somehow managed to look like a dream. She'd find ways to scrape for clothes and makeup when we were younger, and she never failed to look like a million bucks, no matter the circumstances. Steff had a build-it-and-they-will-come attitude.

When she found out that no one had ever read me *Goodnight Moon*, she read it to me every night for weeks. It didn't matter that I was way too old for that book, because Steffi knew that someone should read it to me.

When I changed my clothes in front of her and revealed what she felt was an entirely too lame and boring bra for a fifteen-year-old, she illegally took her foster family's car, drove me to the mall, and used the money she'd made working at a fast-food place to buy me an unnecessarily sexy push-up bra. "It's not okay to be wearing that cotton bullshit!" she'd screamed. "You, my friend, deserve some sexiness."

I still have that bra.

When I woke up with nightmares, Steffi adjusted my pillow and sheets and told me to breathe and to imagine greatness. To envision a glorious and happy future. That's what was coming, she would assure me. This pain was temporary and would soon be in the past.

I never believed her, but she would still lull me back to sleep with her words.

She taught me that no-pulp orange juice was the only orange juice to drink. That deodorant didn't always have to smell like alcohol. That it could smell like grapefruit and lavender, if you looked for the right brand. That thin-crust pizza always won out over deep dish. That memorizing seemingly boring math theorems would be worth it, just to prove that I could. That laughing hard enough to make puking a possibility could happen.

That learning to hate myself less was a real thing.

That water is much, much thicker than blood.

Here on the plane, I squirm in my seat. I don't know whether to lose myself in these memories or shut them out. Maybe I don't have control in that decision.

I am hit with the impending loss I am about to face, and my breathing gets ragged. This was coming—I've known this—but the reality hits me on a new level.

There will never be another Steffi.

The suffering she is dealing with is probably unbearable. It's unclear to me how much physical pain she is in right now, and I imagine she's got to be on a host of meds, so she could be okay . . .

I grip the armrests and make myself take long, deep breaths.

I'm surely tricking myself. Her pain is probably horrific, and that thought is torturous. There is also her emotional anguish, which is surely so much more intense. Her physical pain might outweigh that? I don't know. I don't know anything.

There are no tolerable answers right now.

There are no tolerable thoughts right now.

Every thought that runs through my head feels inadequate or selfish or inconsiderate or frail.

I don't know how to do this.

In a wave of grief, my body involuntarily contracts in a sob, and I begin to cry.

Before even Esben can reach me, the seemingly cold businessman seated to my right sets a hand on my back. This makes me cry harder. "Let it out," he says without looking at me. "Just let it out. It helps." With a shaky hand, he turns the page of his book and doesn't look my way.

So, I let it out, because I can't do anything else. I sob. The man's hand never moves from where it is, even when I collapse into Esben's comforting embrace.

By the time we land in Detroit for our layover, I am drained and covered in snotty tissues. I don't know how I will make it through these many upcoming and interminable hours, but I have to.

From now on, I assert to myself, there is no room for me or what I feel. None. The only thing that matters is getting to Steffi and giving her what I can.

CHAPTER 28

BIKERS AND SURGES

Every second of the flight hurt. The descent was just another step toward Steffi's death, and so my body trembled during the landing in Detroit.

I eat in the terminal. At least I think I do. Esben has gone to get coffee, I'm pretty sure, so I wipe my hands and call Steffi.

I'm relieved when she picks up almost immediately. "You made me a celebrity."

"Oh. I guess we did. I'm sorry about that. Posting was the only way . . . we needed help, Steff. With spring break and—"

"I love it," she says. I know by her tone that she's smiling, but I'm surprised by the strength in her voice. "It's totally badass. I'm . . . I'm following the posts and comments. So awesome. I look hot in that picture."

I laugh genuinely. "You do. You always look hot."

"Not right now. Ignore that when you see me."

"Of course." I check the time. "Our flight to O'Hare leaves soon. I'm going to hang up to help figure out about a next flight. I'll let you know as soon as we find one, okay?"

"Okay. I'm starving. Maybe Rebecca will get me some In-N-Out Burger. A big burger and a strawberry shake would rock. I'm going to ask her."

"You're . . . hungry?"

"Famished. I slept for a while, and I'm feeling much better. You'll have to get In-N-Out when you're here. You'll freak over it. Hey, did you know that all these people are tagging me on Facebook and Twitter? Lots of supercool foster kids. And, like, a gazillion people who have cancer and are rooting for me. So crazy, right? I'm digging this."

"Okay." I'm a little confused. "Love, Esben is back with coffee. I need to see if he's heard from Kerry."

"All right. Tell him thanks for making me famous. I want pictures of everything, okay? And video. Post it all, or at least show me when you get here. I don't want to miss anything. I can't wait to see you. I love you so much, and I've missed you. You'll have to catch me up on you and Esben, but obviously things are supergood." She is rambling so fast that I can hardly keep up. "Oh, one favor? See if he can get Colton Haynes to tweet me. I love that cutie. Oh, oh! Or Norman Reedus! Or Dave Grohl! You know how I love older men! God . . . can you imagine? They're so crazy sexy."

I laugh again. "You got it."

"Off to ask for, like, five burgers. Bye, Allison. Talk to you soon!"

I hang up and look at Esben. "Huh."

"What's up?"

"Something is weird. Steffi is . . . chipper. I'm going to call one of her nurses."

"We're boarding soon, so be quick."

I call Steffi's nurse Jamie, and she answers almost immediately. "Allison," she says warmly. "Steffi gave me your number. I was debating whether or not to call you."

"I just talked to Steffi. She . . . she sounds energetic. And hungry. Sort of happy, even. Is this a good sign? I know she can't really be getting better, but . . ."

There's a brief silence. "This happens on occasion," Jamie explains. "I've seen it plenty. Patients get a burst of energy. A little euphoric. Kind of like an adrenaline rush. It can last a few hours or even a day or longer, but, no, I'm sorry to tell you that it's not a good thing. It's . . . a sign that the end is coming."

"Oh. Okay." I walk numbly into the boarding line.

"But for right now, she's feeling good. This burst she's in, it's because she's very excited to see you. Let's focus on that. It's nice to see her so happy."

"Okay," I say again. "You're going to watch over her?"

"Yes, I promise. Rebecca and I are here all night. Both of us care a lot about Steffi, and we're doing everything to make sure she's comfortable."

"Thank you. That means a lot. Jamie, I have to go. We are boarding now and will land in Chicago at about ten."

"Everyone here is following you guys online. You can do this."

We hang up, and Esben and I work our way to our seats on this second flight.

"Please have Wi-Fi. Please have Wi-Fi," he says over and over.

"Any leads from Kerry or Jason?" I rest my head against the window.

He snatches the card from the seat pocket, and this time he smiles. "Not yet. But we've got Wi-Fi. Why don't you try to sleep a bit, and by the time you wake up, I'm going to have something for you."

I'm too tired and stressed to disagree, so I hand him my coffee. There's no way he's going to do anything but stay online for the duration of this flight, so he needs the caffeine more than I do. "Sleep would be good. Esben?" I can't help but smile. "Steffi would like Dave Grohl and some other celebrities to tweet her."

"Yeah?" He laughs. "I'll see what I can do."

"Also?"

"What is it, sweets?"

I turn my head and look into his eyes. "You're astounding."

He runs the back of his hand over my cheek. "No. The world is astounding. I told you people are mostly good. They really are."

"I just didn't grasp . . ." Words truly fail me. "I couldn't have begun to predict . . ."

"I know," he agrees. "As much wonderful stuff as I've seen before, this outweighs it all. It's the silver lining, maybe."

"It is," I say firmly. "It is."

Just after the captain announces we've reached cruising altitude, I zonk out and sleep dreamlessly, for which I am grateful. I wake to Esben gently shaking me. We've already landed.

"Listen," he says. "The flight attendant is talking about you and Steffi."

I rub my eyes. At the front of the cabin, a woman stands, holding the PA. She catches my eye. "This song goes out to Allison and Steffi. Love and peace from the airline and all of our passengers. We're with you."

Softly and beautifully, she begins to sing "Amazing Grace."

Esben holds my hand, and, together, we listen. I inhale sharply when a few passengers join in and again when I realize that the entire cabin is singing. My heart is simultaneously breaking and soaring. The overwhelming level of humanity and care coming from strangers is simply daunting. Because I know this is important, and that I'll want to see it later, I ask Esben to film it, which he does.

Outside the gate, I find the nearest bathroom, where I splash cold water on my face. I will not cry now. It's not the time.

As I'm drying my hands, I hear Esben call into the women's room. "Allison? We've got to go. Now!"

I move quickly, and I start running beside him without question.

"We have to get to Midway. It's about forty minutes from here," he says. "Flight leaves in fifty-five minutes."

"Oh no."

"We just need to haul ass." He guides us through travelers to a moving walkway where we continue to run and dodge people. "We've got a ride, though, and I think you'll like it."

This airport is frustratingly huge, and it feels like forever before we reach baggage claim. Suddenly, he stops and casts his eyes over the crowd, searching hard.

"What are we looking for?"

He smiles, bends over to both catch his breath and laugh, and then points. "God, this is nuts. But there."

A man in a suit and black chauffeur hat is holding up a sign with our names on it.

"A limo? Is that a limo driver?" This is crazy.

"It certainly is," he says. "It certainly is. Come on."

The man shakes both of our hands quickly. "I'm Leon. The cop outside let me leave the car out front, but he only gave me five minutes. Hurry."

We get outside to the white stretch limo in record time, and even after we pull out of the airport, I'm still not processing what's happening. Dance music is blasting, and I am officially on sensory overload. There are slick black leather seats, colored lights on the ceiling, two bottles of champagne, and . . . garter belts around the bottle necks.

"Leon?"

"Yes, ma'am?"

"This limo? Um, was it scheduled for something else tonight?"

"A bachelorette party, ma'am. The bride-to-be transferred her rental over to you."

"That was very generous of her," I reply. "Please thank her!"

Esben puts his phone in front of me. "You can thank her yourself. She used the hashtag for you and Steffi and wished us safe travels."

I reply to the bachelorette's tweet with a selfie from the inside of the limo. What a crazy sweet thing for her to do. Next, I send a video of me lying down on the seats to Steffi. **Heading to Midway in style!** I write.

Holy crap! she texts back. **I just read about this online. I can hardly keep up with all of the comments. Drink some of that champagne for me!**

"So we have tickets to Los Angeles?" I ask.

Esben nods. "We do. A nice young couple. They just . . . gave up their seats. Just because they're awesome." He sighs with a happiness of sorts. "If you can believe it, the pilot is going to meet us at security and help get us through. He can only wait so long, though. It's going to be tight."

"I can't believe this is working." I'm still in shock.

"I know. I can't either."

We're more than thirty minutes into the ride when Leon says from up front, "Sir? Ma'am? We have a problem."

The car slows to a stop. There are red brake lights everywhere.

Before I have a chance to say anything, Esben is online. He finishes typing and looks at me. "Say a prayer." Then he opens the moonroof and pokes his head out.

"What are you doing? Esben!" I stand, too, and take in the horrendous traffic jam. "Christ. No. No, not now. Please."

"Come on. Come on. Come on." He's facing the cars behind us.

"What are you doing? We're stuck. We're just stuck." I rub my face. "We'll have to . . . hope for a later flight."

"This is the last one out tonight."

"Oh God."

"We're getting on it," he says stubbornly. "Just . . . just wait."

The cars behind us begin to blur into one. This is over. We won't reach Steffi. The honking of horns is deafening, the endless sea of lights depressing. I hear the roar of some kind of engine, but I don't care what it is.

"There!" Esben shouts excitedly. "There!"

I stare in shock as four tough-looking motorcyclists pull up next to us. "You must be Allison and Esben. Heard you two need a lift."

The guys look to be in their midfifties, all with thick graying beards, denim and leather outfits, heavy boots, and bandannas knotted around their heads. Tattoos are everywhere. They're also all wearing sunglasses, despite the time of night.

"Oh boy," Esben says.

"You're definitely posting this insanity," I say with a laugh. "Steffi won't forgive us if we don't."

"You coming or not?" The first biker holds out a helmet.

"We're coming!" I duck down. "Thank you, Leon. Thank you so much." I swing open the door and walk to the biker, who revs his engine. I glance back at Esben, who shakes his head with amused acceptance.

"All set there?" My new driver asks gruffly. "Grab on tight, sweet cheeks. We'll be taking the breakdown lane. Could get a little hairy."

I straddle the bike and clutch on hard to this man's mammoth waist. "Okay. What's your name?"

"Doesn't matter." He revs his engine again. "Here we go."

A surge of fear courses through me, and I shut my eyes for a moment. We are, for sure, speeding, but I'm comforted by the fact that my driver is obviously in total control of his bike as he flies us past unmoving cars. Without these bikers, we'd never make it to Midway. Never.

Just as we pass the area where traffic seems to ease up—there's no sign of an accident or anything, just a damn unexplained traffic clog—a siren rings out behind us.

"Here we go!" my biker cries out rather triumphantly and hits the gas. "Hang on, little lady! Hang on!"

Oh my God.

A motorcycle cop is chasing us.

We bang out a turn, and soon the entrance to the airport is ahead. We screech to a stop, with the police officer's siren still audible but lagging behind.

"Go!" the biker yells at me. "Go, go, go!"

I scramble to get off the bike, and before I can even get my helmet off, he's gone.

I'm still standing on the departure sidewalk when Esben taps me hard on the shoulder. "We need to move. Allison! Now!"

I turn and run with him into the terminal. There's no time to think about what just happened, and we only just make our flight to LAX. After we land, we're picked up by an off-duty Uber driver, then sail to Cedars-Sinai with such ease. Almost too much. Maybe I was secretly hoping for another problem to extend the inevitable, but we are here now. A wave of sadness washes over me.

After hours and hours of chaos, we are here. Our car pulls up at the entrance, and I am unspeakably moved by what I see.

There are at least thirty people outside. Some hold candles, some have signs with **#ALLISONANDSTEFFI**, or **#SCREWCANCER**, or **#BESTFRIENDS**. Some have flowers, stuffed animals, or balloons. They are quiet and sweet and radiating love so entirely that I hardly know what to do as we walk past them. There are hugs and a few soft words. Mostly, there is a circle of serenity. These people are here to guard Steffi against as much pain as they can.

"Will you take a picture for Steffi? She'll want to see this." I am almost numb. The love that has been thrown our way today is immeasurable. And no one wants thanks. No one wants attention for his or her part in getting us here. Every single tag that I've seen today is fueled by nothing but true heart. I stagger a bit as I walk. "Take a picture," I say again.

"Of course," Esben says. "This is beautiful."

When we step through the front doors, I brace myself, preparing to see Steffi soon.

However, I am not prepared to see the two people who call my name from the waiting area. When they reach us, I am breathing hard, seething with anger, rage from past pain that I almost can't control.

"What the hell are you doing here?" I spit out. "How dare you? How *dare* you?"

"Allison," the woman says, with tears in her eyes. She was clearly going to lean in for a hug, but my words stopped her short. "We read about Steffi online. We just happened to be in San Diego. Obviously, we drove up when we heard."

"We were hoping to—" the man starts.

"Hoping to what? What *exactly* were you hoping to do, huh?" I'm near screaming.

"What's going on? Who are they?" Esben touches my arm with concern.

"Cal and Joan Kantor," I say, shooting a venomous look their way.

"Steffi's foster parents?" he says in disbelief.

"Yes. The ones who kicked her out when she turned eighteen." My words are cold.

"Wait, what?" Cal says. "Is that what she told you?"

Joan touches a hand to her forehead. She looks as distraught as I feel. "Oh, Cal . . ."

Her husband takes her hand and collects himself before he speaks. "Allison, that's not what happened. Not at all . . ."

"What do you mean?" My stomach sinks as something clicks.

"We didn't kick Steffi out," he says, struggling not to cry. "We never would have done that."

"She told me . . ." I cannot believe this. And yet I can. "She told me that you didn't want her. Not for the long term. That it wasn't working out."

"Dear God." Joan shakes her head.

"She was scared," I say in a whisper as a new understanding of the past washes over me. "She was too scared to trust you. That was it, wasn't it? Oh, Steff . . ."

"We should have known," Joan says, heartbreak in her voice. "Damn, we should have known. But she was so adamant, so headstrong and sure. Very polite about not wanting to be adopted, but very clear.

249

While we wanted to respect her choice, we tried to convince her. We did everything we could, but—"

I jump in. "But you cannot convince Steffi of anything she doesn't want. And she never wants to feel dependent on anyone else. She *can't.*" I know this all too well. I should have known this would extend to Cal and Joan.

Cal nods. "Yes. Allison, we loved her then, and we love her now. We think of her as our daughter." His face crumples. "She will always, always be our daughter."

I step forward. "I see that. I believe you."

Crushed. I am crushed, because now there is yet another layer of tragedy to Steffi's illness.

CHAPTER 29

TO THE GOODNIGHT MOON AND BACK

The nurses, Rebecca and Jamie, are sweet. Very sweet. They've clearly done this before. So, they do what they can to prepare me before I walk into the room. I hear something about how thin Steffi is, about her coloring being off. About machines and beeps and monitors. About it only being a question of hours. When I press them, Rebecca answers. She's seen enough patients to know, and her guess is soon. Four to ten hours.

Esben waits in the hall, seated on a hard chair. "I'll be here as long as you need me."

I know he will, and it's the only comfort I have.

Cal and Joan are with him. I'm not sure how to tell Steffi that they are here, but I suppose I'll figure it out.

Jamie pushes open the door and walks me in. "I'll be right outside if you need me," she says softly.

"Allison!" Steffi's volume and joy shock and terrify me.

She is sitting up in bed, surrounded by wrappers. The room smells strongly of burgers and fries.

It's all I can do to guard her from my reaction, because the girl before me looks so drastically different from the one who appeared outside my dorm last fall. She is very, very thin, her skin tone near ashen.

Her formerly full blond hair is flattened against her head, stringy and limp. I see bags under her eyes where there were never any.

Everything about her looks totally wrong, and yet it's equally easy to see my best friend. She will always be Steffi, no matter the circumstances.

"Get over here!" She beckons. "God, I can't believe you made it. You've had a crazy day, huh?"

It's the middle of the night, yet she's wide-awake and wired.

"A little bit." I try to sound like a normal human being. "But anything for you."

"I knew you could do it!"

I cross the small private room and lean over to hug her. Seeing how weak Steffi looks is hard to swallow, and I'm hesitant to hold her too tightly. However, she grabs me with more strength than I'd anticipated, and so I respond. It feels so wonderful to hold her after all these months, especially when I didn't think I would ever again.

She pats my back repeatedly until I sit in the chair by the bed. "Now, tell me everything. Tell me about you. And you and Esben."

She makes it hard not to smile, because her enthusiasm is so elevated, and it is so very Steffi to want to talk about me when she's the one in crisis. "What do you want to know?"

Steffi raises an eyebrow in the way that only she can, with a crazy high arch and leering eyes. "Has it happened?"

"What?"

"Have you slept with him?" She says this so loudly that I turn to see if anyone outside the room has heard. Jamie is trying not to laugh.

"Well . . ."

"I'm on limited time, kiddo. Spill."

"Yes."

"And?"

"And . . . it's awesome. He's awesome."

252

"Esben is as cool as I first thought, right?" she says happily. "I was right about him, wasn't I?"

"You were. Very, very right."

For over an hour, she makes me tell her everything that's gone down. So, I update her about Esben and school and Simon. About Simon's care packages, about what's going on with Carmen, Kerry, Jason, and Danny. I tell her much about my new world that she hasn't heard and that I wish she were a part of, could be a part of.

I'm having a hard time keeping my breathing even. Something about having a seemingly routine conversation makes being here all the more frightening. I glance at Jamie, and she gives me a reassuring nod. I should just let this happen; that's what she's telling me.

"Oh, the bracelet!" Steffi says. "Lemme see!" She grabs my hand and gasps. "It's gorgeous. He did so good. He's here, right? Where is he?" She looks over my shoulder. "I know I look like crap, but hello? Hospital. He won't care, right? Also, you haven't commented on my shirt. Simon's doing, of course. Somehow he got this to me today."

I hadn't noticed, but now I look down and smile. She's wearing a red shirt with a Wonder Woman logo on the front. It's perfect.

"They let me change out of that freakin' hideous hospital gown. Or *hospice* gown, if we're being technical. Because that's basically what this is. How depressing, right?"

I don't know how to answer her. How to do any of this. But Steffi keeps talking, so I'm given another moment to pull myself together.

"So, really, where's Esben? I want to see all the videos and pictures he took. Why hasn't he posted more? I've been following everything online. Dude, that limo situation was insane! I can't believe it. Any of it. The only reason I looked away from the Internet was to chow down. You'll try In-N-Out tomorrow, right? Promise me."

"I promise."

"Where's Esben?" she asks yet again. "I want to see more."

Her excitement makes me laugh. "I'll get him."

"Yes!"

It's with caution and nerves that I walk to the door. "Esben? Steffi wants you to come in. To see what other pictures and video you have."

"She does?" He's as taken aback as I am. "Okay. Yeah. Of course."

He follows me into the room, and I see Steffi's eyes fixate on him. She's silent now, waiting until he has pulled up a chair beside me. Steffi leans back against the mattress and looks at him. "Esben," she says softly and reaches out.

"Steffi." He takes her hand.

"It's good to see you." She's quieter now, calmer. "Show me. Show me pictures from today. I want to see . . ." Steffi takes a few shallow breaths that alarm me. ". . . everything. And you have to post it all. This is my moment, right?" She cracks a smile.

"Sure. Whatever you want."

Esben holds his phone up to her and swipes through photos and videos. She asks a hundred questions, and he answers them all. When he gets to the video of the flight attendant singing, Steffi suddenly reaches to her side, but for what, I'm not sure.

"Steffi? What is it?" I ask.

Jamie is at Steffi's side in a flash. "She just needs some oxygen. That's all. It's okay." She moves smoothly as she lifts an oxygen mask over Steffi's mouth.

My hand goes to Esben's leg, and I dig my fingers in.

Steffi holds up a finger, asking us to give her a minute. I nod and rest my hand on her shoulder, letting her know that she can take as much time as she needs. The nervous look she gives Jamie frightens me to the core, but I keep a calm expression. As though it's normal for my best friend, my lifeline, to need help breathing.

It only takes a matter of seconds, a few moments to inhale and exhale, and Steffi nods. She lifts the mask for a second. "Show me more."

Esben seems cautious when I say, "Show her the flight attendant. The singing."

"Yeah? Okay. You sure?"

"Yes. She'll love it." Steffi and I both know that she's dying. That it's close. And this song and its haunting melody will not make her aware of anything she doesn't know.

Steffi puts the oxygen mask back over her mouth and watches. Halfway through, she holds out her arm. I take her hand. I won't let go from this point on. Whatever high she's been on, whatever adrenaline was amping her up, is gone.

We are downhill from here.

"'Amazing Grace.' I love . . . that song. Such a pretty voice." Steffi's words are barely audible behind her mask, but, still, I hear her. "All those nice people."

"Everyone cares about you," I tell her.

She turns her head, and I can see the smile around her eyes.

"Get ready for this one," I say with as much fun in my voice as I can. "You will never believe it. Trust me. Esben, show her what happened getting from O'Hare to Midway!"

For a few minutes, Steffi watches, though her eyes are getting foggy. It's subtle, so subtle, but I see it.

"A motorcycle? You got on a motorcycle?" She lifts the mask to talk.

"I know, right? So cool." More false positive attitude. "It was insane."

"Allison handled herself much better than I did," Esben adds.

Steffi puts her other hand in his and takes a few deep breaths. Then she lowers the mask and speaks to him. "Esben?"

"Yes?"

"You love her?" she asks.

Esben smiles reassuringly. "I do."

"I knew that. But it's good to hear. Good." She breathes again for a time. "Thank you. Thank you. It . . . it . . . makes this easier. Allison?" she whispers.

"Yes, honey, what?"

"It hurts. God save the queen, it hurts." She'd smile if she could, but she can't.

"God save the queen," I agree. "God save the queen."

"I'm, uh . . ." She shuts her eyes for a second. "I'm ready for this to be over. I'm really ready."

"I know."

"I'm sorry. For what I did."

"There's no sorry here, only love."

She nods.

I don't know how to tell her what I have to. But it's time. "There are a few other people here to see you," I say gently.

Slowly, she turns her head, but doesn't say anything.

"Esben? Can you . . . ?" I can't take my eyes from Steff, and I watch him kiss Steffi on the cheek.

He holds his sweet kiss for so long that I know it's good-bye. And his good-bye is very important, because Steffi knows my connection to him and what he's done to get me here. I feel extraordinary pain lingering in my heart, though I block it out. I'll let it hurt later.

Blind now, because I cannot see through my bleary eyes, I hear the door swing open and shut, and then there are footsteps, and I know Cal and Joan have moved into the room.

"These are people who love you," I say. I blink and try to clear my vision. "Please don't be upset with me."

A wash of emotion rushes over her pale face, and she lifts a hand to cover her eyes.

"They love you," I say. "It's all okay. They love you. They want to be here for you."

Steffi starts to panic and flounders for me, yanking her oxygen away. "They're mad." She begins to cry. "They're mad, aren't they?"

"No, no, no." I replace her mask. "Listen to me. You listen to me very clearly. No. They love you. You are their daughter. They are your parents. And they are here."

Her eyes water so much that my heart further shreds. But she nods, and behind her tears, I can see tremendous relief. I can see peace.

"Steffi?" Joan says from the other side of the bed.

"You are our joy." Cal's voice is steady, steadier than it should be.

Steffi turns her head.

Nobody moves, but then, with clear effort, she inches an arm their way. Both sit and lean against the bed so that they are as close to her as possible.

Joan smiles. "We love you, do you hear me? We love you."

Steffi starts to protest and gropes for something by the bed. Jamie again gets to her and hands her something.

"It's a morphine drip," Jamie explains to us quietly. "Steffi can hit it when she needs pain relief."

When Steffi hits that button three times, it's impossible to watch and impossible for my heart and my soul not to feel savagely ripped apart.

"I'm sorry for what I did," Steffi says with a rasp.

"No." Cal shakes his head. "No, you did nothing wrong. No apologies."

It takes a bit, but Steffi nods.

Joan is upset, but she hides it well. "I know that you're apologizing in your head. Don't, okay? We are all together now, and that's what matters. We are your mom and dad, as we have always been. You've never been without us, and you never will be. It's very simple."

Steffi's smile is as broad as she can make it right now, and Cal and Joan both bend over to hold her. It's only then that I notice the IV in her arm, presumably for the morphine.

I feel as though I should maybe step out of the room and give them some time, but I know there might not be much, and I can't stand to leave. Plus, Steffi's hold on my hand, while weak, is steadfast. So, I stay.

For a long time, we all just sit with her. Later, she brushes away the oxygen mask.

"Joan? Remember the . . . curtains you put up for me?" It clearly takes effort for her to say even this. "Sheers. White. With stars."

Joan touches Steffi's face. "I do remember."

"I loved those. You did something . . . so nice. For me." Steffi's face doesn't change, but we all know that she's hitting upon a good memory. "Very pretty."

"I'm glad you liked those." Joan sounds so motherly that it makes my heart ache. "We have pictures of you all over the house. And your room is still your room. We haven't touched it."

"So sorry . . ." Steffi is getting weaker. "So sorry I wasn't better. Smart enough to know . . ." She looks agitated, as much as she can now. "I should have said yes. Chosen you."

"No." Cal's voice conveys only intense sincerity and gentleness. "No. You did what you could. You made the choice that you felt was right at the time, and no one could ever fault you for that. We get why you couldn't trust us. Joan and I get it." He rubs a finger under his eyes. "That doesn't matter. What matters is that we are a family. Okay?" He forces a smile. "Do you hear that we adore you? That you're our daughter? Because that's the truth."

A new level of comprehension and acceptance sweeps over her. I can see it. I can see that Steffi takes in their love.

"Thank . . . you." Steffi shifts a bit, clearly in pain. "I love you both, too. I do." She hits the morphine button.

When she settles and looks my way, I find myself shifting to another emotional state, to a new kind of peace, to a harbor where there is nothing but the two of us. The sterile, monotone, scary hospital room recedes into nothingness.

It's coming.

I crawl into her bed, laying my body next to hers. She has always held me, but tonight, I hold her.

"Allison . . ."

"It's okay, Steffi. It's okay."

"Before I forget . . . there are some things I have to tell you. Final things."

Inside, I scream. I rail against this. But I won't let her hear that. "Anything."

"My ashes. I don't want . . ." She struggles for breath. "I asked for ashes. But I don't want to be in some gross urn. We clear? You scatter my ashes in the ocean."

"I'll do anything you want." Emotionless, I'm about the practical now. I have to be. "California or anywhere?" I touch her hair. "Simon and I are going to the Cape or the Vineyard this summer. Would you want that?"

There's a long pause. "The Vineyard. That's perfect."

"Then that's what we'll do."

"And—"

"And Cal and Joan will come with us, yes," I say for her. "Yes."

"Absolutely," Cal says.

She squeezes my hand lightly. "Esben."

"Him, too," I confirm.

"Not . . . sad. Okay?" Steffi looks at me with hope.

"No, we won't be sad that day, my beautiful girl," Joan answers when I cannot. "We will celebrate how much joy you brought us all. It will be a day of celebration, not of tears."

Steffi looks peaceful after those words, and her eyes grow heavy. "After this. When I'm gone. You'll be okay, though, right?"

"I will," I promise her. "Do *not* worry about me. Please don't. I will miss you forever, but I will get through this. You told me to be brave, and I can do that."

"Promise?"

"Yes." I hate lying to her, but I have to. "The only thing that matters right now is that I love you. And that you trust that I am strong. It's time for you to trust that, okay? Steffi, you are my heart, and I will always love you. To the goodnight moon and back. Always and forever."

She breathes through the mask for a while. "I'm so tired . . . Allison? I just want to sleep for a little," she says behind the flow of oxygen. "Do you mind?"

"You sleep as long as you want."

Slowly, she looks at Cal and Joan and then back to me. "You'll be here when I wake up? I'm so sorry . . . I just need a little nap."

"We will be here when you wake up." Because I have to be a rock right now, I do not cry when I say this. "We will be here. So, you sleep, Steffi. Just sleep. And have beautiful, wondrous dreams."

Steffi smiles a little, then taps her mask, and I lift it. "My mom and dad came," she says in a whisper.

"They did," I agree.

My frame is pressed against hers, and I know what it means that Steffi's nurses don't move me from my position. Cal and Joan are both bent over the bed, their love a blanket, flowing smoothly over her, around her.

Steffi is so devastatingly weak now. "Love you . . . moon and back."

She sleeps, half waking too many times. But mostly she is unaware over the next hours that pass, and it's all that I could ask for. I'd hate for her to be cognizant. *She* would hate to be cognizant. So, Cal, Joan, and I just stay with her. That's all we can do.

When she can't, I adjust her oxygen mask.

When she can't, I hit her morphine drip as much as is allowed.

When she can't, I talk and tell her she doesn't have to. I tell her that I know and feel it all. And that she should, too. That it's okay not to talk anymore. That she is my forever friend. That she is Cal and Joan's forever daughter.

For a time, she just sleeps and breathes. And then, finally, she sleeps and doesn't wake again.

I'm glad that she misses the end. That she's not awake for the moments before her death.

And when the monitor sounds, when her breathing stops, Joan and Cal and I are all holding her.

She does not leave this world alone.

She leaves this world whole.

CHAPTER 30

THE WORLD HAS CHANGED

It's just after eight in the evening when I wake in a hotel room, disoriented and numb. I've been in a hard, dreamless sleep, and it takes me a few minutes to remember where I am and what has happened.

I should be crying, feeling something. But I am utterly emptied. It's some warped form of bliss to find myself in this state. It must be misguided and delusional, I know, but it's a blessing.

Esben is in a small armchair, looking weary as he scrolls through his phone. He glances up when I throw back the sheets and sit up in bed. "Hey. How are you doing?" He comes to sit beside me. "Dumb question, sorry."

"No, it's fine." I rub my eyes. "I'm going to take a shower. Are you hungry? I'm starving. We should eat."

"Sure." He tries to touch my leg, but I move away. "Whatever you want."

"We're supposed to go to In-N-Out Burger. I promised her," I say diligently.

"Okay. Then that's what we'll do."

I plod to the bathroom and shut the door. I strip down and look at the pile of clothing I've left on the floor, resolving to burn it when I get home. My clothes and my body smell like death, and I didn't bring anything else to wear. It's only crazy determination that makes me stand up straight and look in the mirror. I want some idea of what I look like, a baseline from which I must rise. My reflection is shocking. I don't look like me, and not just because of my puffy eyes and matted hair. I just don't look like me. Maybe I won't ever again. Not after last night.

The tile in the shower stall seems off, the water that sprays over me feels too sharp, and the smell of the shampoo and soap makes me want to gag. Everything is wrong. Everything, I know, will always be wrong.

This fact is not alarming to me, though. It's just a fact. Cut and dry. So, when I finish my shower and dress in my tainted clothing, I do so calmly.

When I emerge from the bathroom, Esben smiles weakly at me. "You ready? There are about six locations within spitting distance from the hotel."

"I don't care. Any one is fine." My hair is barely towel dried, and water leaks down my back.

"Okay. We can go outside and see what direction we feel like going in." He waves his phone at me. "The guy who gave us this hotel room wrote to make sure everything is good. Said we should order room service or whatever we want. If you're hungry for breakfast in the morning—"

"Esben," I say flatly. "It was very nice of him. Please thank him for me. But . . ." I take an exhausted breath. I barely have the energy to walk from this room, and I certainly don't have the energy to engage in conversation. "I don't want to talk. I'm sorry. Let's just get this burger thing over with."

He nods. "That's all right. I understand."

The pattern on the hall carpet seems to shout at me, and I look straight ahead as we walk. There are mirrors in the elevator, and I again think how totally unfamiliar I look. Esben also appears a virtual stranger. I know this is wrong, but there is no emotional impact from these revelations, just belief in the truth I've uncovered.

The entire world has changed. *So, there we go. That's all.*

The short walk we take outside feels arduous, as though I am in the final mile of a marathon and not walking a mere few blocks. We order burgers and shakes, and I eat without tasting. Esben is quiet, and I'm grateful for that. Part of me recognizes that I am a zombie right now and that I'm acting strangely, but part of me wants to dive deeper into this nothingness.

The benches and table are hard and unforgiving. I crumple up wrappers, and the noise makes my ears pound. My fatigue hurts. "I'd like to go back to bed now."

Esben looks sad and worried, and he's probably at a loss for how to handle me. I wish I could tell him not to be any of these things. That I'm all right, because I am now half-dead myself and not feeling much of anything. But it would take too much to form these words. I'm not even sure how I'll make it back into bed.

But somehow I do. I get into bed with my clothes on, and then I start neurotically smoothing down the bedding. *I have not lost my skill sets. I can compartmentalize, shut down, and protect myself the way I always have.* The alternative is surely a path to a whirlwind of grief, but I'm going to be okay, because I have managed to rebuild my walls in a matter of hours. This thought makes me smile. I am safe.

I shut my eyes and fall asleep immediately.

At five Sunday morning, I awaken and know immediately that I won't get back to sleep. This is unfortunate, because sleeping is really quite a wonderful escape from life. Esben is out cold, and I hope he can sleep in. He stirs slightly when I kiss his cheek but, fortunately, doesn't wake. I know I love him, and I wish I could feel that right now, but my current vacant heart is an inevitable by-product of my protective armor.

We need to somehow find flights home, and I might as well get a start on that, so I grab my phone and get online. To my relief, the airline strike apparently ended at midnight last night. *Of course.* A day earlier would have been goddamn nice. It only takes a quick search to find a number of flight options for this afternoon.

Although I still have countless people to thank on social media, the idea of going on Twitter or Facebook is daunting, so I drop my phone in my purse. In a haze last night, I asked Esben to post online and tell people it was over and that Steffi was out of pain. The replies will be too difficult to take right now.

Then I remember something.

I have Steffi's phone.

Her nurse Rebecca gave it to me, I think. Robotically, I rummage through my purse until I find it. I'm grateful for the few seconds it takes to turn on, because I have an opportunity to breathe and prepare myself. For what, I don't know. It's just her phone, but it's hers, and it feels monumental. I click on the Internet icon to see what she looked at last. It's impossible not to laugh when I see an Amazon page confirming her purchases to be sent to the girls in her old apartment: a tube of small toy dinosaurs, some cooling hemorrhoid wipes, and a paperback guide to the back roads of Arkansas.

In her photo album are pictures from her trip to see me last fall, and I swipe through these quickly, because I will not drown in images of a life that no longer exists. Not now, maybe not ever. I lazily hit her text messages. I'm hoping she had supportive friends, that she hadn't entirely closed herself off. My messages are at the top, and I swipe past what are clearly confirmation texts for doctors' appointments, but then I stop, because something else has caught my eye.

A name. A name that is so familiar to me that I didn't even see it at first.

Esben Baylor.

My heart pounds when I hit the text thread.

I scan the last messages from just a few weeks ago.

Are you sure she's doing okay? Steffi wrote. **You promise?**

She is, really. This is all difficult still, obviously, but she's honestly doing well. I know it took a while after the call, but Allison is tough.

I scroll up to an earlier point in the thread. From Christmas Day.

Is Allison's Christmas fun? she asks him. Are you seeing her tonight? What did you give her? What did she give you? Did you love meeting Simon?

Esben answered with a long, detailed reply, telling Steffi everything she could possibly want to know about winter break until that point. He told her how beautiful I looked in the red sweater Simon bought me, about the trifle mishap, Christian and their dance, about our plans for New Year's Eve . . . everything.

I scroll up again. There is a picture of the bracelet he picked out for me, and he asked Steffi if I would like it.

The words grow blurry in front of me, and I shut my eyes for a moment. When I open them, I scroll back until I reach the beginning of their conversation.

It takes me an hour to get through all of Esben and Steffi's messages to each other. What I read rips out what's left of my heart.

It's after ten in the morning when Esben wakes, and I am still frozen in this chair. My anger and sadness have had hours to spread their venom into my heart.

"Hey," he says hoarsely. "You been up long?"

Slowly, I turn to him. I cannot hide the pain on my face. I don't want to. "Esben, what have you done?" My voice breaks, but I resolve not to fall apart.

He rubs his eyes. "What are you talking about?"

I lift the phone in my hand. "This."

Esben shakes his head. "Your phone? What?"

"This isn't *my* phone."

It takes a second for this to sink in, and Esben drops his head and takes a big breath before looking at me again. "That's Steffi's, isn't it?"

I nod.

He starts to stand, but I stop him. "No, stay there." My voice shakes.

"Allison, let me explain."

"You don't need to explain, Esben. It's all right here. I read every message. Steffi went to see you when she was with me at Andrews. The night she went out to pick up Chinese for us, I remember that she was gone way too long . . . she went to you then, didn't she? And she told you that she was sick, that she was going to die."

"Yes," he says somberly.

"And then she asked you to look after me. To get close to me."

He hesitates. "Essentially. But it was because she wanted—"

"I know what she wanted. She knew that I was alone, so she wanted me to have someone. She saw the video, and she decided to push us together. Steffi also knew the kind of person you are. That you could never say no to something like this, right? You wouldn't do that." I look out the window at the glaring sunshine. "You wouldn't turn down a dying girl's request," I state factually.

"No, it wasn't like that," he says strongly.

"She set this up. From the minute she saw that video of us, she hatched this plan. So, this supposed relationship you and I have?" Now I turn to him with hurt and unbearable sorrow. "This relationship didn't happen the way I thought. Not at all. It was an obligation that you had to fulfill. You . . . you made me believe in so much, but none of that really existed, did it? It's like this was your biggest, grandest, most selfless social experiment, huh? But I know you . . . that can't be right. Please tell me that can't be right."

"Of course that's not right." Despite my putting my hands up to stop him, Esben crosses the room and kneels beside me. "You know as well as I do that there was something very real that happened between us *before* Steffi came into the picture. You *know* that, Allison. I didn't know how to handle it when Steffi showed up at my door. I mean, what was I supposed to do? I tried to convince her to tell you what was going

267

on, but she was adamant. I just . . . I told her what she wanted to hear, but I only meant that . . ." He shakes his head. "I don't know. You know that I pretty much fell in love with you the moment I met you. And everything we've built together? Steffi could never make that happen. *You and I* made that happen. This is real."

"And this whole time"—I am so confused that I can hardly hear what he's saying, and I can hardly speak—"this whole time, you knew. *You knew she was sick for months before she told me.* If I'd known what she was facing, maybe I could have done something. I might have flown out here and ignored the way she was deflecting me. Simon might have been able to convince her. Something. Maybe you loved me, but you still didn't give me any options." It's so hard not to cry. "You did what the dying girl wanted."

He shakes his head hard. "I would never want to hurt you. I'm so sorry, Allison. I didn't mean to. I wanted to respect Steffi's choice. You saw the texts. You saw how many times I tried to get her to tell you herself."

"You slept with me and—" I stop myself.

Oh no.

Suddenly, my body flips into a panic, and I stand and walk the room while I piece this together. "Maybe Steffi was right."

"About what?"

I stop and look at him. "We get *one*. She always said we only get one. Remember I told you that? She was absolutely right. I had *her*." I laugh in painful understanding, and I am stretching for air. "I had her, and I switched her out for you. Is that why she died? The world wouldn't let me have you both? If I hadn't listened to her . . ." I see what I've done now.

Esben shakes his head hard. "Allison, that's crazy. You know that isn't true. That is *not* how the world works."

"If there hadn't been a you and me," I say, mostly to myself, "Steffi wouldn't have gotten sick again. She'd be alive."

"No, Allison," Esben says sharply. "Steffi was going to get sick no matter what. You couldn't have controlled that. We don't get to make bargains like that."

He's right. Or maybe I'm right. I have no idea. I suppose it doesn't matter, because Steffi is dead, and nothing will change that.

I pick up my purse. "I have to go," I say numbly. "I have to go home."

"No, please don't leave. You're not thinking clearly, sweetheart, you're not." He touches my arm. "Allison, I love you. I love you with my entire heart. Tell me you believe that."

I'm afraid that I'm going to start crying and never stop, so I swallow back my tears when I look up at him with unbearable sadness. "I do know that. And I love you, too, Esben. But that isn't enough now." My entire being aches like I have never felt before. "Or maybe it's too much. You will always remind me of Steffi's death. I'm grateful, more than I can say, for how you got me to Los Angeles. But I will never be able to look at you and not think about Steff. You will *always*"—now I start to break down—"*always* break my heart because of what we've been through. What we had won't work anymore."

"Allison, no. God, please don't say that." Esben has tears in his eyes as he tries to take me in his arms.

"No, no, please don't touch me." It's all I can do to hold myself together the little that I am. "I have to go. I'm sorry. I'm sorry that I'm all screwed up again."

"You're not making any sense. Please, just sit down, and we will figure this out," he pleads.

"I can't. Esben, I told you ages ago that I was broken. Maybe I wasn't then, but I definitely am now. This will be better for you in the end. I love you so much, but this will be better."

I back away from him. Everything is so confusing, so depressing and terrible. Before I can do something stupid, like change my mind,

I turn and leave the room. This is the only smart choice I have. There will be no recovery for me or for us.

Somehow, I am in a cab on the way to LAX. I call Simon, and when I hear his voice, I desperately want to cry again, but I don't.

"Allison?"

It's seven blocks before I can form words, but he waits. "I need to get home. Dad, I need to get home. Please help me. Please help me. Please help me."

"Get to the airport. I'll find you a flight."

"Please help me," I keep saying.

"I will."

CHAPTER 31

BAKED

For two days, I do nothing but cry and take refuge in my bedroom at home. Bruce Wayne barely leaves my side, snuggling and trying to comfort me. He's big on snoring, and I find the sound oddly soothing. By Tuesday, I am out of bed and probably severely dehydrated, but at least the crying has stopped. Simon has taken the week off work, and he keeps trying to talk to me, but I don't want to talk. I want to bake. Cookies, cakes, layer bars, custards, pies . . . everything.

I just want to bake. No matter how inept I am in the kitchen, that's what we do. That's *all* we do.

On Friday, Simon and I are in the kitchen, surrounded by so many sweets that it looks as though we are in a pastry shop. Bruce Wayne is snoring loudly in the corner of the room, asleep in a very fancy dog bed Simon got him. The only thing I will talk about is how to perfect my icing skills or how to properly hold the bag for piping filling into the profiteroles, and Simon has patiently walked me through all of the recipes that I picked out. But as I am obsessively eyeing the sprinkles I've just put on a cookie, Simon slams down a rolling pin on the board in front of him.

"What? Is something wrong with that dough?"

He sighs loudly and takes off his apron. "Allison? Kiddo, you know how much I love you and that I support you no matter what. In everything that you do. Right? You know that?"

"Yes," I say softly, and I sprinkle another cookie.

He braces his hands on the counter and looks across at me. "But right now, I do not support you in how you're handling things, and I am not going to enable this any longer. If my daughter is doing something unhealthy, then I have to speak up, so that's what I'm going to do."

"You read the texts. I told you everything that happened and—"

"Stop it!" he snaps. "Be quiet, and listen to me. Yes, I read the texts. Yes, I heard your asinine theory about only getting one and about how you think you're powerful enough to have caused Steffi's death by falling in love with Esben. It's ridiculous, and it would be irresponsible of me to say otherwise."

He's making me sound crazy. "I didn't say I was powerful enough—"

"Basically you did. It's called magical thinking. And it's garbage." He pulls over a stool and sits. "My dear, you need to pull it together. Steffi's death? It's a massive loss, it is. Your best friend died. A friend with whom you shared a very tight bond. You are entitled to grieve and be angry and sad and a whole bunch of things. I give you that. What I don't give you is support when I see you walling yourself off again. From me, from Esben, from people who love you. I do *not* support letting you go back to an even darker place than before, especially not after all the progress you made. I saw how happy you were, how you came out of your shell in a hundred ways this year, and I am not going to let you throw that all away. Look, honey . . ." Simon takes the sprinkles from my hand and sits still until I am forced to look at him. "Steffi was wonderful in so many ways. Spirited, dynamic, funny—*so* funny, right?—beautiful, smart, and tough as anyone could be. But maybe too tough." He pauses to let this sink in. "Do you agree?"

I think about this for a while. "Maybe," I admit.

"I think she was. So tough that she pushed you away when she could have used your help. That makes me very sad. Yes, we all had to respect her decision, because she was forceful as they come, but it's still sad. And I think that, while she was a role model in so many ways, Steffi also gave you some very misguided ideas about life. About people. She decided that we only get one special person in life, because that's all she could handle. It made allowing you in and no one else sound reasonable. It made rejecting Cal and Joan sound reasonable. It's unfortunate that she did that to herself. But that's not how you have to be, Allison. You don't have to push everyone away to protect yourself."

I stare blankly at him, unable to respond.

Simon's face softens. "Haven't you been happy this year? Hasn't it felt good to be close with people? I can tell you that I've really enjoyed being with you in a whole new way. Don't go backward, sweetness. Don't. It's a huge mistake. Steffi put Esben in a complete no-win situation. What the hell was he supposed to do, huh? You tell me what you would have done if you'd been him. There was no right choice."

"But"—I know this sounds stupid even as I say it, but I have to get it out—"he wasn't loyal to me when he should have been. It's like he chose Steffi over me."

"That's incorrect. You are not seeing this for what it is. At all. Esben was loyal to her because *you* were so loyal to her. It's kind of a big god-damn weight that she unfairly placed on his shoulders. He couldn't violate her trust, and, because of that, he had to violate yours. Esben had to choose the lesser of two really rotten evils. If you'd stop being so nutty," he says, smiling, "you'd see that."

I sit for a while and think about all of this. "I really freaked out, didn't I?" I finally say.

"Yeah. You certainly did." He snatches a cookie from the tray in front of me and eats it whole. "Look, you might be confused about what Steffi and Esben did. Get over it. They both did what they thought was best for you. They both wanted you to get through this with as little damage as possible. Steffi would most definitely not want you disappearing into a squalid shell again, and she would not want you ending your relationship with Esben. She wanted the opposite."

I notice that the cookies in front of me are getting wet. Apparently, I'm crying on them. "Steffi loved me. For real."

"She did." Simon presses a tissue to my face. "You know that. Listen to your heart."

"And Esben loves me. Also for real." The cookies are about to get drenched.

"Very much."

"I really screwed things up. So bad."

"You had a—" Simon clears his throat, obviously trying to be tactful. "You had a bad reaction. An understandable, bad, regressive reaction to a horrific situation, but one that you can fix."

I look at him in desperation. "What if I can't fix it? What if it's too late?"

"My darling daughter," he says with a smile, "it's only been a few days. Nothing irreparable has happened. The kind of magic that you and Esben have does not evaporate because of a freak-out. Even a freak-out as dramatic as yours."

I'm not sure if this is true or not. I've never had a relationship bordering on the one I have—or had?—with Esben. Except, I realize, I sort of do. "What about you and me?"

"What about us?" Simon is rolling dough again.

"Did I hurt us? With how I've acted?"

"The only harm you've done is make me gain a few pounds, which I don't appreciate because I have a date next week."

"You do?"

He waves a hand dismissively. "Oh, someone I met . . . on Esben's feed. A guy who commented."

I perk up. "One of the people who tagged you with *hotdad*?"

Simon blushes. "Maybe. Yeah. He's my age, though. Not some inappropriately young thing. Very handsome man."

Uselessly, I start patting the wet cookies with a paper towel until Simon takes it away from me.

"Give it up. Those cookies are shot."

I wipe my eyes. "So, are we okay? I'm sorry I hurt you. I'm sorry for how I've been since I got home."

"We are always okay. Always. And I'm sorry for snapping at you, but I think I had to."

"Esben probably should have snapped at me."

"He didn't?"

I shrug. "Not really. I'm not sure I gave him the chance." I reach for a lemon bar. "He did say that I wasn't making any sense. Mostly, he was way too nice. And probably way too scared about what a lunatic I'd become." I lean forward and set my forehead on the counter. "I'm so embarrassed. And I feel awful. He didn't deserve a lot of what I said to him. What I did to him."

"Most of it, probably not." Simon rubs my back. "But maybe a little. I'm not sure. Again, he was between a rock and a hard place, and there may not have been any right moves. In the end, I think you *really* know this boy. And you trust him."

Simon is right. I'm not the person I used to be. I do trust Esben. And I do believe in him and in us.

"Goddamn it!" I suddenly scream. "Dad, how in the hell do I fix this?"

Simon busies himself with whipping up cream-cheese frosting for the carrot-cake cupcakes and doesn't say anything.

I strum my fingers on the counter, I cry some more, I fret, I vacillate between drowning in shame and then forgiving myself because of the loss I've faced. Because I am flawed and not even close to being perfect.

Then a bright spot in this depressing spiral hits me.

I sit up. "I called you 'Dad.'"

275

Simon nods but continues furiously whisking the concoction in the bowl.

"I called you '*Dad*,'" I say more emphatically. "That's big."

"You did. And it is."

"When I was in the cab on the way to the airport . . ." I'm rather stunned. "I did it then, too."

"Yes. I wasn't sure if you . . . meant it."

A smile overtakes me. Happiness overtakes me. "I did."

"I like that." Simon's face looks so sweet right now, and it eases my stress and upset.

"I remember asking you to help me."

"Yes."

"And you did. You always do."

"And I always will."

I fiddle with arranging a series of cake toppings, lining up small containers of sparkles, pearls, and shimmery sugars. There are about ten food stains on my sleeves, but I don't care. "I know that. I see now that I haven't ever doubted that. Doubted *you*. Not really. You're my father. My dad."

"Forever."

So, while I haven't questioned Simon, I apparently had a massive failure when it came to trusting Esben. I slump forward. God, he deserved more. "Esben stopped texting and calling on Tuesday morning. That's not a good sign. I could be too late. What if I've lost everything?"

"You haven't," Simon states with conviction as he pulls a perfectly risen chocolate cake from the oven. "It's only been a few days. A few days since you lost Steffi, since you blew up at Esben. Pull yourself together, and be rational, okay? And, really, come on now. You perfected the trifle. How can anything bad happen after such an accomplishment?"

"I called you 'Dad' and made a trifle that didn't make anyone want to puke. Two milestones, right?" I ask hopefully.

"Right." Simon beams as he holds out a spoonful of his cream-cheese frosting for me to taste.

"You're still driving me back to school tomorrow, right?" I ask.

"Yes, why?"

I lean in and taste the frosting. It's perfect, of course. "I need to call Kerry. Get advice and girl talk before I get back to school. Do you mind?"

"Not at all. Run off. Be a college kid who doesn't help clean up the kitchen—it's fine. I will somehow manage . . . without you." He feigns distress, and his act is so over-the-top that I laugh. I actually laugh for the first time in days.

"I'll be back in a few minutes, and I will scour this kitchen, I swear."

"Don't worry about it." Simon suddenly feigns casualness. "Allison? If you'd like, you could . . . just take my old car yourself, okay? I have the new one now."

"Oh, yes. That simple little Porsche. You kept the other one? That I know you don't need?" I eat another five scoops of frosting and try to suppress a smile before Simon grabs the spoon from my hand.

"Just say yes."

Technically, Simon didn't buy me a car . . .

"Okay. Yes."

I don't want to make a big deal out of this, but Simon walks over to Bruce and begins petting him like crazy. "Did you hear that? Our Allison is now the proud owner of a car."

Bruce thumps his tail and pants as though he's actually excited.

"More importantly, what's up with Kerry?" Simon asks as he rubs his nose against Bruce's. "What's this call about?"

I walk over to them and stroke Bruce's fur. "I'm going back to basics." It's nice to feel like myself again. Or, rather, like the new me again. Confident in what I want, even though I don't know how everything will turn out. "Hey, Simon? Dad?"

"Yes, love?"

I move over and lean into my incredible father and hug him. "Thank you. So much. For everything."

"Anytime."

"Sorry about all this insane baking."

"We all get a little bonkers sometimes. Better baking than, you know, burning down the house."

"True."

I hug him for so long that eventually he laughs and begins patting my back. "Go on. Make your call. I'll be here when you're done."

I step away and smile.

I know what I want, and I'm going to do what I can to get it.

Bruce Wayne stretches and pushes his nose against me in what I take as a sign of approval. I'll take positivity wherever I can right now.

CHAPTER 32

TIME AND AGAIN

The drive back up to Andrews College the next morning was interminable, and more than once, Kerry clapped her hand over my fingers as they drummed over the steering wheel. I couldn't help it.

My phone call with Kerry was embarrassing and awkward and full of my apologies, but she's on my side. And she's not particularly thrilled with the fact that Esben wouldn't speak to her about what happened between him and me, so she was glad that I filled her in. After telling Esben that she was fed up with his silence, she drove back to school with me instead of with her brother.

Now, it's a beautiful evening in picturesque Landon. Kerry and I sit together on the same bench where I sat last fall. As I did then, I stare at the lake; only this time, I am not trying to escape, to drown.

Tonight, I am trying to live.

She puts a hand on my back to ease my trembling. "It's going to be all right."

I watch the ebb and flow of the lake. This past week is too much to take in, and while I have lost Steffi, and I temporarily lost the new person I'd become, I cannot lose everything. The water is beautiful, absolutely beautiful.

After a while, I say, "I am so in love with him."

"I know," she says. "Just breathe, Allison. You can do this."

At six o'clock, I look at Kerry. "Now?"

She nods. "Now. He got back to school an hour ago. He'll get the notification for sure."

My hand shakes as I type out a tweet and tag Esben: Ran when I shouldn't have. If you can forgive me, meet me at 7. Same place, same 180 seconds together. #thiskissthiskiss2.

I couldn't pull my plans off without Kerry's help, and she's convinced this will work. "He's hurt," she says, "but he's mostly angry at himself for his part in this. I know that without him telling me anything. Also? I've seen how he's been since he's been home from LA. Allison, he's hopelessly lovesick. You can practically see his heart bleeding all over his shirt."

"That's an attractive image."

She shrugs. "Today's a good day for drama."

"I left him there, Kerry. I left him in Los Angeles." I rub a hand anxiously over my upper arm. "He did everything, and I went totally crazy. I left him. That is not okay."

"You were strung out. You . . . Allison, you were not thinking clearly. We all get that. *Esben* gets that. He's got to. He's scared right now. Just like you are."

For forty-five minutes, I neurotically check Twitter, desperately hoping for a reply, for something to tell me that he's coming, but there's nothing. There are, however, over six hundred retweets of my post.

"Let's go," Kerry says confidently. "Jason, Danny, and Carmen have everything set up."

I nod, but she has to drag me from the bench.

The short walk to the center of town feels too short, and the cobbled streets, iron lampposts, and cute shops all take me back to September. Kerry leads me by the hand to the blocked-off street that is filling with people on this warm night.

"You ready?" she asks.

"No." But I force a smile. "Yes."

"Then take a seat."

She pivots me toward a very familiar table with a set of two chairs. Slowly, I walk to my spot and sit down. I look around. There's a bit of a crowd, I notice. In fact, it is a much larger crowd than the first time we sat across from each other. My heart starts to pound, but I can't help smiling a little. Apparently, my Twitter post attracted a few followers. There are so many strangers here, but I relax a hair when I see Jason and Danny, who both give me goofy faces and thumbs-up signs. They've each got a phone in their hand to record this, and my stomach knots. Out of the corner of my eye, I see Carmen waving at me, and she smiles with support. I cast my eyes back over those people who have become part of my life and for whom I am so grateful.

At least this time, I am not alone. I may be even more scared, but I am not alone.

There is a clock at the top of one of the shops, and I see it's two minutes before seven. I look at Kerry, and she motions for me to be patient.

I adjust myself on the seat and then run my hands through my hair and exhale deeply. I shouldn't panic yet.

But minutes tick by, and I cannot stop myself from glancing up at the clock repeatedly.

Soon enough, it's ten after.

Dammit. I shake my head and look down, unable to face Kerry or anyone else.

A few people clap and call my name. I hear someone say, "It's okay, Allison! You got this! He'll show!" More encouraging applause lifts my eyes, and I try to smile at the crowd, even though my eyes are brimming.

At seven eighteen, my heart really begins to sink. *He's not coming. Esben doesn't forgive me.*

I think about how awful it will be to never again hold him, kiss him, laugh, or fully live. To never again be allowed to love him.

What if he never again sets his hand on the back of my neck, grounding me the way his touch always does?

What if those amber eyes of his never again sparkle with mischief when they see me?

What if I never again get to trail my fingers over the curve of his lower back in a way that drives him wild? There's a certain gasp he makes when I eventually inch under his waistband and then stroke my fingers to the front of his body. I want to do that over and over.

What if our bodies are never again joined together, moving seamlessly and smoothly in the way that we've learned makes magic and romance and bliss come true?

What if there are no more blueberry kisses tasting of intense cold and even more intense heat?

What if there are no more phoenixes, sand timers, mismatched socks, or microwaveable mac and cheeses?

What if we never again help shelter dogs find homes or reconnect long-lost friends or create princess parties for children? We've become a team, and our partnership has strength and healing. We can change the world. We can find more good. I *know* we can. I do.

And what—oh God—what if I never get to prove how much harder and better I can love him? How I can fall in love even more deeply with this sincere, giving, undeniably everything boy who has rocked my world to its core?

What if this romance has ended?

What if, what if, what if . . .

My heart is filled with terror at all that I might have destroyed.

Seven twenty-five. I'm sure that I look visibly distressed, because people around me begin to chant the hashtag I'd made. *"Thiskissthiskisstwo!"*

I am done. I can't take this anymore, and I push my chair back. I glance at Kerry, and she nods in sad agreement. It's time to give up.

I'm about to stand and end this hell, when the crowd erupts in such applause that I'm scared to even hope why. My heart clenches when Esben flings himself breathlessly onto the chair across from me.

I'm not sure how I manage to speak, but I do. "You're here." I make no attempt to conceal the relief or the emotion that rings through my words.

He nods slowly, and I see undeniable love in his eyes. "Always," he replies through his panting. "Always." His face is flushed, and he has to catch his breath before he continues. "I saw your tweet. My phone died . . . that's all. Baby, *that's all.*" He runs a hand through his hair as he slowly settles. "So, I couldn't reply. Then I went to drive here, and . . . my car needed another jump. So I ran." He swallows hard and tries to slow his breathing. "But I ran to you." Esben locks eyes with me. "I'm here. I am completely here."

"That's all that matters." I smile at him and take a big breath, calming my nerves that were fried a few moments before. "And you want to do this?"

He smiles back and begins to settle in. "I do."

He's sweaty and perfect and intolerably gorgeous. He is everything.

Esben will never have to jump through hoops for me again.

After we've both found a measure of stability, and when I know it's time, I raise an eyebrow. "You ready? A hundred and eighty seconds."

"A hundred and eighty seconds," he agrees.

I turn to Kerry and nod. She is about to burst, and it's a fraction of a second before she silences the crowd and calls out, "Time starts now."

Ten seconds. Right away, Esben is intense, his eye contact direct, and I know he will not flinch, not waver, for even a moment. Unlike the last time, today, I welcome this from him. Whereas I did everything I could to block out Esben that September evening, now my mind and body are relaxed and open, feeding and refueling from this experience. It's easy to bask in these first moments of reunion, and, based on his expression, he is feeling exactly the same.

Thirty-six seconds. I have missed Esben so profoundly. It's only been a week since we've seen each other, but it's felt like a century. I cannot believe how bananas I went.

I left him in Los Angeles. After everything he did for me. I give Esben an apologetic look. *I am so sorry. I am so goddamn sorry. You didn't deserve to be treated so terribly. Not at all. I hate what I did, and I wish I could take it back.* I press my lips together, and Esben leans a mere inch to the side, then shakes his head almost imperceptibly. He's telling me that it's okay, that I was in turmoil, that I was allowed to have a meltdown.

You're too forgiving, I think. *You're too generous and too good and too patient. But I admire those things about you, and I am learning from them. Slowly, but I am. I won't screw up like that again, I promise. This was more about hurting myself, about those fragments of my past that still cut sometimes. But now I am stronger. Because of you, because of Simon, because of Steffi.* My smile comes from my trust in myself and in the future.

Sixty-eight seconds. Esben's expression has changed a little. It takes me a while to guess what he's feeling. While it's somewhat difficult for me to accept, he wants me to understand that I have helped him also. Our relationship is not as one-sided as I sometimes think. His serious face and his unwavering stare have us frozen together. It's important to him that I believe him. He *needs* me as much as I need him. He *wants* me as much as I want him. I am reminded how long he went without a girlfriend or any kind of real relationship, so I must pay attention to the fact that he fell in love with me. There's a reason for that, and it has nothing to do with Steffi's part in pushing us together.

He's right. I will not forget my worth in this romance again.

Ninety-nine seconds. As we continue to move through this experience for the second time, another thought occurs to me. As much as Esben has helped me to transform myself, there is another person who deserves as much, if not more, credit. Simon. My father. *Dad.* Long before Esben came into my life, Simon was there, slowly and painstakingly building a foundation of trust for me to build on. I've spent a lot of time vaguely acknowledging this and feeling guilty about it, but I'm done with guilt. This is the time to appreciate and absorb all that he's offered, to do something smart and healing with his love. And I will.

Even when I've tried to shut him out, Simon's lessons have permeated my walls. He's the reason I was so unsettled at the beginning of this year, even when I'd never heard of Esben Baylor. Some part of me was responding to Simon's love and devotion, and it was making me itchy to be able to accept that and to reach for more. I owe my father so much. Instead of feeling like a burden, this feels like an opportunity and one that I will run toward.

One hundred and twenty-two seconds. The intimacy and comfort I share with Esben brings up too much. I won't shut it out this time, but it hurts. I miss Steffi. I knew this was coming. *Her death.* I cannot stand those words, but I think them anyway, because I have to get used to them. *Steffi is dead.* To pair my best friend with death is such a grotesque and unimaginable association—a reality that I'm trying to assimilate, even though I've known this was coming for months. I take in Esben's strength for comfort. I lift my chin and try to rally. *I miss her already. I don't think I'll ever have a friend like her. No one will replace her. But . . .* I almost lose eye contact when I yet again tear up. I want to fall to pieces, but I don't. *But I can find other relationships, other friendships, new and different and wonderful. They won't be what I had with her. But that is going to have to be okay. Cherishing her and what we gave to each other will hold a sacred place, and that's okay. It's not a competition.* I begin to cry freely. But I do not veer from my eye contact with Esben. I can't. He's my lifeline.

When Steffi told me to be brave, she meant it. She wanted me to have what, in some ways, she couldn't allow herself. As strong and ferocious as she was, she couldn't embrace this life, because she was too afraid, because she'd built too many walls. And before she could discover another way to live, a savage cancer goddamn ripped through her body and killed her.

There wasn't enough time for her to heal from her past, but I have that time, so I will take it. I will revel in the opportunity to find rebirth and rejuvenation. To find myself completely.

One hundred and forty seconds. Esben has followed my every move over the past few minutes, every flinch, every tiny change in facial expression . . . I've circled back to a place of peace and love. To a place where all I want is a reunion with this boy who has helped me find myself. I send pure love and romance his way. And desire. I can't ignore that. Esben, it seems, is feeling what I do, because, to my surprise, he breaks his own rule and, just for a second, dips his eyes to the spot on my neck that I know he loves to kiss before resuming our eye contact. He's got lust in his eyes. For sure. I raise my eyebrows and send him a flirtatious look while I adjust my pose.

One hundred and fifty-nine seconds. He still looks at me directly, with a steadfastness and fortitude that I adore. Then he mouths three perfect words to me. It doesn't matter when or how we've said this before. It only matters what we mean now.

I love you.

There is no delay as I reply silently, *I love you.*

A whooping "Woot! Yeah!" comes from everyone around us. The lustful and heated looks we send each other are apparently not subtle. Everyone sees what's going on between us, and I welcome the mass cheering in this moment.

Almost there, I want to tell him. *Hold on. Hold on for me.*

One hundred seventy-two seconds. Both of us may explode. The people who encircle us start counting down. ". . . Eight! Seven! Six!"

I stand. Esben stands. We're ready. We follow the rules and don't break eye contact, but we're ready.

These last seconds are excruciating and gorgeous. Esben is so exceedingly handsome and strong and shattering on all levels. All of his beauty used to break me, but tonight, it empowers me. It assures me that I can create a life that will let me be whole.

"Time," Kerry calls out.

We are so lost in each other that neither of us hears her. His shoulders are broad in a way that fits my body so perfectly, his focus on me so great that I cannot break from this moment, and my devotion to him is so overwhelming that my head and heart are not in my control.

"Time!" Kerry yells forcefully. "Time!"

I snap back to reality and give him a flirtatious, daring look.

Esben grins back. *Do it,* he's silently telling me. *Do it. Let me hold you again.*

With nothing but confidence, I slam my foot back, kicking the chair out from under me. It takes a fraction of a second more for me to lower my hand under the table and upend it onto its side. There's a stop in time, during which we look at each other and do not move. I begin to break, because I see that all we fought for has endured.

"Time! Goddamn it, time!" Kerry is screaming now.

We cannot reach each other fast enough, and tonight, I am the one to hold him up, because Esben is falling apart, burrowing his face into my neck, his tears wetting my skin. So, I reach for his lower back and pull him in.

"Please don't cry, love," I say. "Please don't."

His arms wrap around me, and I savor his perfect embrace. "Did I understand you right? You're totally in this? You won't leave again?" he asks, his voice wobbly.

"Yes," I confirm. "I'm sorry. I'm so sorry. God, I was a wreck in Los Angeles. I made every mistake and then some."

"Stop," he says while he holds me securely. "It's going to be all right. God, Allison, just kiss me."

This is easy to do. In seconds, we re-create our kiss from months ago, but with even more sincerity and so many more layers of feeling. There is nothing from the wreckage of my past that invades my need for him this time. There is nothing but pure, raw love. So, when he pulls me harder against his mouth, I respond by lifting up on my toes and meeting the power of his kiss. *It is allowed,* I remind myself, *to be whole-heartedly in love. To devour this wonderful boy and to celebrate the future.*

There is no reason to ever stop kissing him, and it's seriously possible that I could stay like this for the rest of my life. But when his tongue crosses my lips . . . and trails to my neck . . . and then when I arch into him too hard, I remember that we are so, so not alone. There are camera clicks and flashes and more whoops from the ever-growing audience here. These are sounds I would have shunned before, but tonight? Tonight, they flood me with happiness.

When a particularly loud whistle floats our way, we both ease back and laugh.

I run my hands over Esben's chest and rapidly get lost in too many wonderful ways. The feel of him and the shape of him are so familiar and so needed. "Do you want to get a coffee?" I finally whisper. "And later, maybe some oysters?"

His hand touches the back of my neck. "Absolutely."

It takes a few breaths to gain my composure, but I look at him. "And then, do you want to talk about some crazy social experiments that we could do together and post online? Because I have some ideas."

He takes time to gaze down at me and let his mouth travel gently over mine once again. "Absolutely."

"But first"—I start with no shame and no hesitancy—"but first, before any of that, do you want to go back to my room and be crazy in love?"

"I do." Esben's lips play down my neck, and he takes my hand. "More than anything."

"And then?" I press my body against his. "And then, how about we never stop?"

"Agreed. Never." Esben grabs me by the waist and spins us around, raising our hands to our audience so that we can take in the support and joy from so many who have been rooting for us. Then, in one swift move, he bends me back and dips me so smoothly and so romantically that I can hardly breathe. His mouth grazes against my neckline.

"The Internet is gonna love this," I say over the crazed cheering.

"They certainly will," he says, laughing into me. "And I assume that, this time, I have your full permission to post?"

"You know it."

"I love you so much, Allison." He breathes these words not just over my skin but over my heart.

"And I love you so much, Esben."

There is no more white noise in my head or soul.

There is no longer the belief that I only get one.

I get way more than one. I get as many as I will allow, and I plan to allow many.

I'm going to live a beautiful life. In honor of Steffi, in honor of Simon, in honor of all the glorious, giving, caring people online, and—most importantly—in honor of myself.

I hold on to Esben. He still smells like cookies and love.

ACKNOWLEDGMENTS

Tremendous gratitude to Courtney Miller at Amazon Skyscape for her support, enthusiasm, and hard work bringing this book to publication. In addition, she also connected me with my outrageously talented editor, Amara Holstein. She worked wonders on my messy first draft and helped me sculpt this book to shine the way I'd wanted, and I am crazy thankful for her skill and care. Skyscape's Jason Kirk has been nothing but supportive and tuned in to me and this book, and I throw huge love his way!

In order to be my agent, one must have the patience of a saint, and Deborah Schneider certainly has that, as well as a sharp sense of humor and knockout publishing smarts. I am incredibly lucky to be in such good hands.

Rebekah Crane, Tracey Garvis-Graves, Tammar Webber, and Rebecca Donovan all cheered me on when I needed it, and I could not ask for smarter or more loving author friends. Hugs and curtsies to Michelle Odland for reading an early version of this book and offering insightful feedback and unfailing belief in me. Also, mad love to Cara Leuchtenberger for sharing difficult information from her years of oncology nursing and for doing so with great intelligence and compassion.

As they have done with every book I've written, Tom Cullinan and Alexa Longley read and provided valuable feedback, along with much love and laughter.

Once again, my husband, Bill, and my son, Nicholas, get major credit for putting up with me during intense writing days and for handing me tissues when I needed them.

As always, Andrew Kaufman was my rock while I wrote this book. Some friendships nearly knock you over with their strength, their timelessness, and their true reciprocity. Ours is one of those, and I don't forget that for a second.

Danielle Allman is one in a million. She read every single chapter within hours after I'd finished it, and, together, we laughed and cried and swooned and problem solved. Together, we made it through this book.

And to those who share, take risks, trust, and give so much of themselves online, thank you. What you do matters, and you remind us that—in what can feel like a very dark world—there is endless genuine light and love.

ABOUT THE AUTHOR

Photo © 2016 Cara Vescio

Jessica Park is the bestselling author of more than fifteen novels, including *Flat-Out Love* and *Left Drowning*. She grew up in the Boston area and attended Macalester College in Saint Paul, Minnesota. After spending four years in the frigid North, including suffering through one memorable Halloween blizzard, she decided to set out for warmer climes. She now lives in the relatively balmy state of New Hampshire, with her husband, son, two dogs, and a cat. She admits to spending an obscene amount of time thinking about rocker boys and their guitars, complex caffeinated beverages, and tropical vacations.